BETRAYAL

IN

BLACK

MARK M. BELLO

A Zachary Blake Legal Thriller

Published by 8Grand Publications
Printed in the United States of America

ISBN: 978-1732447172

Betrayal in Black is dedicated to innocent victims of police violence—America *can* do better . . .

About the Cover

Special Thanks for Park West Gallery and Artist Dominic Pangborn for their contributions to the cover of *Betrayal in Black*.

Park West Gallery is the world's largest art dealer, bringing the experience of collecting fine art to more than 2 million customers since 1969. Park West has gallery locations in Michigan and Florida and is famous for bringing its knowledge and customer service to art auctions on cruise ships and fine hotels, as well as its gallery locations.

Dominic Pangborn was born in 1952 and is a celebrated Korean-American artist and designer. Critics have described his style as 'evolutionary' because it is continually changing. As a result, change has become a consistent theme in his works.

The color red is seen in the majority of his works. After a collector observed that red must be his favorite color, Pangborn decided to consciously focus on red, making it one of his most predominant themes.

His work and accomplishments have been celebrated at the White House and the 2018 Winter Olympics, and his art is collected around the world

Prologue

"Sixteen calling fifteen. Come in, please. What is your current location?"

"Vinewood and Ninth, possible B & E. Currently waiting on key holder. What's up. Sixteen?"

"Copy. Pulling vehicle over—Michigan plate number 272-BLM. That's 272 BRAVO, LIMA, MIKE. Got that?"

"Copy that."

"Going to check ID. Two male occupants matching description of Burger King robbery suspects . . . Occupants appear to resemble the suspects but did not get a good look."

"Copy that. Wise to await backup. Where are you now?"

"Cedar, just south of Pennsylvania, heading north. The stop should be north of Pennsylvania, heading north toward Eureka."

"Will come to your location ASAP. I see where you are."

"Will await your arrival. Ten-four."

"Ten-four. Will be there shortly."

***

"The kids sure enjoyed the fair. I'm glad we came. The people were nice, considering. Want to get something to eat?"

"Sure, I'm hungry if you're hungry."

"It's all about me, right? It's always about me. You are the sweetest man."

He really is. After all of these years together, he still always puts me first.

"Your happiness is my happiness, baby," he coos. "You know what they say?"

"No, but I know you'll tell me," she giggles.

"Happy wife, happy life."

"And don't you forget it," she warns.

"Marcus, please roll down the window for me?"

"Sure. Whoa, what the fuck?"

"What?"

"There's a cop coming up on us, with lights and siren flashing. The whole nine yards." He's in a panic.

"Maybe there's an emergency up ahead. There's a hospital nearby."

"I don't think so."

"What's the speed limit?"

"Thirty-five. What are you doing?"

"Thirty-two, thirty-three."

"Okay. Stay calm. Let's see what he does."

"He's right up my ass. I smoked a joint on my way home from work. Can you smell it?"

She sniffs at the air. "No, I don't think so." She is pissed off.

How can he smoke weed, then get into a car and go for a drive with his family?

She'd let it slide, at least for now.

"Stay calm, baby. You weren't speeding. We got the kids in the car, and even if he smells weed, we can tell him it was me, not you."

"Like a cop will care. He'll make me walk a straight line or something."

"Please don't give him attitude."

"I won't. What about the gun?"

"Make sure he knows you have it. Do you have the permit?"

"In the glove box."

"Let him know you have the gun and a license to carry."

"I will. Here we go . . . pulling over right now."

"Aisha, sweetheart?" She turns to her six-year-old daughter strapped in her car seat.

"Mommy and Daddy are going to talk with the nice policeman. Keep an eye on the baby, okay?"

"Yes, Mama. Are we going to get something to eat? I'm hungry."

"After we talk with the nice policeman, baby. Please stay quiet back there. It's quiet time now."

The woman pulls an iPhone from her purse and enables the video function.

***

"Good evening sir and . . . uh . . . ma'am. License and registration, please?"

"What's the problem, officer?"

"License and registration, sir."

"I heard you. Am I entitled to know what I did wrong? I wasn't speeding. When I last checked, my rear lights were working okay."

"License and registration . . . now!"

"Talkative fella', aren't you? All right. I'm getting them out. I want to make sure that you are aware that I have a gun and a permit to carry."

"Don't get them out! Don't even move! Put your hands on the dash!"

"Okay, calm down now. My hands are on the dash."

"License and registration, *now!*"

"Hands on the dash or license and registration? I can't do both, officer."

"Raise your hands in the air and slowly step out of the car."

"Why? I haven't done anything wrong," Marcus pleads.

"Did I stutter? Raise your hands in the air and step out of the car. I need to see your license, registration, and permit."

"Stop pointing that damned gun at me! You are scaring my children. See, they're crying. You've upset them. It's okay babies. Daddy is talking to this nasty policeman. I'm sorry he is being such a mean man. We'll get something to eat in a few minutes."

Marcus tries to stay calm for the sake of his family.

"I'm not asking. Step out of the damned car!" The officer is becoming unglued.

"I'm getting out, damn you, but, here, let me just show you my—"

"Don't reach. *Stop!*"

"I'm getting what you requested, just going to show you my—"

"Put your hands where I can see them!" The officer snarls.

"Jesus H. Christ, officer. I'm not—"

Thunderous shots ring out, and Marcus slumps away from the dash, back toward the driver's seat.

"Oh my god! You just shot my husband," screams the front seat passenger.

"Marcus, hang in there, baby. Call an ambulance. *NOW!* Why did you do that? He was just doing what you told him to do. Oh my god! He's unconscious!"

The woman shakes the unconscious victim. She screams and turns to her children, hysterical in the back seat. She turns back to her husband.

"Marcus, can you hear me? God, the children!"

"Mommy! Mommy!" Aisha cries.

"Mommy is right here, Aisha, baby."

"Stay where you are, ma'am. Don't move."

"Is he dead? *Noooo!* He needs an ambulance. *NOW!*"

"Fuck, oh, fuck! I can't believe this shit! Why did he reach for—"

The woman is livid.

"You *requested* his license and registration! All he was trying to do was show you! What's the matter with you? Are you crazy?"

"Fuck! Don't move!"

The officer is now pointing the gun at the female passenger.

"Nobody's moving," she cries, raising both hands in the air. "What about our children? Don't move, Aisha."

"Fuck!"

"Whatever you do, don't hurt our children," the woman pleads.

"I told him to put his hands on the dash. I told him not to move his hands. I told him to raise his hands and exit the vehicle. I told him to keep his hands where I could see them. Why didn't he do what I ordered? Fuck!"

The kids are still screaming in the back seat.

"My kids are terrified! I need to get them out of the back seat."

"Keep your hands where I can see them, ma'am."

"Absolutely. I'm not moving a muscle. Is someone else coming? I need to tend to my babies. Did you call for an ambulance? You need to get an ambulance out here! Dear God!" she cries. "Tell me he isn't dead! Blood's everywhere! He didn't do anything! Why? Why did you shoot him? For no damn reason, *that's* why!"

"Shut up! Just *shut-the-fuck-up*!"

The cop hovers over her in a shoot-to-kill stance.

The woman defies him.

"You don't get to talk to me like that! Where is that damn ambulance? Marcus, Honey? He's dead. I think he's dead!"

A squad car pulls up. Officer Alex Mickler gets out of the driver's seat.

"What's the problem, here, Randy?"

"Glad you're here, Alex."

A second officer exits his vehicle. The two cops engage in a whispered conversation as they walk toward the victim's car. The second officer peers into the driver's side window and recoils in shock.

"This guy is dead, Randy. Did you call for a bus?"

"Not yet."

"Fifteen to central. We have an officer-involved shooting. One male adult with multiple gunshot wounds. We need a bus, stat, to Cedar, about a half-mile north of Pennsylvania.

"One female adult is being taken into custody. There are two minor children in the back seat in need of attention. Call social services.

"We need multiple squads to block off Cedar from Pennsylvania south to Eureka north. We need supervisors here, *STAT*! Page everyone within earshot. Do you read?"

"Loud and clear."

"Randy, take a seat on the curb. Ma'am, please exit the car and make sure I can see your hands," Mickler commands.

"My children, what about my children?"

"They're fine where they are, ma'am. Now, please exit the vehicle."

"They are *not* fine! They're *scared*, officer! I need to be with them."

"Mommy!"

"They'll be fine."

"How can my kids be fine? That bastard shot my husband in cold blood, right in front of us!"

Mickler points to the trunk. "Hands on the trunk, ma'am."

"*Please* get my kids out of the car and bring them to me, *PLEASE*!"

"Follow my orders, please, ma'am. Help is on the way. Just keep your hands where—"

"My hands are right here! I'm not moving! I haven't moved an inch! I've got the whole thing on video on my phone! That cop killed my Marcus in cold blood! He killed my husband! He killed their daddy!"

She shakes and points her finger at the first officer.

"Stay calm and don't move, ma'am. The ambulance is here."

An ambulance driver approaches the scene.

"What's the situation?"

"Victim's in the driver's seat with multiple gunshot wounds. He's not moving. Jones claims there's a gun in the car, so proceed with caution. I believe he is deceased."

"Okay, I've got it from here."

"The car is a crime scene. Make sure the emergency brake is engaged."

"Got it."

"Tell me what happened, Randy? I thought you were going to wait for me before approaching the vehicle."

The woman interrupts.

"He shot my husband for no reason, *that's* what happened! Will you please get my kids out of the car? They're frightened."

"Patience, please, ma'am. You will get your turn. I'm talking to Officer Jones right now. Randy?"

"I don't know, man. It was a routine traffic stop. There were infants in the car for Christ's sake! I demanded to see his license and registration. I might have smelled marijuana, not sure. He told me that he had a firearm and a license to carry. I told him not to reach for it. His hand was behind the driver's side door. I couldn't tell what he was holding. I told him to put his hands on the dashboard where I could see them. I didn't know where the gun was, and he wouldn't put his hands where I could see them.

He would not comply with my instructions. I couldn't see the fucking gun!"

"Okay. Then what?"

"He was staring into space, like he was high or something. It was getting tense and I was nervous. I kept telling him to keep his hands on the dash because I had no idea where the gun was."

"Okay, Okay. And?"

"He reaches down and . . ."

"How many people were in the car?"

"Four, counting the victim. The female states she's the wife. Her I.D. indicates her name is Sarah Hayes, same last name as the driver, one Marcus Hayes. There are two kids who she claims are their children."

"Deep breaths, man, just take deep breaths. There were four people in total? One male suspect, one female, and two minor children?"

"Correct."

"Why were they pulled over?"

"The vehicle and occupants matched the description of the Burger King robbery perps."

"The Burger King guys are both males."

"I couldn't tell the passenger was female until I reached the vehicle."

"Where were you relative to the suspect?"

"I was at his side-view mirror with my gun drawn pointing down diagonally at the driver."

"Are all rounds still in the vehicle?"

"Is the suspect still in the vehicle?"

"What about the woman?"

"She was a pain in my ass. She kept screaming. 'You shot my husband. My babies. My babies.' She claimed she's got the whole thing on her cell phone."

"Was anyone else at the scene besides these four?"

"No. Well, not that I know of, anyway."

"Did you run the plate?"

"The car belongs to the driver. No outstanding warrants."

"Where do they live?"

"Detroit."

"What were they doing in Cedar Ridge?"

"I didn't ask. They seem out of place for this area."

"The boss is on his way. Hang in there. We'll sort this out."

Chapter One

"What do you think?"

Cedar Ridge chief of police Warren Brooks has convened a task force to conduct a special inquiry into this officer-involved shooting. The most experienced law enforcement officials from city and county are named to the task force.

The press will have a field day with this!

The chief and the task force listen to the transcript of the audio and review dash cam video. They review copies of a disturbing iPhone video the victim's wife captured.

Officer Randy Jones is suspended pending completion of the investigation. He faces state charges and a possible federal civil rights investigation and prosecution. The victim was African-American. His name is Marcus Hayes; he resided in Detroit. Officer Jones is a veteran Cedar Ridge resident and cop.

"This is off the record, correct?" A task force veteran wonders.

"Absolutely," assures Chief Brooks.

"Doesn't look very good to me. I didn't hear or see anything to suggest that the officer was in danger at any time."

"Any time a citizen utters 'I have a gun' to an officer, that officer is in danger," counters Brooks.

"True enough, I suppose, but why would the victim tell the officer he had a gun if he planned to use it? The victim did exactly what he should have done under the circumstances. We can't go shooting every citizen who is carrying and has a legal right to carry."

"Hayes should have complied with Jones' orders to the letter, don't you think?" Chief Brooks is naturally inclined to defend his officer.

"We can't tell whether he complied or not from the audio or the angle that the video provides. Furthermore, Jones requested, at least twice, to see the guy's license and registration. How was Hayes supposed to do that without reaching for something? At

best, he was given inconsistent commands. Which ones should
he have complied with? Close call."

"You think Jones will face charges?"

"From the city or county, maybe. From the feds?
Absolutely."

"For now, any investigation of Officer Jones will be handled
in house," Brooks orders. "Internal Affairs needs to get Officer
Jones in here for a confidential interview. We need to get his
statement on the record. The audio and video tell us some, but
not all of what was going on out there.

"Monday morning quarterbacking is easy. We all have
opinions about what we see in the video, but what was Jones
seeing? What was going through his mind? What was the guy
doing inside the car that caused Jones to react the way he did?
We've got our work cut out for us. We may need to get another
police department involved so that the investigation is
completely independent. I don't want any civil rights marches in
our city—they are not good for our image."

"Neither is an officer-involved shooting of an innocent black
man who was pulled over for no apparent reason."

"There *was* a reason, dammit. The officer thought that driver
and occupant looked like the Burger King suspects."

"Because the driver was a black man? Any other reasons
come to mind?"

"Jones claimed there was a resemblance."

"That's absurd, Chief. The Burger King guys were much
younger, and, by the way, both male. This was a male and female
with young children in car seats. There was no traffic violation.
Jones admits on tape that he could not see the suspects well
enough to tell that one was female. This so-called robbery
suspicion was hardly probable cause for the stop.

"But, let's assume for a second that there *was* probable cause.
These people did nothing wrong. He pulls them over, approaches
the window, and sees a man, a woman, and two children. They
are some twenty years older than the Burger King suspects.
Officer Jones knows, then and there, he's made a mistake. Why
not simply apologize for pulling them over, tell them it was a
case of mistaken identity, and to have a nice day?"

"Because he might have smelled marijuana?"

"That's weak, Chief. He pumps four bullets into a guy over a possible joint? This smells like a case of driving while black through a predominately white community."

"I know; I get it. For now, we defer to Internal Affairs. Let's reconvene once they've completed their investigation. Anything else?"

"Yeah, Chief. I don't know Jones well, but this case is a powder keg. What if we have to sacrifice him, right or wrong, for the greater good of the community?"

"Not close to considering *anything* like that yet. We'll cross that bridge if or when we come to it. For now, we let Internal Affairs do their thing. Anyone else? No? Okay, meeting adjourned."

Chapter Two

"This is Lieutenant Douglas Kelly, Internal Affairs Division at the Cedar Ridge Police Department. For the record, this is an IA interview with Officer Randall Jones, who understands that this is a formal inquiry and that his statement is being recorded. Have I stated things correctly, Officer Jones?"

"Yes, you have."

"And you understand this interview is being recorded with your permission, is that correct?"

"Yes."

"Also present is Officer Jones's union representative, Thomas Fowler, and his attorney, Robert Olson. The time is 10:37 a.m. This interview is about case number BIA-2018-437. We are here today with Officer Randall Jones, Badge number 2431, who has consented to this interview and will identify himself for the record. Sergeant Fowler and Attorney Olson, do we have your permission to tape and proceed with the interview?"

"You do," Fowler agrees.

"Yes," Olson concurs.

"Great. Let's proceed. Is Randall Jones your full name? First name R-A-N-D-A-L-L. Last name J-O-N-E-S?"

"Yes, sir."

"When were you born, Officer Jones?"

"April 16, 1990."

"And you work for the Cedar Ridge Police Department?"

"I do."

"Please confirm your Badge Number for the record."

"2431, sir."

"In what capacity do you work for the Cedar Ridge Police?"

"I am a patrol officer."

"And how long have you been a patrol officer for the Cedar Ridge Police?"

"Three and one-half years, sir."

"Did you work anywhere else before Cedar Ridge?"

"Yes. Before Cedar Ridge, I worked for the City of Ecorse as a patrol officer trainee."

"For how long?"

"Two years, sir."

"And you are currently assigned as a patrol officer?"

"No, sir."

"No?"

"No, I am temporarily suspended," Jones sighs. He stares at the ground, embarrassed to maintain eye contact with Kelly.

"Right, of course. I meant before the suspension."

"Before the suspension, I was assigned as a patrol officer."

"On which shift?"

"The evening shift. 6:00 p.m. until 6:00 a.m."

"How long have you been working that shift?"

"Two years, sir. Sometimes we rotate, but I mostly work the evening shift."

"What shift did you work when you were hired?"

"By Cedar Ridge, sir?"

"Yes, sorry, Cedar Ridge."

"I was a trainee for six months, even though I had completed training in Ecorse. Protocols and procedures are a bit different between the two cities. They wanted me to get up to snuff, retraining, so to speak. So, I worked days with Officer Gil Dunham."

"Gil is a good guy."

"Yes, he is."

"Tell us about your training."

"I earned a two-year criminal justice and law enforcement certificate from Wayne County Community College. As I stated earlier, I completed two city training programs in Ecorse and Cedar Ridge. I'm certified by Cedar Ridge to work as a patrol officer."

"Did you receive use-of-force training, Officer Jones?"

"I did."

"Where did you receive that training?"

"Originally in Ecorse. In Cedar Ridge, we do a use-of-force training session once a year, with both firearms and Taser. We also have a once-per-year department training shoot."

"When was the last training session?"

"About four months ago. Gil was my training officer at that time, too. He has been kind of a mentor to me. We've known each other for a long time."

"Have you had any specialized training?"

"No."

"You are a patrol officer in uniform, is that correct?"

"Yes, sir."

"Please describe your uniform for us."

"It is a fully marked uniform with a badge on the left with my badge number, a name tag that reads 'R Jones' and stitching that identifies me as a police officer."

"Go on."

"I wear a visible exterior bulletproof vest and a full utility belt that is also quite visible. It is pretty obvious out there that I'm a police officer. I also have patches on both arms identifying the Cedar Ridge Police Department."

"What color is your uniform?"

"Navy blue."

"And you indicated you wear a gun belt?"

"It's a 'utility belt,' but it has a gun in it."

"What equipment is carried in this belt?"

Jones pauses to think. "I carry my gun, a Sig Sauer P20 45-caliber, on my left side because I am left-handed. I have two sets of handcuffs, a Taser, a baton, a portable radio, and a set of keys."

"And you wear this belt every time you go out into the streets on patrol?"

"Yes, sir, every time, and in the same position so I can react to situations on instinct."

"Does your department use body cameras?"

"We don't have body cameras, but our squad vehicles have dash-mounted cameras."

"Do these cameras record both audio and video?"

"Yes. And, they have a remote microphone."

"That's the kind you wear on your person, right?"

"Correct."

"Is it a departmental policy that the microphone is worn at all times?"

"Yes. Except when I am in my vehicle and the microphone is holstered, I wear it at all times on the job."

"For a clear record, were you wearing the microphone at the time of the incident that we are here to discuss?"

"Yes."

"Do you know whether it was operational or not?"

"It was the last time I checked, sir. Internal Affairs has my utility belt and all of my accessories, including the remote mic. They'll know better than I do.

"I know I had it on that night. I assume it was working. But I don't know whether I pulled it from the holster or not, or what I did, exactly. I was so focused on the vehicle and its occupants . . ." Jones wipes sweat off his forehead.

"While it's in the car, it sits in a holster?"

"Well, it's more of a charging cradle."

"And unless you take it out of this charger, the remote mic stays in the car?"

"Only if I forget to take it out of the charger and take it with me when I exit the vehicle."

"But you remember having it with you on the day of the incident on Cedar?"

"Yes, I do, but I didn't check it right then."

"Are you the only officer assigned to this squad car?"

"No, others drive it."

"Are the others responsible for charging the equipment before you take possession of the vehicle?"

"They are responsible for placing it into the charging cradle. Sometimes, when you need it, it's not fully charged."

"Was it fully charged that night?"

"I believe so, sir, but I'm not positive."

"What does this mic look like?"

"It's a two-inch or so square device that you can place anywhere on your person. Top pocket, pants pocket, perhaps clip it on something; the idea is to not obstruct it so it can pick up clear audio signals."

"Do you test the microphone to make sure it's working when you start your shift?"

"Yes, although there is an assumption that the previous officer placed it in the charger, and it will have enough juice for an eight-hour shift."

"Was the day in question a routine day, at least until this incident occurred?"

"Yes. I made a few traffic stops before this one, so I'm pretty sure the microphone was working."

"Have you reviewed those other stops?"

"No, I haven't, but I do know that I had the mic on my person and that it was showing activated on the video screen." Jones furrows his brow. His voice crackles with hostile agitation. He takes a deep breath and expels it slowly.

"Let me make sure I understand what you're telling me. The two pieces are synched, and the video monitor tells you if the audio's on and working?"

"Yes."

"Is the vehicle marked or unmarked?"

"It is a fully marked squad car, displaying Cedar Ridge Police on both driver and passenger side doors. It has a light bar and siren on the top and a push bumper in the front. The car is equipped with LED lights and red and blue flashing lights. The exterior is navy and white with a navy interior. If the lights are on, on a clear night, they are visible from as long as a mile away."

"Are there prominent back lights?"

"Yes, sir, and they blink on and off. They're very hard to miss."

"When you're pulling someone over, do you activate all the lights?"

"Yes."

"Between the marked vehicle and the uniform, no one could mistake you for anything other than a police officer?"

"I can't see how, sir."

"What other equipment in your car helps you with your job?"

"There is a mounted computer with an AT&T wireless internet connection. We can reach the department offices in Cedar Ridge and Wayne County offices in downtown Detroit."

"The computer and all other equipment were fully functional

on the night in question?"

"To the best of my recollection."

"Let's talk about the incident that night, shall we?

"Sure."

"Tell us about your day before this incident occurred."

Jones's attorney, Robert Olson, interrupts questioning.

"The record should reflect that Officer Jones is answering questions to the best of his recollection. We are post-incident here. Jones has been under a great deal of stress and has had a difficult time sleeping. He's doing his best, but I reserve the right to supplement or modify any mistakes of omission or commission. Clear?"

"Clear. We can also reconvene if the record needs to be corrected or supplemented. For the record, the person who just spoke was Robert Olson, Officer Jones's attorney. Now, back to your day, Officer Jones?"

"I clocked in around 5:15, 5:20. I went to my locker and changed into my full uniform. There isn't always a roll call, but there was that evening because of the Burger King robbery. We were told about the robbery and given a verbal description of the perps. We were told to be careful and vigilant because the suspects were armed and considered dangerous."

"Go on."

"I cruised the city for most of my shift, making contact with citizens, setting up speed radar locations, and looking for vehicles to pull over." Jones's tone softens as he discusses more mundane matters.

"You mentioned earlier that you stopped a few vehicles. Can you be more specific?"

"Yes, I pulled over four speeders and one person for defective equipment."

"How is it that you remember this?"

"I checked my logs before coming here today."

"Did you give out citations?"

"Yes, to all five."

"Might you have pulled someone over that you did not cite?"

"No. I am a by-the-book police officer. If I pull you over for a violation, you're getting a ticket."

"Well, I hope you never pull me over."

Kelly smirks. Jones doesn't see the humor.

"Continue, please."

"I drove by the Burger King at Cedar and Pennsylvania several times during my shift. I wanted to keep an eye on it, if you know what I mean. The owner is the former mayor of Cedar Ridge, so catching these guys would have been nice."

"What did you know about the robbery?"

"Two teenaged black males robbed the cashier. One pointed the muzzle of a firearm at the head of the cashier and demanded all of the money from both registers. After the cashier emptied the registers, the one with the gun dragged the guy into the back and demanded he open the safe. The cashier told him he didn't have access to the safe and didn't know the combination. Only the manager could actually open the safe. The perp pistol-whipped the guy so severely that he had to be hospitalized."

"And the description of these two was 'African American males,' and that's it?"

"No. They were described as teens, maybe early twenties. One had long dreadlocks and the other an Afro."

"You reviewed the incident video before coming today?"

"Yes, sir."

"What do you remember about the vehicle and its occupants?"

"The vehicle was a relatively late-model Ford Escape, a small SUV. I was sitting at the intersection of Cedar and Pennsylvania watching the Burger King when it drove by. I saw what I thought were two African American males who matched the physical description of the robbery suspects. Both had hats on, but the driver had an Afro, and the passenger had dreadlocks poking out from the sides of the hat, almost shoulder length."

"What did you do next?"

"I followed them, sir. I took their plate number, which came back clean. Then I called for backup."

"Who did you call?"

"Officer Alex Mickler, car fifteen."

"Did backup come?"

"Not until it was all over."

"And it was Officer Mickler?"

"Yes, sir."

"What did you tell Mickler when you first called him?"

"That I was tailing a vehicle that I suspected was being driven by one of the Burger King robbers. That the driver matched the physical description of the suspect, but that I couldn't see the passenger very well."

"What did he say?"

"He told me he was waiting for a key-holder and that he would be there as soon as possible. He suggested I wait for him in case these people were the suspects and were armed."

"And did you wait for him?"

"Well, no, I didn't. I decided to pull them over." Jones squirms in his seat and continues to stare at the floor.

"Without backup?"

"Yes."

"Why?"

"Because Officer Mickler was tied up waiting on a key holder, and I didn't want to lose these guys," Jones grumbles.

"You decided to pull them over without backup, correct?"

"C-correct," he stammers.

"Had they done anything wrong up to that point? Were they speeding? Did they have an equipment problem? Anything?"

"No, sir. But, they matched the description of the Burger King suspects."

"Because they were black?" Kelly charges.

"Absolutely not!"

Jones slams his palm on the table.

"Fine." Kelly dials it down a notch.

"What did you do next?"

"I turned on my lights and siren and pulled the driver over."

"Did he promptly pull over as commanded?"

"Yes, Sir."

"What time was this?"

"Around 8:30 or 9:00 p.m."

"What happened next?"

"I scanned the area to see if there was other traffic, pedestrians, joggers, residents on porches, things like that.

Traffic was light, and no citizen activity could be seen, so I decided to exit my vehicle and approach the suspects, about half a mile north of Pennsylvania on Cedar."

"You did everything to make sure things would be safe except wait for Officer Mickler. Is that correct?"

"Yes, sir. That is correct."

"Just so we're clear, the only reason you called for backup was the Burger King thing, right? Without the robbery, this would have been a routine traffic stop, right?"

"But this was *not* routine. I called because of the Burger King robbery. On a normal stop, I would notify squad partners I'm okay. In this case, since the robbery suspects were considered armed and dangerous. I wanted to make sure traffic was as light as possible and innocent bystanders were at a minimum. The driver pulled the vehicle over, and I issued a code four."

"What's a code four?'

"That I'm safe and don't need assistance."

"Why would you do that before the stop?"

"I don't know. It seemed safe to me. I can't explain it." Jones grimaces and shifts his position.

"But then, it wasn't," Kelly suggests.

Jones stares at the floor. Silent.

"Officer? Then it wasn't?"

"I turned off the siren but kept the flashers and emergency lights on. I had my eyes focused on the driver, which is my habit. I exited my vehicle and approached, looking inside, looking for any sudden movement.

"As I got up to the car, I noticed a slight odor of marijuana. In this case, it hadn't been smoked recently. I observed two car seats occupied by small children in the back seat and also noticed that the person in the passenger seat was not a man. She was a black woman with braids under her hat. The driver was a black male with an Afro under his hat.

"Ages?"

"Driver and passenger?"

"All occupants."

"Driver was forty or so, maybe late thirties. The passenger was about mid-thirties. The kids were young, in car seats, both under ten. The driver had his seat belt on. His right arm rested on the steering wheel; his left was not in plain view. When I walked up to the window, he immediately demanded to know what he did wrong."

"What did you tell him?"

"I requested his driver's license and registration."

"Then what?"

"He again inquired what he did wrong, and I again requested his the license and registration."

"What did he do or say at that point?"

"He started reaching for something. Initially, I presumed it was his license and registration. That's when he told me he had a gun and a license to carry. He offered to show both to me. He started to reach the left hand, the one I couldn't see, down to his side around the left leg area. I told him to show me his hands, not to reach for anything. I believe I told him to put his hands on the dash."

"And did he?"

"He kept saying he was, but he wasn't. He was reaching down, and I couldn't see his hand. He kind of turned his body toward the passenger seat as he reached down. This blocked my view of his right hand, so I couldn't see either hand. I kept telling him to stop moving and to put his hands where I could see them. He did not comply.

"He seemed to have no regard for what I was saying or for the danger he was putting himself and his family in. At that point, I was fearful for my life and the lives of all occupants in the vehicle. His left hand began to come up. As it did, it appeared to be holding something. I was trying to see his hand and what was in it as clearly as possible. I was not sure what I was seeing, and he was not following my directions. He continued to pull his curled left hand out of the darkness. I thought, at that moment, I might die.

"Remember, after demanding to know what he did wrong a couple of times, the next thing he tells me is that he's carrying. What does that mean? 'Fuck with me and I'll kill you.' I didn't know and sure as hell didn't want to find out. If his hand comes up and there is a gun in it, I'm a dead cop. I felt that I had no option, sir. My gun was pointed at him. His hand was coming up. I shot him. I don't remember how many times. I aimed center mass because I was focusing on the safety of the passenger and the children. I was worried about ricochets."

"You were at the driver's side window?"

"Yes, sir."

"Facing toward the back seat?"

"Yes sir, up by the side-view mirror. I was trying to see the suspect's left hand."

"And the kids were in car seats in the back seat?"

"Yes, sir."

"You indicated you were worried about a ricochet, but you fired anyway?"

"He gave me no choice, sir." Jones is defiant.

"Were the children boys or girls?"

"They were both girls, I believe, sir."

"And one child was directly behind the driver, correct?"

"Correct."

"And it appeared to you that this man had his hand on the gun and that hand was coming up toward you?"

"Yes, sir."

"And it also appeared to you that this man was the Burger King robbery suspect?"

"At what time, sir?"

"When you pulled him over."

"Yes."

"At any time after that?"

"I don't understand what you mean, sir."

"You pulled them over because you thought they resembled the suspects, right?"

"Right."

"You approach the car?"

"Yes."

"Instead of two black males, you see a family man, woman, and two children?"

"Yes, sir."

"At that point, do you abandon suspicion that they are your suspects?"

"The man fit the description, sir. That's all I can tell you."

"But this man was in his late thirties with his wife and kids. Is it likely that he robbed a Burger King?"

"No, sir. I guess not."

"When would you abandon suspicion that he might be the suspect?"

"When I approach the car? I don't know . . . he had a gun. He fit the description . . . I feared for my life!" Jones squints in pain. Tears run down his cheeks.

Olson interrupts.

"Don't let him put words in your mouth, Randy," he warns.

He leans over and pats Jones on the hand.

"For the record, that was attorney Olson again. Yes, Officer Jones, Mr. Olson is correct. Don't let me put words in your mouth."

"Okay."

Jones takes a deep breath, trying to regain lost composure. He wipes his eyes with his sleeve.

"You approach the car; you see a family, not two black suspects. Why not say 'Sorry, my mistake. Have a nice day' and let them go?"

"Because of the marijuana smell and because he advised, almost immediately, that he had a gun and began reaching his left hand downward."

"A faint smell of marijuana is punishable by death these days?" Kelly snarls.

"Of course not, sir," Jones mutters. "But driving under the influence is dangerous and worth investigating. The slight odor of marijuana became insignificant after he told me he was carrying and began reaching his left hand down toward his body. At that point, all I could think about was the gun."

"Let's move on. After you shot him, did he say anything?"

"I don't remember. I remember the woman started screaming. She was hysterical."

"Well, you had just shot her husband. Were you surprised that she reacted as she did?"

"No."

"After you shot the man, did you ever see the weapon you

thought he had?"

"No, at that point, I was focused on whether the passenger might be a threat."

"Did you ever, at any point, see the weapon the man admitted he possessed?"

"Not that I saw, no."

"What happened next?"

"Officer Mickler arrived at that point and took over the scene."

"Do you remember what the woman was screaming?"

"Yes, something like 'why did you shoot him?' She claimed to have the whole thing on video on her cell phone." Jones stares at the ceiling and reflects on the events.

"Did you engage her in conversation?"

"I told her to keep her hands where I could see them. She complied."

"Did you call for EMS or an ambulance?"

"I believe Officer Mickler called, sir."

"Did one come to the scene while you were there?"

"An ambulance came to the scene."

"Did the attendant tell you anything?"

"That the suspect was deceased, sir."

"What happened to the woman and the children?"

"Officer Mickler ordered me to sit on the curb while he secured the woman and the children."

"How did he do that?"

"He removed the woman from the front seat at gunpoint. He detained her, placed her in handcuffs, and escorted her back to the station."

"And the kids?"

"I'm not sure, sir. Alex handled that."

"And what happened to you?"

"I was escorted to an unmarked squad car by Officer Brian Jenkins."

"And then?"

"I was taken to the station and told to go home. The captain put me on administrative leave."

"Did you interact with Officer Mickler afterward?"

"No, sir. In fact, I haven't discussed this matter with anyone before today except my union rep and my attorney."

"You are fully firearms qualified, correct?"

"Correct, sir."

"Have you had any personal issues lately, officer?"

"No, sir."

"No stress in your personal life?"

"No, sir."

"Did you have any personal knowledge, Officer Jones, of the Burger King robbery?"

"Yes, sir. I was one of the back-up officers following the robbery."

"I understand there was a security camera that captured video of the suspect."

"True."

"Did you see the video?"

"Yes."

"Before or after this incident?"

"Before."

"And you viewed the suspects?"

"Yes."

"Upon reflection, does the driver of the car you pulled over look anything like either of those suspects?"

"No, sir. I guess he doesn't. But I thought so at the time."

"How is your dash cam video triggered, Officer Jones?"

"It is triggered as soon as I activate my emergency lights."

"And you did that in this case?"

"I did."

"And, to your knowledge, there is dash cam video of the incident?"

"Yes."

"When you first observed the vehicle, where was it?"

"On Cedar, one block south of Pennsylvania."

"How long did you follow before you pulled the vehicle over?"

"About half a mile or so."

"And you called in the plate?"

"Yes. It was clean."

"Did the driver do anything wrong while you followed him?"

"No, sir."

"When did he become aware that you were following him?"

"I'm not positive, but I believe he became aware when I first put on the flashers and siren."

"He took no evasive action? He didn't try to get away?"

"No, sir."

"And he pulled over immediately after the flashers and siren were engaged?"

"Yes, he did."

"I want to go back to his left hand. You thought the driver was holding something?"

"Yes, as he was bringing it up."

"Did you actually see an object?"

"No, but I couldn't see any reason for his hand to be in that position unless he was holding something."

"Could he simply have been clenching a fist?"

"Uh, well, I guess that was possible," Jones concedes.

"In fact, that is what has been determined."

"Yes, sir."

"How was the lighting out there?"

"Not great, but I could see. However, from my position at the driver's side door by the side-view mirror, and the position of his right hand reaching down and then up, I could not see his hand. That fact, coupled with his statement that he had a gun, placed me in fear." Jones shifts. Beads of sweat are visible on his forehead.

"Was there anything about the victim's attitude that made you suspect he might be dangerous?"

"He wouldn't follow my instructions. He kept putting his hand down where I couldn't see it despite my commands to show me his hands. He wouldn't make eye contact, and his body language was defensive. He began to mumble things I couldn't hear, and there was, as I indicated earlier, a slight odor of marijuana." Jones nods and folds his arms.

"By the way, Officer Jones, what was this man's name?"

"I don't know."

"Did you ever discover his identity?"

"Briefly, when I checked the plates."

"What was the woman's name?"

"I don't know."

"When you discharged your weapon, what were you aiming at?"

"Center mass, directed down, as low as the midsection and as high as the chest, to avoid the kids." Jones locks eyes with Kelly.

"One more question Officer Jones. In your professional life as a patrol officer, have you ever been involved in any other incidents where deadly force was used against a citizen?"

"Yes, sir."

"What were the circumstances of those incidents?"

"One incident."

"Tell me about it."

"A traffic stop."

"Was the suspect guilty of any traffic offense on that occasion?"

"No, sir."

"Why did you pull him or her over?"

"There had been a B and E in the neighborhood. My partner and I thought they might be the perp."

"Was there a working description of the perpetrator on that occasion, Officer Jones?"

"No."

"What made you suspicious of this person?"

"He seemed out of place."

"How do you mean?"

"He didn't fit the profile of a resident."

"Was he white or black?"

Jones breaks eye contact and stares at the floor.

"He was black, sir," Jones admits to the floor.

"Thank you, Officer Jones. We'll be in touch."

Chapter Three

"It does not appear Officer Jones appreciates the gravity of the situation. I just listened to a man in total denial of the fact he gunned down an innocent man. In my judgment, 'I think I smelled marijuana' or 'I couldn't see his left hand' are hardly justifications for lethal force. This seems pretty cut and dry to me, Chief."

Lieutenant Brian Bigalow is reporting findings to Cedar Ridge police chief Warren Brooks. Bigalow is Brooks' first lieutenant. The two men are part of the task force charged with investigating the officer-involved shooting incident on Cedar and Pennsylvania.

Brooks is angry. He doesn't care for the transcript of Officer Randy Jones's Internal Affairs statement.

"Jones believes it was a good shoot, Brian. He believes Hayes refused to comply with instructions, putting lives at risk. With all due respect, I believe this was a judgment call for the officer. I'm not sure there's a right or wrong in this scenario," offers Bill Lane, a task force investigator.

"That's ridiculous, Bill," Chief Brooks grumbles. "The stop was not justified. These people were pulled over for no reason. Jones observes a late-model Escape, becomes suspicious, and decides to follow. Why?

"If that isn't bad enough, Jones stops the vehicle without cause and approaches. If you give Jones the benefit of all doubt, at that point, we can assume he suspects these people might be the Burger King guys.

He approaches the suspects' vehicle. What does he see? A family of thirty or forty-somethings with small children—*that's* what he sees!

"Why not acknowledge his mistake, right then and there? Apologize and walk away! The right solution here was that simple."

Brooks paces the room and continues to rant. He's beyond angry.

"Why did Jones suspect them in the first place? The Burger King robbery was committed by a couple of black kids, so that fact justifies pulling over *every* black guy? People who don't know our city or our officers might conclude these people were targeted *because* they were black. That's a problem we need to acknowledge and handle.

"Jones compounds the problem when he gives the so-called suspect conflicting commands and leaps to unfounded conclusions," Brooks fumes.

"I understand Chief. So, what do you want to do?" Lane inquires.

"I want to take a long vacation and hope to God this blows over before I get back. Jones is currently on leave. From my point of view, we need to make sure it becomes permanent. And that goddamned interview is *toxic*. Let's hope Internal Affairs formally declares Jones unfit to serve and rules for a permanent suspension.

"Send the case to the Wayne County prosecutor and let him decide what to do with it. This whole mess should go to the grand jury. We get political cover and our officers won't think we don't protect our own."

"You call your suggestion an example of 'protecting our own?'" Bigalow chides.

Brooks lets it go.

"No, Brian. But is Jones's behavior worthy of our protection? Jones executed that man. And for *no damn reason*!

"Which leads me to the painful, yet simple conclusion that the shooting was the act of a racist cop. At the very least, granting the officer every benefit of the doubt, there are clear racial undertones at play in this case. We can assume some percentage of rank and file members won't agree. That's why we need a grand jury."

"Okay," Bigalow agrees. "I'll talk to Bialy."

***

Lawrence Bialy is the Wayne County prosecutor. Many recent high-profile cases have catapulted his career. The most recent was the Arya Khan case. A young, East Dearborn Muslim woman was falsely accused of murder. Her attorney, Zachary Blake, proved her innocence, and Bialy joined Blake in assuring that a judge formally exonerated her. Because of his smart politics, Bialy ended up a hero rather than the idiot who tried to prosecute an innocent young Muslim woman. He scored major points with East Dearborn voters.

Today, Brian Bigalow is entering Bialy's office with a political powder keg. An innocent black man was gunned down by a police officer in the predominately white downriver community of Cedar Ridge. Bialy recalls his brief conversation with Chief Brooks and ponders the position Brooks is putting him in. *Real nice Brooks—punt and dump this shit in my lap. Black Lives Matter will have a field day with this. I'm not touching this case without some political cover of my own. This crap goes to a grand jury. Let the jury decide whether or not to recommend an indictment and, if they don't issue an indictment, well, sorry, it was a grand jury and not the Wayne County prosecutor that made this decision.*

Brian Bigalow taps on Bialy's office door, startling the prosecutor from his thoughts.

"Good to see you, Brian," Bialy whispers. "I talked to your boss. What's your pleasure? I'm not sure how I can assist."

"Good to see you, too, Larry. Wish I were here under better circumstances. The chief told you about the Jones-Hayes shooting case?"

"He damned sure did."

"The chief feels an investigation and possible prosecution of Jones should be considered. He doesn't buy the reason for the stop, and even if the stop was kosher, he believes Jones should have left these people alone once he saw they were not the Burger King suspects. The chief believes if Jones had done that, none of this would be happening now."

"With all due respect to what Chief Brooks *thinks*, what does the evidence *say*?"

"We've got dash cam video and the deceased's wife's iPhone video, which she posted on Facebook as the incident unfolded. We also have Officer Jones's recorded statement to Internal

Affairs. Together, these pieces of evidence are not exactly favorable to Officer Jones.

"Chief Brooks feels, and I agree, that the evidence suggests that Jones racially profiled these people. Many people will conclude this is a textbook 'driving while black' case."

"I agree this isn't a pleasant situation for Cedar Ridge or Wayne County. Perhaps we should punt."

"Punt?" Bigalow looks confused.

"Send the case to the US Attorney's office. Let's see if they'll pursue this as a civil rights violation."

"Chief Brooks doesn't mind that idea, but as an *included* endeavor, not *instead of* one."

"So that's how things are? We could let a grand jury look at the case. There's a panel convened for a racketeering case in front of Judge Fenkell. I'll see if he's willing to let the jury hear the evidence on this one."

"Great idea, Larry. Chief Brooks will be very appreciative."

"Get me the evidence you have compiled so far, as soon as possible, and I'll shoot it over to Fenkell, okay?"

"More than okay." Bigalow is smiling.

"Tell Brooks he owes me one. This is the kind of case that can derail a career."

"I'll tell him, Larry."

"Anything else?"

"No. That's it."

Bialy stands and looks toward the door, a clear indication that Bigalow is being dismissed.

"I get it. I've been thrown out of better places."

"I'm not throwing you out. I'm asking you nicely to get the hell out of here. I have work to do and a grand jury to impress." Bialy nods toward the door.

"I'm gone."

"Then why am I looking at your face rather than your ass?"

Bigalow rolls his eyes.

"Bye, Larry."

He walks out the door.

Bialy stops him at the door and grimaces.

"This case could be a political disaster. I need everything you have. Get me the goods on this guy, and we'll get it done. I'll keep you guys posted."

***

A grand jury, unlike most judicial proceedings, conducts its business in secret. A prosecutor uses a grand jury for a variety of reasons, one being the political cover that Lawrence Bialy seeks in the Jones-Hayes case. A grand jury has broader powers than the police or the district attorney. The jury can subpoena reluctant witnesses or anyone who has refused to speak with investigators. It can also subpoena documents it discovers were previously withheld from its consideration. A grand jury also serves as a testing ground for the evidence. At its core, it is a group of ordinary citizens that investigates whether a crime has been committed and attempts to determine whether there is probable cause to take a case to trial. It delivers a prosecutor a 'strength of the case' analysis. Is an indictment achievable? What more is necessary?

Grand jurors serve for eighteen months and can investigate more than one case at a time. They may meet at odd hours, only as necessary. They may meet several times a week, during the day, in the evening, or not at all on some days. The prosecutor directs the presentation of evidence and asks most of the questions, but grand jurors may also question witnesses. In most cases, proceedings, meeting places and time, are secret.

The only people allowed into a grand jury room are the jurors, the prosecutors, the court reporter, a particular witness, and, sometimes, the witness's attorney. The attorney's role is limited to providing advice to the client. Attorneys don't ask questions and, in many cases, cannot even sit in the jury room with their witness-clients—witnesses are required to step out whenever they wish to consult with their attorneys. Everyone is sworn to secrecy. From time to time, a judge might be called in to resolve legal issues.

Bialy is ambivalent about using this grand jury in the Jones case. He likes the political cover it provides for him in the community. However, if the jury issues an indictment, and Bialy is reasonably certain that it would, the case becomes his to try. The jury will need only probable cause for an indictment. At trial, the prosecutor must prove guilt *beyond a reasonable doubt*, a much higher standard of proof.

Baily senses that the Jones case is no easy win and a political nightmare. Wayne County's largest city, Detroit, has a predominately black population. Many suburban Wayne County cities are predominately white. So, regardless of the outcome, Bialy will be pissing off some segment of his voters. If a grand jury fails to indict or indicts Jones and Bialy fails to secure his conviction, civil rights protests are likely in an already divided Wayne County. If Bialy secures a conviction, he becomes anti-cop or anti-law and order. It's a classic lose-lose situation.

Secretly, Bialy hopes that a grand jury gathers tons of evidence, fails to indict, and allows Bialy and his team time to review and perhaps supplement the evidence. After review and supplementation, he might reopen the case in front of another grand jury.

But the chances are slim to none.

Having watched video footage and read the transcript of Jones' interview with Internal Affairs, Bialy fully expects a 'true bill' to issue a full indictment of Randall Jones.

Bialy sits back in his executive chair and gazes out his window at the Detroit skyline.

Tough city with tough people, but we've made a nice comeback from some very tough times.

Out his window are signs of economic development downtown. White and black-owned businesses are re-establishing a Detroit presence, and seeds of racial harmony are being planted. However, now that this evidence has been turned over and a grand jury is involved, Detroit and its Wayne County neighbors might be headed for a racial confrontation, unlike anything the Detroit area has seen since the 1967 riots rocked the city. The community doesn't need this Jones-Hayes debacle.

Chapter Four

Zachary Blake is a prominent Detroit area civil trial lawyer. His practice is focused on high-value personal injury cases. On occasion, because of his trial skills, he commands six-figure fees representing high profile criminal defendants. His most recent successes were criminal cases where he proved his clients' innocence to judges and prosecutors, getting all charges dropped before the cases went to trial.

Blake is now a legend in the Detroit legal circles, but it wasn't always this way. Once a highly effective trial lawyer, Zachary experienced a series of personal and business setbacks that caused him to spiral downward, ignore friends and loved ones, and give up his dream of championing justice. Less than five years ago, he was working out of a one-room office on Eight Mile Road, hustling misdemeanors, juvenile and traffic cases.

After his recent high profile courtroom successes, Blake's practice is booming. He's not only in high demand and frequently tapped to handle the highest-profile civil and criminal cases, but also offers his opinion on all matters that had legal issues or implications. The Jones-Hayes matter is undoubtedly one of those. Blake has made sure that the media knows he's available for comment.

Today, Blake and his family are having breakfast at the Original Pancake House on Woodward Avenue in Birmingham. They've traveled to the restaurant in separate cars because Blake is scheduled to appear on a Sunday morning talk show to discuss the legal ramifications of the Jones-Hayes case.

His adopted sons, Kenny and Jake, both order the Big Apple. This pancake is akin to eating an apple-cinnamon pie. These culinary beauties are cooked to order and take twenty to thirty minutes to prepare.

As his family members wait for their masterpieces to arrive, Blake gazes at his breakfast companions. His wife Jennifer and her two boys are bent over their iPhones, distracted by Internet news or texting marathons. Blake's mind wanders to the time they first met.

With a single phone call to his office, Jennifer changed his life. She wanted him to obtain justice for her sons against a powerful church and a predator priest. Blake took a hard look in the mirror, dusted off long-forgotten trial skills, and won a nine-figure trial verdict, the highest ever achieved in a Michigan courtroom. Several years later, the verdict is still the Michigan record.

The icing on the cake was that Zachary and Jennifer fell in love. They eventually married, and Zack adopted Jennifer's sons. The three are the loves of his life, but at this moment, he is annoyed.

Suddenly, Blake claps his hands together. He startles his family up from their phones. They look around apologetically at startled patrons sitting nearby.

"What Zack? You're embarrassing us!" Jennifer exclaims.

The two boys look at him like he's from outer space.

"Can we all put down our cell phones and enjoy each other's company for a few minutes while we wait for the food?" Blake requests.

"Sure, Dad," Jake agrees. "What would you like to talk about?"

"Yeah, Dad, sure," Kenny mimes, staring at his iPhone screen.

"Kenny, Dad's right. Put down the phone for a minute, would you?" This was not a request. *My mother used to say: Pick your battles.*

"Sure, Mom," Kenny grouses. He puts down the phone but continues to glance at the screen.

"Do you guys know *why* I'm appearing on Channel Four this morning?"

"No, Dad, but I'm sure you're dying to tell us."

"I've been summoned to give my legal opinion about the Jones-Hayes situation."

"Which situation is that?" Kenny inquires.

"Jones-Hayes," Blake repeats.

"What's it all about, Dad?" Jake wonders aloud.

"What's it all about? *Seriously*? Don't you guys read the news?"

"Is it on Snap Chat or Instagram?" Kenny wants to know. He steals a glimpse at his iPhone screen.

"Jenny, help me out here, dear," Blake rolls his eyes and turns to his wife.

"Boys, Randy Jones is the police officer being accused of shooting a black citizen in Cedar Ridge. Seriously? You guys haven't heard about this?"

"I think I saw the video on Instagram. Is that the one?" Kenny murmurs.

"Is the guy okay?" Jake is concerned.

"No, dammit, he's not okay! He's dead!" Zack chastises a bit too harshly. His family and other stunned patrons glare at him. Blake gazes at his boys and sees hurt in their eyes.

"I'm sorry, guys. I didn't mean to snap at you, but if what I have seen so far is true, this case and this cop really piss me off."

"What happened, Dad?" Kenny's suddenly interested.

"A young black couple with two small children in the back seat got pulled over in Cedar Ridge."

"What did they do wrong?" Jake is now into the story.

"Nothing, Jake. The officer claims that the driver looked like a suspect from some earlier robbery in the same community." Blake explains.

"Did he?" Jake asks.

"Did he what?"

"Look like the guy?"

"No, not even close. I have no idea what this cop was thinking. It's difficult to even give him the benefit of the doubt. That's how much they didn't resemble each other. The bottom line is the driver was twenty to twenty-five years older than the robbery suspect. Both husband and wife were college-educated, middle-class American citizens, like you and me."

"Except that they were black, and we are not," Jennifer states the obvious.

"So, what happened?" Jake is intrigued.

"Apparently, the officer approaches the driver's side window and asks for license and registration. The driver starts for his pocket and mentions, 'I want you to know officer. I have a gun and a license to carry.' The cop tells him to show his hands at the same time he asks for the license and registration, the rest gets kind of fuzzy, but the officer ends up shooting and killing the guy."

"Oh shit!" Kenny exclaims.

"Oh shit' is right," Blake huffs.

"Language, Jennifer scolds, ever the mom.

"What does this have to do with you, Dad?" Kenny wonders.

"I'm a guest on the *ViewPoint* program this morning. They want me to comment on the case."

"What do you plan to say?"

"It depends on the questions. But I can tell you this—no white driver, whether he matched a suspect's description or not, is going to be pulled over in Cedar Ridge on a routine traffic stop, unless he disobeyed some traffic law."

"That's pretty cynical, wouldn't you say, Zack?" Jennifer suggests.

"No, Jenny. The boys need to know this. This reads like a classic 'white cop pulls over black guy for no reason' situation," Blake grumbles.

"What does that mean?" Jake doesn't understand.

"It's what sometimes happens to African Americans in predominately white neighborhoods. It's a form of racism."

"And you think that happened in this case?" Kenny is now ignoring his iPhone.

"Yes, and I'm not the only one. Wayne County and Cedar Ridge city officials are considering charging the cop with murder. They're sending the case to a grand jury."

"Aren't those proceedings secret?" Jennifer inquires.

"They are, but I have inside information."

"From who?" Jake whispers.

"I could tell you, but then I would have to kill you," Blake deadpans.

Jake studies him. *Is he serious?*

Blake chuckles, and they all share a nervous laugh. But this is no laughing matter.

"Why do we care?" Jake inquires.

"Because we care about justice and fair play, Jake. I'm Jewish, which means I'm a minority. While I don't wear my ethnicity on my face like a black man does, I would not want to be targeted by police officers simply because I am Jewish. That's what the Nazis did to the Jews in Germany during World War II. White Christians, the majority, have a responsibility to care about equal justice and fairness for all, including minorities. Don't you agree?"

"When you put it that way, of course, we do," Jennifer rescues her youngest son.

When Zachary Blake is passionate about an issue, everyone, including loving family members, must get with the program or get out of his way.

"We'll be watching Dad. Will you be home in time for the Tigers game?" Kenny attempts to lighten the conversation.

"They're awful. Why would you want to waste an afternoon on them?"

"Because I love baseball! You know that. I thought you did too. Plus, it's a *bonding* experience. We get to spend some time together, Jake too. What do you say, Dad?"

"When you put it that way, how can I refuse? I should be home in plenty of time. Want me to bring anything?"

"Buddy's Pizza," exclaims Jake.

"What a surprise," Blake smiles.

Buddy's is a favorite in the Blake-Tracey household.

"How can you think of lunch when we haven't even had breakfast yet?" Jennifer remarks.

"Smart people always plan ahead," Kenny boasts.

Blake smiles. The boys are growing up. He wants them to have a social conscience and recognize the importance of what was going on in the country and around the world. These are troubling times in America. Kids today get news and ideas from social media. *Newsweek, Time, the Detroit Free Press and Detroit News* are publications that only 'old people' read. Zack doesn't care how or where his kids get the news. But he is concerned about misinformation on social media.

Disparate treatment of minorities should be discussed in every school in the country. Do the boys understand the

*difference between news and propaganda? Misinformation is
rampant on the internet, and the biggest provider of 'fake news'
is the President of the United States, Ronald John.*

Blake winces at the fact that his sons are unaware of the
Hayes-Jones case. The president, while unpopular in most
circles, is dividing the nation along racial and religious lines.
America hasn't seen this type of ethnic polarization since the
days leading up to the 1964 Civil Rights Act and Dr. Martin
Luther King, Jr.

This toxic environment, fueled by President John, is what
caused his last two criminal cases to escalate as they did. Blake
is also convinced that the mood of the country is partially
responsible for the Hayes shooting. At least, that's what he plans
to say during the interview.

The family's discussion takes a light-hearted turn toward the
misfortunes of the Detroit Lions and the Detroit Tigers. The
Tigers recently fired their manager and traded their best players.
Blake, an avid baseball fan, laments the loss of the Tigers' long-
term star players, the nucleus of a once solid baseball team. The
long-suffering Lions hired a new coach, but the team is still
mired in mediocrity.

The Big Apples arrive along with an oversized vegetarian
omelet Blake and Jennifer are sharing. Blake studies his omelet
then gazes, longingly, at the two Big Apples sitting in front of
him. He grabs a knife and fork and begins to carve a piece out of
one of the tasty delights. He gets his hand slapped for the
gesture.

"It is not polite to take someone else's food without asking,"
Kenny scolds, mimicking his mom.

Jennifer stifles a giggle with her hand over her mouth.

"Yeah, Dad, how would you like it if someone stuck his dirty
fork in *your* breakfast?" Jake lectures, spouting another
'Jennyism.'

Jennifer can't stifle her laughter this time.

"But look how big those things are. I only want a small bite.
Come on!" Blake pleads. He scrunches his face to look wounded.

"But, you need to ask first," Jake mocks. "Right, Mom?"

"Right, Jake," laughs Jennifer, spitting out omelet pieces and holding her hand over her mouth.

"Fine! I'll ask for a bite of one of the Big Apples that *I'm* paying for!" This is no laughing matter for Blake. He's losing his temper.

"We're waiting. Ask politely and nicely." Kenny indicates, looking to Mom for support.

"Alright, I'll play along. May I please have a bite of one or both of your Big Apples, boys?" Blake cajoles.

"Maybe we'll save you a bite, right, Jake?" Kenny taunts. He gazes, longingly, at the pancake.

"Right, big brother. Maybe we'll save you a bite, Dad. Don't count on it, though. Bad manners are not usually rewarded," Jake teases.

Blake scowls, returns to his omelet, and begins to devour it. Jennifer and her two boys eye each other, shrug, and start eating. The family continues their meal in virtual silence. Blake hopes to taste some leftover Big Apple, but the two boys devour both of them. As they place their knives and forks down, they sigh and pat their stomachs. Blake is simmering.

"Boy, that was outstandingly delicious, wasn't it Jake?" Kenny sighs.

"Delightfully tasty," Jake agrees.

Jennifer glances over to a bewildered Blake, who looks from one boy to the next. *This man can take anything some tough litigator throws at him, but these two teenagers are surprisingly successful at getting his goat.*

Blake rises and slams his napkin down on the table. He grabs the bill and exits the booth. "Payback is a bitch," he mutters.

"Zack, you're acting like a child," Jennifer scolds.

"That goes for you, too, lady."

Blake walks away, leaving behind another round of laughter from his family. He stalks over to the cashier, pays the bill, and storms out of the restaurant.

Blake is waiting in the Range Rover as Jennifer and the boys exit the restaurant. He is still steaming as his family approaches. He pops the locks.

Jennifer hand motions him to roll down his window.

"Good luck this morning. We'll be watching. Please drive carefully."

"Sure. Thanks for sharing, boys. And thanks for the support, *Jennifer*," he snaps.

He guns the engine, squeals the tires, and speeds off.

Eat my exhaust!

He glances into his rearview mirror and observes his family doubled over with laughter, a few feet behind the vehicle. He looks at himself in the rearview and sees an angry scowl. Gradually, he begins to smile, then laughs; a slight chuckle at first, but eventually, it morphs into full-blown bellows.

Simply conceding to himself that his behavior was inane, and the boys' behavior was funny doesn't change his attitude about exacting revenge.

Payback is indeed a bitch!

Chapter Five

Blake is still plotting his 'food revenge' as he arrives at WDIV studios on Fort Street in downtown Detroit. Devon Harlan, the host of *ViewPoint,* greets him in the lobby. Devon introduces him to her other guests. Blake already knows Lawrence Bialy, the Wayne County Prosecutor. The other guest is Stacey Schwartz, a reporter for the *Detroit News.*

The four discuss the segment, topics which they will offer expert commentary and what questions to expect. All three experts are frequent visitors and familiar with the process. All agree to follow Harlan's lead.

Showtime!

"Good morning, everyone. Thanks for joining us on this beautiful Sunday. I'm your host, Devon Harlan, and this is *ViewPoint.*

"Today's discussion is controversial but long overdue in our town. How far has our community come in its battle against racism? Are we yet a colorblind society? Has Detroit and its suburbs succeeded where others have failed?

"My guests today are Wayne County prosecutor Larry Bialy, attorney Zachary Blake, and *Detroit News* columnist Stacey Schwartz. Good morning to all of you."

"Good morning, Devon," the three chirp, almost in unison.

"Most of our viewers are aware of the recent shooting in Cedar Ridge, which claimed the life of a young father and husband Marcus Hayes of Detroit. A Cedar Ridge police officer, Randy Jones, faces disciplinary action and possible criminal charges for shooting Hayes during a traffic stop.

"Larry, let's begin with you because you will face the difficult decision of deciding whether or not to pursue criminal charges against Officer Jones.

"Law and order advocates argue the officer shot Mr. Hayes in self-defense out of fear Mr. Hayes was reaching for a weapon after repeatedly failing to obey the officer's commands.

"Civil rights activists and others believe this is a case with racial undertones. Those activists opine that Officer Jones targeted Mr. Hayes and pulled him over solely based upon his race.

"Other critics argue Officer Jones issued inconsistent verbal commands that confused Mr. Hayes. Larry, please tell our viewers: What is the status of your investigation?"

"Thanks for inviting me, Devon. The honest answer to your question is that we are still investigating. No decision has been made. What I will say to your viewers at this point is that, whether or not Officer Jones is innocent, Marcus Hayes' death is a tragedy.

"A woman lost her husband. Two small children lost their father. A dedicated law enforcement official is devastated; his career and reputation hang in the balance. There are no winners here.

"What I can assure your audience is that a thorough investigation will be conducted. If the evidence supports an indictment, one will be issued. I want everyone to know that in Wayne County, no one is above the law."

"We are also pleased to have prominent Bloomfield Hills attorney Zachary Blake with us," announced Harlan, turning to Blake. "Zack, can you please give us a perspective from the other side of the case? How would you assess this case from a defense point of view?"

"It's nice to be with you today, Devon. Like any other case in the beginning stages, the prosecutor holds all of the cards. The defense learns things as the case progresses and evidence is revealed. In this case, since we are still early in the process, I don't know much more than anyone else. I only know what I read in the *News* or *Free Press*, and I am hesitant to comment without knowing all the facts.

"However, I was discussing the case with my family this morning. The circumstances are indeed tragic. If I were the lawyer counseling the officer, I would advise him to shut up, assert his Fifth Amendment rights against self-incrimination, and make Larry and his office *prove* he violated the law."

"Good advice for Officer Jones, Zack, but in this case, we have the two infamous videos: One was captured by the dash cam of the officer's patrol car and the other by Marcus Hayes's wife, Sarah, on her cell phone. I cannot imagine filming an event that results in the death of my spouse. What a tragic circumstance."

"Nor can I, Devon. But if I'm representing Officer Jones, I'm cautioning *everyone* that video evidence is inconclusive. Both videos are graphic and clearly depict the *officer's* actions and inactions. However, neither video demonstrates, at all, what the officer saw," Blake comments.

"What do you mean?"

"Devon, the officer's principal defense is that he acted in self-defense, for his safety and the safety of others in and around the suspect's vehicle. Fortunately, or unfortunately, depending on the truth of this situation, the viewer cannot see what Mr. Hayes is doing in either video.

"Most important, viewers cannot see his hands, which Officer Jones alleges were reaching for a gun. On the other hand, the eyewitness, Mrs. Hayes, claims her husband's hands were *not* reaching for a gun. He was reaching for the license and registration Officer Jones demanded. This case is an officer's worst nightmare, a damned-if-you-do, damned-if-you-don't situation. Giving the officer the benefit of every doubt, a case for self-defense might be made. In my professional judgment, however, this will be a very tough burden for Jones."

Devon turns to Stacey Schwartz. "But, Stacey, what about the stop of this family in the first place? Cedar Ridge is a downriver, blue-collar, predominately white community. Here comes a black family driving through town. According to nearly every account I've read, Mr. Hayes is observing all traffic laws. Still, he is pulled over. Why?"

"The officer argues the couple matched a description of two robbery suspects. Civil rights activists say this is a clear case of murder by cop and for no reason other than the fact that the driver was a black man. I know you have been a principal reporter for the *News* on this incident. What have you learned so far?"

"As your viewers probably know, the stop, in this case, is most controversial. We know there was an earlier robbery at a nearby Burger King. According to witnesses, the robbers were two young black guys, one with an Afro and one with dreads. Apparently, Mrs. Hayes has dreads and Mr. Hayes has an Afro. The officer alleges they resembled the suspects. The problem is that the Hayes couple was twenty years older than the robbery suspects. If you look at the composite drawings of the suspects and compare them to photographs of Mr. and Mrs. Hayes, they look nothing alike. Even the dreads and Afro are dissimilar.

"So, why the traffic stop when the officer *admits* that the driver did nothing wrong? To this impartial observer, those facts suggest Mr. Hayes was pulled over for driving while black and the shooting was the worst result of a bad stop.

"Worse, my investigation has uncovered a startling number of similar incidents in similar communities across the country. This demonstrates that these types of cases are far more prevalent since Ronald John was elected president."

"That statistic is interesting and *terrifying*, Stacey."

"Well, Devon, terrifying or not, it's accurate. This is not a great time to be black in America."

"Devon, may I add something to Stacey's comments?" Blake chimes.

"Sure, Zack, by all means."

"Whether Stacey's reporting relative to national trends under the John administration is true or not, it is not evidence of Officer Jones's guilt. Those who know me know that I am a staunch defender of civil rights. However, I am also a staunch defender of the concept of innocent until proven guilty and the right to a fair trial. I sincerely hope Officer Jones does not get tried and convicted in the press before an indictment is issued and an untainted jury decides his fate."

"I can promise you that he will get an unbiased review from my office," Bialy stresses.

"An indictment will only issue if the facts and the law support it, Devon. No one will be railroaded for the sake of political correctness on my watch."

Blake smiles to himself. *Larry lies extremely well with a straight face.*

"Good to hear, Larry," Devon praises.

"By the way, rumor has it that a grand jury might be taking up this case. Care to comment?"

"Devon, the Wayne County Prosecutor's Office does not discuss or confirm grand jury proceedings in public forums. I have no comment."

"Okay, my friends, that's all the time we have for this segment. We'll keep an eye on this controversial, high-profile case and report any and all interesting developments.

"Thanks to all of my guests for lending their expertise today. Up next, while downtown Detroit is experiencing a development boon, its neighborhoods are suffering. What is Detroit doing to address the issue? We will be talking with some urban development specialists and urban beat reporters when we come back."

After the show, Blake approaches Bialy.

"Good to see you, Larry. How is this thing shaking out, off the record?"

"Are you asking as an officer of the court, someone who can keep his mouth shut?"

"Absolutely."

Bialy checks the hallway and sees no one. "On the q.t., the case is going to the grand jury tomorrow. I don't know who Devon's sources are, but they're spot on."

"What evidence do you have?"

"Let's take this outside, Zack."

They step out into the late morning sunlight.

"You've seen the two videos, I presume."

"I have, Larry. They're fairly damning but inconclusive. I wouldn't hang a prosecution on those alone."

"Officer Jones gave a statement to Internal Affairs. He virtually admits to stopping these people for no reason and killing the husband out of baseless fear. That and a previous, similar incident are presenting Officer Jones in a bad light."

"Good for justice, bad for Jones. I hope you get the bastard if that's what the evidence shows."

"One never knows, but it looks like this officer's policing days are over. It also looks like he will be indicted for and convicted of second-degree murder in the death of Marcus Hayes."

"Don't count your chickens before they hatch, Larry. You thought Arya Khan was guilty, too, remember?"

"I remember. I'm happy that we righted that wrong in the end. How's she doing, by the way?"

"Fine, last I heard."

"Give her my best if you talk to her. She's quite a woman. Say, Zack?"

"Yes?"

"Can I count on your confidence one more time?"

"It depends on what you tell me, but, generally, of course, you can. What's up?"

"I'm certain I can get the indictment, but probable cause is a lot easier to prove than guilt beyond a reasonable doubt."

"What are you driving at?"

"These are strange times in America and in Detroit, Zack. If we were reviewing this case under a previous administration, *any one of them*, I would have suggested that we had a ninety-five percent chance of a conviction. Today, with the racial and religious divisiveness of President John, the chances are reduced to, like, fifty-fifty."

"Okay?"

"I want to hedge my bet."

"And the hedge, Larry?"

"I'm going to recommend that the feds file a civil rights case against the officer."

"And?"

"I want to *privately* recommend that the family hire an attorney and file a civil case against the officer and the city of Cedar Ridge. And I want to recommend you as the plaintiff's attorney. Are you interested? No referral fee expected or anything. I'm just looking for justice for the Hayes family."

Blake can't believe his ears. He and Bialy were often adversaries; this is the ultimate compliment. The case is in

Zack's sweet spot. It's a *very* high profile civil case involving serious damages and an important societal issue.

"Sure, Larry." He tries to mask his excitement. "I would certainly consider it."

"Thanks, Zack."

No, thank you!

"You're welcome, Larry. I'm happy to help."

Chapter Six

"Good morning, ladies and gentlemen of the grand jury. It is 8:30 a.m. on Monday, July 30, and the Wayne County prosecutor's office and the Cedar Ridge Police Department are seeking an indictment against Cedar Ridge police officer Randall Jones for murder in the second degree. My name is Rochelle Lynch. I am a Wayne County assistant prosecutor and the lead prosecutor for this case. Adam Rock, seated to my right, is my second chair and will be assisting me throughout these proceedings.

"This investigation seeks to answer the question of criminal liability on the part of Officer Jones in the shooting death of Marcus Hayes. We will cover a lot of ground during these proceedings. However, there will be no parade of witnesses or numerous exhibits. Officer Jones will not testify, but an Internal Affairs officer will, and he will provide an audiotape and transcript of his thirty-five-minute interview of Officer Jones. You will first hear the interview in its entirety. Following this presentation, the Internal Affairs officer will testify and be available to answer any questions that you may have.

"You will also see graphic dash cam and iPhone video of the traffic stop and shooting. I apologize in advance for the content, but this video evidence must be viewed to understand why we feel charges are appropriate in this matter.

"You will also hear an audio recording of Officer Jones's call to Officer Alexander Mickler requesting back up. Officer Mickler and the victim's widow, Sarah Hayes, an eyewitness to the shooting, will also testify live. You may ask them questions.

"We will be presenting a use-of-force expert who will testify about national standards that apply to police officers during traffic stops, appropriate causes for such stops, and, most importantly, the policies and procedures to follow when confronted with a citizen who indicates he is carrying a weapon, as Marcus Hayes did in this case.

"This expert witness will then apply those standards to this case and opine whether or not Officer Jones acted reasonably under the existing circumstances. With these preliminaries out of the way, do any of you have any questions before we begin?"

Lynch pauses and waits on the jury.

"No questions? Let's begin with dash cam and *iPhone* video. They've been marked as Exhibit Numbers One and Two, respectively. We will follow this with Officer Jones's statement to Lieutenant Douglas Kelly from the Cedar Ridge Police, Internal Affairs Division, Exhibit number three. You will each be provided with a transcript of the statement so you can follow along. After the statement is presented, we will hear from Lieutenant Kelly in person. Will someone dim the lights, please?"

The lights dim as a computer and video projector are placed front and center. A portable white screen is erected in front of the jurors.

A technician plays the two videos. The lights come back on, and the technician plays the audiotape. The entire presentation lasts an hour and a half. Lynch studies the jury during the audio presentation. Jurors are engaged, reading the transcript as the tape rolls along, and flipping pages as the audio reaches the end of each page. When the audio ends, Lynch calls Lieutenant Kelly to the stand.

"Would you state your full name and spell it for the court reporter, please?" Lynch begins.

"My name is Douglas Kelly."

"Where are you employed?"

"Cedar Ridge Police Department, Internal Affairs Division."

"And how long have you been a police officer?"

"Thirty-eight years."

"Have you spent the entire thirty-eight years in Cedar Ridge?"

"Yes, ma'am."

"Where did you receive your training to become a police officer?"

"I attended Wayne County Community College and obtained a two-year certificate in criminal justice. Then, I attended the

Downriver Police Academy and graduated in 1980. While I was working as a patrol officer during the day, I finished my studies with a Bachelor's in Criminal Justice at Wayne State University. Afterward, I attended law school at Detroit College of Law, graduating in 1990. I was promoted to the detective squad, where I worked for fifteen years. In 2005, I was transferred to Internal Affairs as a senior investigator and promoted to lieutenant until I was named Director of Internal Affairs in 2012."

"Impressive resume, lieutenant. Is it unusual for you to be conducting these types of interviews at this stage in your career?"

"Chief Brooks requires my direct involvement when there is an officer-involved shooting."

"Internal Affairs is the branch of the police department that investigates the misconduct of police officers; is that a fair statement?"

"It is."

"You are not a squad commander or anything like that? You do not directly supervise patrol officers, right?"

"Correct."

"How did you become involved in this case?"

"Cedar Ridge chief of police Warren Brooks assembled a task force to look into the matter. That task force included Officer Jones's squad commander, Richard Farnsworth, as well as other elite members of the department. "

"And did the task force conduct an investigation?"

"It did."

"Did it publish findings?"

"It did."

"Lieutenant, I want you to look at what has been marked as GJ Exhibit number four. Do you recognize this document?"

"I do. It's the task force's final report."

"Are you one of the signatories on the report?"

"I am."

"Please review the report and confirm for the jury that it is the full report of the task force."

Kelly calmly and casually flips through the pages. When he finishes, he remarks, "This is the full report with all official signatures at the bottom."

"You were present during the audio presentation of Officer Jones's Internal Affairs interview, were you not?"

"I was."

"Did the jury hear a full and accurate presentation of the interview you conducted?"

"Yes."

"Was this the only formal interview conducted with Officer Jones?"

"Yes. Jones also made a brief statement to Officer Mickler at the scene, and that statement is part of the record, as is Officer Mickler's account."

"Before we admit the report into evidence, please explain the concept of qualified immunity as it applies to officer-involved shootings."

"Sure. If an incident occurs on duty, as it did in this case, an officer receives the benefit of qualified immunity. Simply stated, a police officer is permitted to use deadly force in many more situations than civilians are. Since an officer is trained to use a firearm, and if he or she discharges a weapon while on duty, the officer is *presumed* to have used it for a lawful purpose.

"In investigating this matter, Officer Jones is not only presumed innocent, a constitutional right that all citizens enjoy, he is also presumed to have acted lawfully, in his capacity as a police officer. What person—"

Lynch interrupts Kelly, turning to the jury.

"Ladies and gentlemen, you will be specifically instructed on the details of this qualified immunity standard toward the end of these proceedings. Sorry for interrupting you, lieutenant. Please continue."

"No problem. I was going to explain the standard this way: Who would become a police officer if they were subject to arrest and prosecution every time they discharged their weapon? That's why we try to give an officer every benefit of the doubt."

"Move to admit exhibit number four."

"I won't ask you to regurgitate all of its contents. I believe this report speaks for itself, in volumes. However, I *will* ask you to publish the task force's final conclusions."

"The task force concluded that Officer Jones acted without justifiable cause. We have suspended him from active duty and are currently negotiating his permanent departure from the Cedar Ridge Police Department."

"Is your investigation a criminal or administrative investigation or both?"

"Both. We primarily function as an administrative body, determining an officer's fitness for service. However, if our investigation reveals what we consider to be criminal wrongdoing, we publish our findings and refer those findings to your office for consideration of criminal charges."

"The Wayne County Prosecutor's Office, correct?"

"Correct."

"And have you referred this case to the Wayne County Prosecutor's Office?"

"Yes."

"Despite the qualified immunity that applies to police officers, your report concluded that Officer Jones might have committed a crime, is that correct?"

"Yes."

"What crime would that be?"

"That is for you to decide."

"I understand, lieutenant, but you referred the case. What crime does Internal Affairs believe occurred during this incident?"

"My review of the tapes and the results of Officer Jones's interview suggest Officer Jones is guilty of second-degree murder or perhaps the lesser crime of voluntary manslaughter.

"However, whether a crime was committed and the degree of criminality that applies is decided by your office or by this grand jury, not by the police."

"Please define second-degree murder for the grand jury."

"Second-degree murder is an unplanned intentional killing or a death caused by a reckless disregard for human life. My review of the evidence suggests the second definition applies to this case."

"And an explanation or definition of voluntary manslaughter?"

"Voluntary manslaughter is an intentional killing where the offender had no prior intent to kill. It is often referred to as a killing that occurs in the heat of passion. The circumstances leading up to the killing would be such that a reasonable person might become emotionally or mentally disturbed at the moment of the act that results in death."

"That definition sounds more 'heat of passion,' correct?"

"Correct. A case might be made that Jones's irrational fear that Mr. Hayes was reaching for a gun was the 'heat of passion' that triggered his behavior in this case. If this jury agrees, then voluntary manslaughter will be an appropriate finding."

"Any other possibilities?"

"Sure. If Officer Jones can convince the jury that he saw Mr. Hayes pulling a gun and *rationally* feared that Hayes was about to shoot him, his conduct could be considered reasonable and a righteous kill or justifiable homicide."

"Do you believe the evidence supports that finding?"

"No."

"Did your investigation include a look at Officer Jones's prior record?"

"It did."

"Is there anything in his prior record you consider relevant to the inquiry and to your conclusion that the officer's conduct should be referred for charges?"

"Yes."

"Please describe these considerations for this jury."

"The jury may recall from his formal statement that Jones graphically describes a previous similar incident."

"Please refresh our memories lieutenant."

"I questioned Officer Jones about previous, similar incidents."

"And what did he tell you?"

"He indicated he'd been involved in a similar incident involving a traffic stop."

"Please tell the jury what happened."

"In a similar situation, Officer Jones pulled over a vehicle when no traffic violation was committed and no equipment issues were noted. When I queried Jones about why he pulled the driver over, he told me there had been a B & E in the neighborhood. He and his partner thought this might be the perpetrator.

"I inquired whether there had been a working description of the perpetrator on that occasion. He told me, 'no.' I wondered what made him suspicious enough to pull the guy over. He said the guy seemed 'out of place.' Those were his exact words.

"What did that mean? He told me the driver did not fit the profile of any resident in the community. Finally, I asked Jones if the driver was white or black. He indicated the man was black.

"It is apparent that Officer Jones has some issues with black men driving in the city limits. Jones feels that black men in Cedar Ridge are 'out of place.'"

"What is known on the street as *driving while black*?"

"In my opinion, yes."

"Thank you, lieutenant. We may recall you at a later date. Do any of the jurors have any questions?"

No questions. Kelly steps down; Lynch calls Officer Alex Mickler to the stand.

Lynch establishes Mickler's professional qualifications and replays the call between Mickler and Jones.

She displays the portion of the dash cam video from the time of Mickler's arrival at the scene. The video concludes, and Lynch approaches the witness.

"Officer Mickler, do the video and audio accurately depict the scene as you arrived?"

"Yes, ma'am, they do."

"Officer Jones called you to provide back up for his traffic stop of Mr. Hayes, is that correct?"

"Yes, it is. But I was tied up with another situation, waiting for a key holder on a breaking and entering situation. Officer Jones's traffic stop was not an emergency. I told him that I would be there as soon as I could."

"His call for backup expressed no urgency?"

"No, it didn't. In retrospect, I'm sorry it didn't because my other call was really no big deal."

"This non-urgent transmission came on your mobile walkie-talkie?"

"Yes, ma'am."

"How much time transpired between the call for backup and the notification that there had been a shooting?"

"Not long. Between fifteen minutes and half an hour at most."

"What did you do when you got the second call?"

"I jumped in my squad car and raced to the scene, about three-quarters of a mile away from my starting point."

"So, you were close to the scene and familiar with the area?"

"Yes, ma'am. I have spent my entire ten-year career with the Cedar Ridge Police Department."

"When you arrived at the scene, what did you see?"

"I saw Officer Jones standing in the street arguing with someone inside the subject vehicle, the Hayes vehicle, passenger side. The vehicle, a Honda as I recall, was still running with lights on. The driver appeared to be unconscious."

"Did you come from the same direction as Officer Jones?"

"No. I came from the opposite direction. I pulled up alongside his vehicle and left plenty of room between the two cars to block them from view. I wanted to prevent passing traffic from gawking or interfering. I left my flashing lights on, exited my vehicle, and approached the scene."

"What happened next?"

"Jones instructed me to deal with the passenger, who turned out to be a black woman. I inquired whether Randy, uh, Officer Jones, if he had called for an ambulance. He told me that he had not. The driver looked to be in bad shape, so I immediately called for an ambulance.

"I was surprised an ambulance had not been summoned before my arrival. I suggested to Jones that he allow me to handle things, invited him to take a seat on the curb, and I instructed the woman to exit the vehicle with her hands raised. She kept asking about her children, her 'babies,' she called them, and I told her they would be fine as long as she complied with my instructions."

"Did she comply?"

"Yes, she exited and walked to the back of the vehicle, as I instructed. The whole time she was screaming that the 'bastard,' referring to Officer Jones, shot her husband in cold blood in front of her and her children. It was difficult, but I managed to place her in handcuffs. She appeared to be in shock."

"Why did you need to place her in cuffs?"

"Because, in my opinion, she was belligerent and somewhat irrational. I felt the situation required more officer control."

"What happened next?"

"I called central, advised them of an officer-involved shooting, and told them to send the cavalry."

"The cavalry?"

"Sorry, it's an expression. I requisitioned multiple squad cars to secure the scene and told them we needed supervisors. I believe I summoned everyone within earshot of my voice. The passenger kept screaming, 'he killed my husband! He killed their daddy!' I urged her to calm down. She calmed slightly and advised that she captured the whole incident on her cell phone."

"What did you do next?"

"Well, the ambulance arrived, and I pointed to the driver and told the attendants he was unconscious. Then I began to question Jones. First, I wondered why he didn't wait for me before approaching. Jones claimed it seemed routine. He mentioned the kids in the car and the smell of marijuana. He said when he requested the driver's license and registration, the guy told him he was carrying. And during my questioning of Jones, the woman kept screaming something like 'he shot him for no damn reason.'"

"Please explain to the jury what Jones meant when he mentioned 'he was carrying.'"

"That means that the driver had a gun in his possession."

"Does a citizen usually tell an officer that he is carrying a weapon if he intends to shoot the officer?"

"No. That would be very unusual."

"Please continue."

"Jones contends the suspect would not comply with his instructions. He wouldn't put his hands where Jones could see them, and he wouldn't tell him where the gun was. The female passenger disputed that account. She claims Officer Jones accused the victim of noncompliance, when he was, in fact, complying. Jones argued that the guy looked like one of the Burger King suspects, was high, and kept reaching down. I pointed out the two Burger King suspects were both young and male. Randy indicated he couldn't tell the passenger was female."

"Anything else, Officer Mickler?"

"Yes. I questioned where Randy was standing when the shooting took place. He advised me that he was standing on the driver's side near the side-view mirror, gun drawn, pointing down at the driver. I inquired whether he ran the plate and what it showed. He indicated he had run the plate and that the vehicle came back as belonging to the driver. The driver lived in Detroit and had no outstanding warrants."

"Is that it, Officer Mickler?"

"In a nutshell."

"Do you want to offer the jury your opinion about potential criminality?"

"No, I wasn't present at the time of the shooting. I'm confused why he decided to proceed without backup."

"Any questions from the jurors?"

"Yes, I have a question," Juror Number Eleven raises her hand.

"Thank you, Number Eleven. What's your question?"

Lynch is apprehensive—surprised a juror has a question.

"You are an experienced patrol officer, correct Officer Mickler?" Number Eleven begins.

"Yes, ma'am."

"Would you have done anything differently than Officer Jones did?"

Rochelle Lynch smiles and busies herself with paperwork. She *loves* this question.

"As I indicated previously, it wasn't my stop, so it's hard to say. In retrospect, however, a routine stop does not typically have deadly consequences. The plate came back clean; Hayes had no previous record."

"Can you elaborate for us, please?"

"Officer-involved shootings at traffic stops are unusual, but they do happen from time to time. I've always thought of Randy Jones as a good officer, but if you requested research on the issue, I'd bet the vast majority of previous officer-involved traffic stop shootings involve suspects with a criminal past.

"Not so in this case. The victim had no previous record. Other than the fact that he admitted he had a license to carry and a weapon in the vehicle, there was no indication that he posed a threat to Officer Jones.

"Mr. Hayes didn't have to tell Randy he was in possession of a weapon. The victim provided that information voluntarily. His admission strongly suggests that he wanted no trouble and had no intention of using the firearm. Jones seemed to panic when he discovered that Mr. Hayes possessed a gun.

"His fear may have been race-related. You'd have to ask him. To me, a law-abiding citizen is a law-abiding citizen, regardless of race. So yes, I believe the result would have been different had I been the officer. I don't believe I'd have pulled this couple over in the first place."

"Any other questions from the jury?" Lynch scans the jury. No takers.

"Ladies and gentlemen, you're excused for the day."

Lynch begins checking her calendar and talking at the same time. "We will adjourn and reconvene on . . . let me see . . . Thursday. Have a good evening."

Chapter Seven

"I'm tired, Mama. I'm tired; I'm frustrated and sad. I'm very lonely, but most of all, I am *damned* angry."

Sarah Hayes' face twists in anguish. She and her mother, Lula Clarke, are seated in the kitchen of the Hayes' refurbished brick colonial in the upscale Indian Village neighborhood of Detroit. The girls are watching cartoons in the living room. Sarah drifts off in thought. *All the work we put into making this our home and Marcus will never get to enjoy—*

"Sarah? Sarah, honey. Where have you gone? Knock, knock."

Lula Clarke's face registers the concern that any mother would have for a daughter in pain. Lula was the first member of her family to graduate from high school and attend college. She married her high school sweetheart and had planned to finish school at Wayne State to become a teacher.

Her husband, Theo Clarke—short for Theodore—also planned to go to college and dreamed of becoming a civil rights lawyer. Vietnam ruined all that.

Theo was drafted and shipped to Nam. He was killed by friendly fire just as America began withdrawing her troops. Suddenly widowed in her twenties, Lula was forced to raise two small children alone. Her dreams of college, a better life, and growing old with the man she loved were laid to waste in the jungles of Vietnam.

After Theo's death, Lula was forced to find a job to support her young family. She knew the pain and heartache of losing a husband and lover, the father of her children. Now, watching her daughter live through a similar tragedy is ripping her heart out. The difference between the two women is that Sarah *did* complete college. She has a bachelor's degree in history from Wayne State University.

"Sorry, Mama. Marcus will never enjoy our beautiful home. We had such hopes and dreams . . . They're gone. All gone . . . "

Tears form. Sarah wipes them with her sleeve.

"You must be careful, sweetheart," Lula warns.

"You have two beautiful babies to consider. The girls need their mama now, more than ever."

"How do people stand for this? How many people have to die before we rise up and say, 'enough is enough?'" Sarah's words are uttered with more force than she intends. She's mad at the world, *not* at her mother.

"That's a difficult question with no simple answer, sweetheart. I've lived in this country and in this city much longer and through tougher times than you have. Every time our people take two steps forward, it seems that we take a step and a half backward. Things are changing for the better, but when you wear your difference on your face, when the color of your skin defines who you are to others, change doesn't come easy," Lulu laments.

"Whatever!" Sarah growls. "It can't do Marcus any good now, can it?"

"That's true, baby. I'm so sorry about Marcus. He was a good man, a great husband, and a wonderful father," Lula reminisces, holding back emotions.

Her heart aches for her daughter. She is doing the only thing a mother can do under tragic circumstances. She sits by her daughter's side and listens as the younger woman pours her heart out.

"A good man," Sarah begins. "A good man. Yes, he was a good man, but he was also a black man. And when you're *black*, being good isn't always enough."

"No, sweetheart, it isn't. A black man walks a different line, a tightrope. Sometimes that line is hard to see. That seems to be what happened here."

"What do you mean, Mama?"

"Because Marcus was a good man, he wanted the officer to know that he was carrying a gun. He wanted no misunderstandings. He didn't have to tell the man he had a gun, but he told him anyway. His honesty was his undoing. Why would he tell the officer that he had a gun if he had intended to use it?"

"God help me, Mama. *I told* Marcus to tell the officer about the gun!" Sarah convulses in despair. "*I* got Marcus killed!

Marcus tells him about the gun, and suddenly this cop flies into a panic, barking out all kinds of orders, pulling his gun and pointing it at Marcus, ready to shoot. Why couldn't the cop listen to what we were saying? Why was he so impatient? Aren't cops trained to be *patient*, to use their weapons as a last resort?"

"But this was a *white* cop, Sarah. And to a *white* cop, a black man and a gun don't mix. Do you understand where I'm coming from?"

"If Marcus hadn't told him about the gun and the cop saw that he was carrying, would that have been any better?"

"No, baby, and that's why this is not on you. The fact is that this happens in a white community, with a black man, a gun, and a cop who claims he can't see the black man's hands. That combination is a recipe for disaster. It doesn't matter who tells who what to do."

"I know you're right, Mama. These days, just getting pulled over in a white neighborhood can be a recipe for disaster. These types of stops are not unusual. Black people *know* this.

"But not everyone is shot to death. There's something about *this* guy, *this* cop. Trigger-happy or something; racist more than likely. This cannot stand. I want justice for my husband, and I'm not going to get it in Cedar Ridge."

"I agree, honey. But Marcus is gone, and you're still here. You must be careful. You feel me, Sarah? What do you plan to do?" Lula's concerned, not only for her daughter but also for her granddaughters' safety.

"I'm not sure yet. I watched *Viewpoint* on Channel 4 Sunday morning. That prosecutor guy, Bialy, was on with another attorney, you know, the famous one, the Jewish guy."

"Zachary Blake?"

"That's the one. He's supposed to be the best, right?"

"That's what they say. Why?"

"I'm going to march myself into Bialy's office and find out what the hell is being done to get justice for my Marcus. The cop's suspended with pay. With *pay*, Mama! My husband is dead, and his killer gets a paid vacation? What kind of justice is that?"

Sarah's rage is building.

"It's no justice at all, sweetheart, but you need to think about this," Lula cautions. "I'm not suggesting you stand down. Go talk to Bialy, but be *respectful*. Don't go to the man's office accusing and demanding. Don't be telling him what he has to do or threatening what you're going to do.

"Make an appointment to see him. Go in there and politely ask something like, 'how is the investigation going, Mr. Bialy? When can we expect to see an arrest or a trial?' Do you understand?" *Are you feeling me, Sarah?*

"I wouldn't have to do this if I was white, now would I, Mama?"

"Maybe not, sweetheart. I don't know for sure. If you and Marcus were white, maybe the country is just as pissed as you are. But knowing that it's wrong doesn't make it any less true. And your kids need their mama."

"But Bialy is the prosecutor for Wayne County, Mama. Marcus was a Wayne County citizen. This guy should be in Marcus's corner. He should want justice, too."

"You're right, Sarah, my sweet Sarah. But, we don't know that he *doesn't* want justice for Marcus. You are only speculating. Also, you must remember two very important things."

"What are those?"

"Bialy is a white guy *and* a politician."

"What's that got to do with anything? He's the damn prosecutor for crying out loud!"

"But, he's the *white* prosecutor, honey. What does *he* know about being black in America? What does *he* know about being pulled over for driving while black? What does *he* know about living with discrimination every day of your life or being a descendant of slaves?

"He works in Detroit but lives in *Northville*. He works with black people and probably knows some socially. But what does he really know about the black experience? Every day, he leaves work in his BMW and drives it to his beautiful white suburban Northville home.

"He probably doesn't even think about black people unless he's at work. Maybe because he's prosecuting one, but who knows? But what real connection does he have? Has *he* ever experienced discrimination? Has *he* lost a loved one to senseless violence? Can *he* hear gunshots from a lounge chair on the front porch of *his* fancy-ass home? Are drugs being sold on a street corner somewhere close to *Northville*? Of course not!

"Still, this is a man who you need on your side if you're going to get justice for Marcus. A black woman challenging the system and taking on a white man—especially a white *cop*—is not going to have an easy time.

"And that damned man in the White House doesn't help things any. He represents the type of political hatred I'm talking about. Guys like him play to the worst fears of white men. Are you having a bad time of it right now? Lost your job? Having difficulty making ends meet? It's not my fault or your fault. It's the black man's fault.

"It's the Muslims' fault. Blame a Mexican immigrant. Man's got everyone lining up, taking sides, white people versus people of color, different religions arguing their way is the right way.

"This is a bad time in America. It's an especially *terrible* time for a black woman to be taking on a white cop or the white establishment. Bialy will take this case in whatever direction the political winds blow."

Lula Clarke is a wise and experienced woman.

"So, what would you have me do, Mama? I won't sit back and do nothing,"

"I'm not saying that you should. All I am saying is that you're going to be locked in a political game. To get what you want, you're going to need to learn how to play the game. That's what I'm talking about.

"Lose the attitude, respect the man's position and his politics, and ask how he intends to handle this matter. He may *not* fully understand the black experience. Maybe you can help him out. Describe the terror of that night for you and your kids. Help him understand how the officer went so terribly wrong. Make him see the world through your eyes, through Marcus's eyes, through a *black person's* eyes."

"Do you really think that is possible, Mama?"

"It's what I have prayed for every day since the day you were born. I prayed that things would be better for you than they ever were for me."

"That's not happening, Mama."

"No, baby, it isn't, but you have an opportunity to shine a positive light on a very negative situation, and you need to take advantage of that opportunity. That's why you have to go about this the right way."

"What if Bialy won't do anything, Mama, won't bring charges or anything?"

"That would be where this Zachary Blake comes in. He can file a civil rights lawsuit, police brutality, or whatever they call it these days. He's not afraid of taking on the man, that's for sure. You might want to see Mr. Blake in *addition* to seeing Bialy. Hedge your bet some. Do you understand what I'm telling you, honey?"

"That's what I'm talking about. I love you, Mama. You always give me good advice." Sarah *loves* this idea of a two-pronged attack.

"I love you too, precious. And speaking of precious, where are those beautiful grandbabies of mine?"

Lula shouts and alerts her grandchildren that the tickle torturer is in their midst. She creeps into the living room on tiptoes and wiggles her tickle fingers. The kids screech with delight and take off down the hall with Lulu hot on their trail.

Sarah smiles to herself.

They were watching cartoons and minding their own business. Why did she have to go and rile them up? Amazing woman, my mother, I'm so lucky to have her in my life. The kids and I need her now, more than ever.

Sarah rises, clears the coffee dishes, and yells.

"Mommy's here, sweet babies! I'm coming to save you from the tickle monster. She's in deep doo-doo!"

She runs into the bedroom, where she finds her mother on the floor, two kids crawling all over her, and laughing hysterically. The vision before her quickly turns to memories of life growing up without a father.

It's a long row to hoe, sweet angels, a long row indeed. I'll do what Mama suggests. I'll be "politically correct" as Mama calls it, for you, my darlings, not for me, but for you.

She dives into a pile of hysterical laughter.

Chapter Eight

Three days later, Sarah Hayes sits in the lobby of the Wayne County prosecutor's office. She called two days earlier, identified herself to the receptionist, and was immediately connected to Lawrence Bialy. Bialy agreed to the meeting with a politician's grace. He offered sincere condolences for the loss of her husband and vowed to investigate the matter vigorously.

Sarah surveys the lavish office environment. *Tax dollars are spent on things like this, but not to train better police officers or make our citizens safer.*

She is nervous, but not sure why. She closes her eyes and hears the calm voice of her mother. *Don't let him get to you, Sarah. Speak your peace and listen to what the man has to say. Don't antagonize him. Whether he's helpful or not, he's the one who must decide to pursue justice for Marcus. Don't get angry. Stay calm.*

"Mrs. Hayes?"

Sarah jumps at the sudden sound of her name. *Did I doze off?*

"Sorry, I must have been daydreaming," she manages, recovering her wits.

"No, *I'm* sorry. I didn't mean to sneak up on you. Would you like something to drink, water, coffee, soda?"

Is he from around here? In Detroit, we don't call it 'soda.' We call it 'pop.'

"No, I'm fine, thank you. I won't take up too much of your time. I just want to find out how my husband's case is coming."

"No problem at all. Come on in."

They walk past the reception desk and an attractive white receptionist. Because Bialy's office is at the end of a long hall, they walk past numerous offices, occupied by the many assistant prosecutors that work under Bialy. Some offices are empty. Sarah notices the occupied offices are staffed with white attorneys, staff members, or assistants.

Can a black man get justice in a sea of white?

They reach Bialy's office. It is, without question, the most beautiful office Sarah has ever seen. Beautiful courtroom paintings adorn the walls. Bialy's desk is carved wood with a matching executive chair and a gold bar nameplate that reads 'Lawrence Bialy, Wayne County Prosecutor.'

Bialy invites Sarah to sit in one of the matching side chairs, smaller versions of his executive chair. Her thoughts return to the expenditure of tax dollars.

"It is a pleasure to meet you, Mrs. Hayes. My profound condolences for the loss of your husband."

"Thank you."

"How may I help you?"

"What you are doing about my husband's death? Is the police officer being investigated? Are charges being considered?"

Bialy opens his mouth to speak, but Sarah continues.

"If charges are being considered, what charges are they and, if not, why not?"

She exhales, realizing that she's held her breath for the entire speech.

Bialy smiles a politician's smile.

"That was many questions in one. First of all, the officer is suspended. You know that, right?"

"Yes. He's suspended with pay and my husband's dead. Marcus is six feet under while his murderer is enjoying his damned vacation!" *Relax Sarah. Listen to Mama. You're coming on too strong.*

"I'm sure this is frustrating, Mrs. Hayes, but there is a *process* we must follow. Officer Jones is protected by a union and qualified immunity. And like any other defendant, he is considered innocent until *proven* guilty.

"He hasn't been charged yet. That's why he's still on the payroll. Not much I can do about that. If he is charged with a crime, there's a whole lot I can do."

"What is going on with the investigation?"

"I'm not supposed to share this with members of the public—"

"In this case, I'm not just another member of the public, now am I?"

"I suppose not." Bialy paused. "Say—can you keep a

secret?"

This gets her attention.

"Sure, what is it?"

"We have turned this case over to the grand jury."

"Uh, okay. What does that mean? Is that a big deal?" Sarah does not understand the significance of this critical development.

"I'm *so* sorry. I thought you knew." Bialy is condescending. "The grand jury is assigned our most important cases. It has independent power. It can subpoena people and records and do things that we prosecutors couldn't do without a judge's order.

"The grand jury can indict a defendant or choose not to. If it doesn't indict, we can go find more evidence and have them look into the case again. All of this can happen without broad public knowledge. You were an eyewitness in this case and will be required to testify. Your testimony will go a long way toward obtaining an indictment and a conviction. This is a significant development. Understand?"

I'm not a child. "I do. I'm a college graduate," she chides.

"Obtaining an indictment is the process of being *charged* with a crime, right? There is already enough evidence to take this case to trial, isn't there?"

"That's exactly right," he concurs, eyebrows raised. "It's simply a fancy term for formally charging the defendant with a crime. He would be charged or indicted, arrested, and jailed. He probably posts bail and is out while his case goes to trial. And if this case goes to trial, I will have my best people on it. I may even try this one myself."

"How many cases do *you* try, Mr. Bialy?"

"Not as many as I used to. The district attorney is more of a political position than a courtroom one."

"With all due respect, Sir. If you don't try cases, why would I want you to conduct my husband's trial? Give me some of those 'best people' you mention."

"Okay, Mrs. Hayes," laughs Bialy, surprised at her candor. "I can do that. Not a problem."

Bialy stands, subconsciously signally that the meeting is over, and tries to dismiss Sarah from his office. Sarah stands her ground.

"Mr. Bialy?"

"Yes, Mrs. Hayes?"

Bialy turns his back and faces the window. He visibly inhales and rolls his eyes.

"What can you tell me about Officer Jones? What's his deal? Does he have some problem with black people?"

Bialy turns back to her. A bead of sweat appears on his forehead. "We are checking and re-checking his background information, previous employment, and encounters with people of color. I assure you that we will leave no stone unturned in conducting this investigation."

He walks to the door and opens it. "If there is nothing else," he utters. "I need to get back to work."

Again, Sarah is not easily dismissed. She sinks into her chair and smiles. She studies Bialy.

"I'd like to meet some of these fine people that you are considering to handle this trial," she demands.

Bialy breaks eye contact in a classic game of chicken. The big-time prosecutor silently recoils at Sarah's request. To his credit, though, he recovers nicely.

"Excuse me a minute."

Bialy walks out of his office and leaves Sarah alone. She rises and begins to study some of the beautiful courtroom paintings. Minutes later, Bialy returns with a well-dressed, thirty-something black man.

"Sarah Hayes, meet Jacoby Maynard."

"Nice to meet you, Mrs. Hayes. My profound condolences."

Maynard approaches her and offers her his hand. Sarah shakes it firmly.

"Thank you, sir. May I ask? How long have you been a lawyer?" She inquires somewhat more acerbically than she intended. *Is he the office token? Why him?*

Maynard ignores her attitude. "I've been here for twelve years. I'm not into politics, like Mr. Bialy here. I like to try cases and see that justice is done for victims of crime."

Jacoby Maynard could not have given Sarah Hayes a better answer if he had known she was coming and prepared his remarks. *He's perfect, except, perhaps, for one thing.*

"Tell me, Mr. Maynard, how many cases have you tried? What percentage of those have ended up with the bad guy in jail?"

"I have a ninety-seven percent conviction rate. That means that only three out of a hundred don't do jail time on my watch," he boasts.

"And what percentages of defendants that you send to prison are white?"

"Huh?" he stutters. The question was unexpected.

"Please take a stab at it."

Jacoby thinks about it. "Not many, five percent or so."

An honest answer, I like that. "Why do you suppose that is?"

"Black people are the majority population in the Detroit area, and Detroit is where the largest percentage of Wayne County crime is committed. I suppose that's the major reason. Wouldn't you agree?"

"Do you think black citizens are arrested by cops at a higher rate than white citizens?"

Sarah is studying him, working him over with her eyes. Jacoby looks uncomfortable. He glances over to Bialy for rescue or permission to respond. Bialy gestures to him to continue.

"Honestly, Mrs. Hayes? Yes. I *do* believe that cops arrest black people at a greater rate than white people."

Sarah turns to Bialy. "Mr. Bialy, Mr. Jacoby Maynard suits me just fine. Keep me posted, please. It was nice meeting both of you. Thank you for seeing me, gentlemen. May I have a number where I can reach you, Mr. Maynard?" She stands, strolls toward him., and holds out her hand.

"Sure. Here's my card." Maynard reaches into his suit jacket pocket, extracts, and extends his business card.

"Mrs. Hayes," Bialy interjects. "Rochelle Lynch, who's not here right now, is handling the case in front of the grand jury. If an indictment is issued, Jacoby will take over."

Bialy again walks to and opens his office door, inviting an end to the meeting.

"Okay." Sarah pauses for effect.

Maynard heads back to his office, leaving Bialy alone with Sarah. As he watches her approach the door, he whispers. "One more suggestion, Mrs. Hayes."

"Yes, Mr. Bialy?" Sarah's intrigued.

"A criminal conviction is not the only way to obtain justice. I've talked to the feds. They're looking into pursuing this as a hate crime. I've also reached out to a friend of mine, and he thinks you should consider pursuing a civil rights case for money damages."

"Like a police brutality case?"

"Yes, a different name for the same type of case. These cases can be filed in a circuit court or in federal district court here in Detroit."

Bialy hands her a business card.

"Take this lawyer's card. He's the best civil lawyer in town. Tell him I sent you."

Sarah stares at the name on the business card. "Zachary Blake?" *Interesting that Bialy recommends the same lawsuit and the same lawyer I'm already considering. What are the odds?*

"Isn't he the guy I saw you with on *ViewPoint* the other day?"

"That's the guy."

"He'll take my case?"

"We've already discussed it—he's *very* interested."

"Thank you, Mr. Bialy."

"You're welcome. Good luck, Mrs. Hayes. Feel better about things?"

"Yes, thank you. Have a nice day. I can find my way out."

Sarah Hayes turns and breezes out the door. She glides down the long hall toward the reception area. She feels Bialy's eyes watching her but refuses to turn back and look.

Sarah salutes the receptionist, exits the office, and presses the elevator button at the bank of elevators directly outside the office suite. An elevator door opens. Sarah enters, leans against the back wall, and waits for the doors to close before she lets out a sigh of relief and pumps her fist.

"Good meeting, gentlemen," she huffs aloud. "I'll be in touch." At that moment, Sarah Hayes begins to laugh, hard, so hard, in fact, tears roll down her cheeks. With little to laugh about since her husband's passing, this feels good.

She glances down and stares at the business card Bialy handed her.

Zachary Blake is an extremely successful lawyer in this town, and he wants to talk to me about my husband's case. This is good news, Sarah, good news indeed.

Chapter Nine

The intercom buzzes in Zachary Blake's office. "Yes, Kristin?"

"There's a Sarah Hayes on the phone, Zack. She has a new case for us. She insists on talking only to you."

"Thanks, Kristin. Patch her through, please."

The call is automatically patched through to Zack.

"Zack Blake, may I help you?"

"Mr. Blake? My name is Sarah Hayes. Lawrence Bialy referred me. My husband was Marcus Hayes. He's the man who was shot and killed by the Cedar Ridge policeman."

"I know who you are, Mrs. Hayes. I spoke to Larry. I'm so sorry for your loss."

"Thank you. I saw you on the television a couple of weeks ago with Mr. Bialy. He referred me to you. Bialy told me the criminal case is only one way for us to get justice for Marcus and recommended you as the man to call for a case like this. Are you, Mr. Blake? Are you the lawyer who can help us?"

"I have handled several police misconduct cases in my career. I haven't seen all the evidence Larry has, but it sure looks like you have a compelling civil rights or police brutality case against the cop and the City of Cedar Ridge."

"Why would there be a case against the City of Cedar Ridge?"

"Because the city employs and supervises the police officer who shot your husband and because, based on what I've heard, some Cedar Ridge police officers have a history of handling black citizens poorly. I think the department might have a *systemic* race problem."

"Systemic?"

"Yes. The Cedar Ridge Police Department may have problems with people of color that are broader than any one case. There might be a race issue in the entire department."

"You mean they're all racist?"

"I don't know that, Sarah. We have to investigate. Based on

how they handled your husband's traffic stop, and how they've handled other people of color in the past, we may have a deeper problem in Cedar Ridge, a *pattern* of bad behavior."

"How does that help my kids and me?"

"Good question. I can't bring Marcus back. I wish I could, but obviously, I can't. The law provides for a family to get a financial reward, compensation, for the wrongful death of a loved one. Money can't replace your husband, but it is the only means the law provides to compensate you for your loss. The more serious or systemic the problems, the more serious the compensation."

"I've lost my husband and my husband's income. I was a stay-at-home- mom. I'm a college-educated woman, but I've got to look for a job for the first time in years. I've been out of the job market for quite a while. I'm sure I'll be fine eventually, but compensation would certainly be helpful. Frankly, I can use the money. How much is something like this worth?"

"I wouldn't predict the value of any case without seeing the evidence, but assuming the evidence breaks our way and assuming the City of Cedar Ridge is a reasonable negotiating partner, this could be a substantial case."

"You talk like a lawyer," she chuckles.

Zack laughs. "I'm sorry, Sarah, you're right. I can speak 'legalese' with the best of them. Allow me to rephrase. If we can prove that this guy was a bad cop and the city knew he was bad and did nothing, this case might be worth a lot of money. If I can prove there is a *systemic* race problem in the City of Cedar Ridge, the case might be worth a *whole lot* more. Is that better?"

"Much better. How much is a 'whole lot?'"

"Sarah, honestly, it's way too early to answer questions like these. I can't promise specific amounts. I *can* promise that I will do the absolute best job I can for you and your kids. Are we good to go?" *She's straightforward—I like that in a client.*

"Good to go, Mr. Blake." *Smart man. Knows his stuff.*

"Please call me Zack."

"And you can call me Sarah."

"I already have. Now, I need you to do a few things for me, a bit of homework before you come in."

"Okay?"

"I want you to get out a piece of paper and write down all the reasons you and your kids miss your husband and daddy. I want to know everything there is to know about Marcus. I want to see cards, letters, emails, and texts he might have written to you or you to him and anything else that can show a judge or a jury what kind of guy he is.

"Do you have videotape, audiotape, or photos of you guys having a good time together? Ask his employer for a letter indicating he worked there and how much he was paid. Do you have recent paystubs? Bring those.

"Ask friends and family, church members, and co-workers to write a page or two about what your husband meant to them. I need to get to know Marcus, Sarah."

"Okay. Anything else?"

"Yes. You were in the car with him when this happened?"

"Yes, I was." Sarah begins to cry.

Zack doesn't wait for her to regain her composure. "I want you to write down everything you remember about that night; I mean *everything*. Don't leave anything out. It is *all* important."

"I have a cellphone video of the whole incident," Sarah reveals, trying to remain composed.

"That's right, Larry told me! I'd forgotten. I understand the police bagged the phone as evidence. Have they returned it?

"Yes."

"Please bring your phone to our meeting. The video is a vital piece of evidence. My computer guys will duplicate it. That was unbelievably good thinking under terrible circumstances.

"Still, write the synopsis, please. Tell us how you felt as all of this was unfolding. Obviously, the officer mistreated your husband; that is a foregone conclusion. How did he treat you?"

"It was *terrible*, Zack." Sarah sobs.

She pulls a tissue from her purse and dabs her eyes and cheeks as she continues.

"He wouldn't listen to either of us. He shoots Marcus to death in front of us, then another cop arrests me and takes me in handcuffs to police headquarters.

"I'm not permitted to go with my kids or with my husband.

I'm terrified. It's the worst night of my life, hands down. I will never forget it," Sarah moans.

"Write it all down, Sarah. These memories are vital. I'm going to give you back to Kristin. She'll make an appointment for you to come in."

"I don't have a car. The police consider our car a potential crime scene and are still processing it."

"Then I'll come to you. Have Kristin check my schedule for enough time to make a house call. Give her your address and the nearest major crossroads."

"That is so nice, Zack. Thank you. I appreciate it. Mr. Bialy might have mentioned you were a good guy."

"You don't want a good guy representing you in situations like this one. You want a *barracuda* when it comes to dealing with bad cops, negligent police departments, and attorneys who represent them. They are afraid of me; they think I'm a bad guy. Please don't give away my secret."

Sarah chuckles through her tears. *He has an easy way about him. I hope he's an ass-kicker in court.*

"Your secret is safe with me, Zack. Thanks for the advice."

"No problem, Sarah. We'll get to the bottom of this. I promise. Hang in there. See you soon. Here comes Kristin."

Zack turns the call over to Kristin. He feels terrible for Sarah and her kids. *What a nightmare! Based on everything Larry told me, this case is a keg of dynamite for the City of Cedar Ridge. These people have one chance and one chance only to make these bastards pay. And I can't wait to begin.*

Chapter Ten

"My dad was a cop. His dad was a cop. All I ever wanted to be was a cop. In an instant, my career is over, flushed down the toilet."

Randy Jones grimaces and hangs his head. His wife, Brenda, tightly grips his hand.

"You don't know that, Randy. Not yet, anyway," she reassures.

"Oh, but I do. I not only know that my law enforcement career is over, honey, but I'm almost positive I'm going to get charged with murder. The tables have completely turned. Even my friends on the force are calling me a criminal. I'm going to prison, Brenda," he agonizes.

Brenda turns to him and holds both of his hands. "Now, you look at me, Randy Jones."

He hangs his head and avoids her eyes. She tries to turn his head toward hers, but he resists.

"Alright, don't look at me, but you *must* listen. You are *not* going to prison. People think it's so easy out there, dealing with all different kinds of people, good people, bad people, people on drugs, drunks, people with weapons, people who might want to hurt or even kill you. Let these people try being a cop. Just once, let all these politically correct critics try working the streets. I see how you are when you come home. If you are charged and this goes to a jury, the jurors will see what I see, a good and kind man who was just trying to do his job, trying to keep our streets and our people safe," Brenda insists.

Slowly, Randy raises his chin and permits his eyes to meet hers. He appreciates her strong, heartfelt words. "Being a cop is an *honor*. I'm proud to protect and serve my city and my fellow citizens. That's why I chose the academy in the first place. I don't go out on patrol thinking, 'who can I push around today?' or 'I wonder if I will get to use my gun?' I try to do the right thing out there. Protect the good guys and put away the bad guys. I deal with a lot out there. I try to keep people safe, even when there is anger and violence.

"Cops put their lives on the line, every day. To have my career end like this, in disgrace—I didn't mean to shoot that guy, Brenda. But he's got these dreads, looks like a hoodlum. He's threatening me with a gun, his wife is screaming, and his kids are crying. On a damn *traffic stop*! I was *frightened*, dammit! Wouldn't you be? No one thinks to walk a mile in *my* shoes. Oh my God, Brenda! How in the hell did this happen?"

Randy Jones buries his wife's lap and sobs. His wife cradles his head and begins to rock him back and forth.

"What is the department psychologist telling you? You're meeting with him, right? Is he helping?"

Randy pulls away from her, wipes his eyes with his sleeve, and attempts to regain his composure. "I'd rather talk to you! These guys don't understand what it's like to deal with these people on the streets," he groans.

"You need a *professional*. If you don't like the guy you're seeing, Cedar Ridge has other people for you to talk to, don't they?"

"Yeah, I think so. I've never really checked. Never had the need."

"Well, I think you need someone you are comfortable talking with now."

"You know, this is all comes down to a lack of respect for law enforcement and police officers."

"What do you mean?"

"There is an element out there that doesn't show cops the respect that they deserve. Some think we're as bad as criminals, maybe worse. I'm not saying there aren't bad cops out there, cops on the take, selfish or abusive cops. There are, but I'm not one of them. I'm not like that, and the vast majority of cops aren't either. Most of us are honest, hard-working people. Are all blacks criminals? I'm sure some are terrific people. Are all white cops racists, all Hispanics drug dealers? These are similar stereotypes. All cops are bad all right—until you need one."

"I don't think very many people feel that way, Randy. I agree there may be some problems with the black community and police officers right now, white *and* black, but those things have been going on for a long time. It didn't start with you, honey."

"But I wanted to be *different*. I wanted to *make* a difference. You know how some people think all cops are dicks? Well, I wanted to buck that stereotype. I wanted to be that one good cop people respected."

He gazes into his wife's eyes, looking for compassion and understanding.

"You *are* that one good cop, honey. One incident doesn't define a whole career. You'll see. We'll get through this." She smiles and pats his hand.

"I love you, sweetheart, but you don't know shit about these things. One incident can, *absolutely*, define a whole career, Brenda, my dear, sweet Brenda. And *this* is that incident.

"I will never recover from this. I will never be a cop again. I'll be lucky to stay out of prison. I know what's going on. I've talked to my lawyer and my union rep. The department is scapegoating me. I'm the racist cop, don't you know? I'm the sacrificial lamb on this new altar of political correctness.

"There is no blue wall anymore. The brass wants me gone so they can say 'see—we got rid of that racist cop. Aren't we grand?' They're up at city hall, right now, plotting to make me look like shit without it rubbing off on the department. Charges are a foregone conclusion."

"Come on, Randy. Lighten up. You don't know whether or not you're going to be charged," Brenda consoles.

Randy's eyes steel.

"Look, Brenda, I love you for what you're trying to do. But criminal charges are a foregone conclusion. In the meantime, I have to find a way to make a living in a community that's going to hate Randy Jones with a passion while more news breaks and the case develops. We have to face reality. Watch, you'll see. Our friends won't be inviting you to the next community event. And wait until you see the looks we get from these so-called friends. It's so damned unfair, Brenda."

"If you say so, Randy. I'm in your corner, no matter what."

"I know you are, and I appreciate it, honey. I honestly do."

They sit together in anguished silence. Brenda attempts to change the subject, lighten the mood.

"Do you want anything to eat?"

Randy ignores her. He's deep in thought. Brenda's not sure he's heard her.

"Randy?"

"Being a cop is a hard job," he continues, staring into outer space.

"When people ask kids, 'what do you want to be when you grow up?' Most kids used to say 'policeman' or 'fireman.'

"Today, why would any kid want to be a cop? People disobey the law, and *I'm* the terrible guy who hands them their well-deserved tickets.

"I pick up some under-aged kids who've been drinking, and they say 'come on officer, give us a break, huh? You were a kid once. We're just trying to have a good time.'

"Or worse, try dealing with a chronic drunk driver. 'Yeah, officer, I've had, maybe a couple of beers.' His Breathalyzer reads 0.18! Or, how about arresting that same drunk at the scene of a fatal accident where he doesn't have a scratch on him, and the other guy is wrapped around a tree? 'What did I do? What did I do?' And people think the *cops* are the bad guys?" Randy is suddenly furious.

"Not all citizens feel that way, Randy—you *know* that honey," Brenda coos, attempting to assuage his growing rage.

"Do I? Do I really? How do you feel when I leave the house at night, Brenda? How do the kids feel when they wake up in the morning and I'm not home yet?"

"Scared." She admits.

"Scared why?" He probes.

"Scared that this will be the last time we see you alive, scared that the kids will grow up without a father," she whispers.

Tears begin to trickle down her cheeks.

"Exactly. You wouldn't believe some of the things I see on the street. Fatal auto accidents with people who are so mangled they are unrecognizable. Drug busts where dealers are employing children to sell for them, shootouts with dealers, robbers, and murderers.

"I ask myself the same questions every time I leave the house. 'Will I ever see my family again? Will I make it through the day without being hurt, without being killed?' This is the life of a cop. Most of us are husbands and fathers with wives and children at home asking that same question: 'Will I ever see him alive again?'"

"So, maybe it is time to move on to something else." She resumes eye contact.

"As long as it isn't prison," he wails.

Brenda explodes.

"Stop that, Randy Jones, you stop that! You are not going to prison!"

"Do you think I'm a bigot, Brenda? For Christ's sake, I'm part Hispanic! Some people consider *me* a minority! I try to treat everyone the same. A colored guy threatens me with a *gun*! Do I care what color he is? I'm going to *defend* myself!

"I pull over a colored guy who's driving, probably stoned, *with his kids in the car*! I smell marijuana! Out of the blue, this scumbag tells me he's got a gun and a license to carry. Why does he tell me that? Does he plan to shoot me?

"Show me your hands, I tell him. He *ignores* me, Brenda! He reaches down into his pocket. Is he reaching for the gun? Why won't he show me his hands? He's not 'the black guy' or 'the white guy,' dammit! *He's the guy with the fucking gun*!" Randy Jones bellows in anguish.

"Why can't anyone understand that? What was I supposed to do, let him get off the first shot? I keep replaying the whole thing in my head. It's driving me crazy. How did it go so wrong?"

Randy pounds his fists on the table, rests his head on his arms and sobs. Brenda can do nothing to console him. She grasps his forearm and holds on for dear life. *How will we get through this?*

Chapter Eleven

Rochelle Lynch parks her car around the block and approaches the front entrance. A storm of protestors greets her as she turns the corner toward the building. It's Thursday morning. The grand jury inquiry into the death of Marcus Hayes is about to reconvene for another round of testimony.

The last thing any of them need is an encounter or confrontation with a protestor on either side of the debate. Obviously, and unfortunately, someone has leaked the location and subject matter of the grand jury.

There are multiple television cameras and reporters present, broadcasting live reports on location. A television reporter from Fox2 News sees Lynch round the corner and approaches her. A camera light flashes in her eyes; suddenly, she is the subject of a live broadcast.

"Ms. Lynch . . . Ms. *Lynch* . . . Rochelle, what are you doing here? Is it true the grand jury is in this building to hear evidence in the Jones-Hayes shooting?"

The aggressive reporter sticks a microphone in her face.

"I have no comment," Rochelle huffs.

She avoids eye contact with the camera lens, pushes aside the microphone, and attempts to brush by the reporter and cameraman.

"Will Mrs. Hayes be testifying?"

"No comment."

She continues to move forward, followed, step-for-step, by reporter and cameraman. The latter struggles to keep pace.

"Will Officer Jones be testifying?"

"No comment."

"What do you think of the evidence in the case?"

"No comment."

"Is there any truth to the rumor that the county wants Jones indicted as soon as possible? Where are you in the process? The public has a right to know. The people are demanding information."

"No comment."

Rochelle tries to keep walking, but the cameraman steps directly in front of her and blocks her path. He moves the camera in and settles it inches from her face. Lynch glares into the camera.

"This looks like an expensive piece of equipment, sir. You would be wise to get it out of my face."

The experienced cameraman holds his ground.

"Come on, Rochelle, give a girl a break. Is there anything you can tell us?" The reporter pleads.

Rochelle adopts a calmer demeanor. "No comment. Looks like a nice rally, though. I'd like to watch. Thanks very much."

She turns away from the reporter and the camera and watches the show of unity and counter-unity. From what Rochelle knows of the official position on Randy Jones, the reporter is correct. Wayne County wants a quick indictment. Rochelle is surprised at the number of police officers on the front lines of this counter-protest. They are demonstrating in support of the officer, providing stern opposition to the protestors. *But who leaked the focus of this grand jury?*

Black Lives Matter is present in full force. A black man stands on the building steps. He holds a portable microphone and is riling up an already raucous crowd of protesters. Crowd size is increasing by the minute. Pedestrians, curious about what's going on, are joining in, looking to get themselves on television.

Oddly, on-duty police officers have been tasked with the responsibility of keeping counter-protestors, including off-duty police officers, at a reasonable distance from protestors, to avoid confrontation. Their goal is to promote a civil exercise of First Amendment rights *and* crowd control.

The black man taps the microphone head and begins his speech. The crowd settles and quiets down to listen.

"I am an American citizen. Marcus Hayes was an American citizen, born and raised right here in Detroit. Mr. Hayes lived and worked in his community as a master computer technician. He could fix whatever was wrong. Mr. Hayes was a devoted husband and father. He helped out at local churches and schools. He was a fixture at the YMCA and a soccer coach for local kids.

He was, by all accounts, a very nice guy and a community asset. However, even this master computer technician, this man who fixed things for a living, was powerless to fix the scourge of systemic racism that cost him his life!"

The crowd boos and jeers. Protestors push forward straining temporary chains that separate them from counter-protesters.

"But what happened on that evening in Cedar Ridge? Marcus Hayes was not simply a man who was shot to death during a routine traffic stop. He was a man who legally owned a gun. He was a man who was driving through town at lower-than-posted speeds. Had he committed a crime?" The man holds the microphone out to the crowd. The crowd shouts out an emphatic, "NO!"

"Marcus Hayes was lawfully armed. According to most reports, this was the reason he was shot and killed. So, my brothers and sisters, I ask you, where is the outrage from the group that usually protests situations like this one? Am I referring to *Black Lives Matter*? Is that what you think?" He again points the microphone toward the crowd. Again, the people shout, "NO!"

"Am I referring to the ACLU?" Again, he points the microphone. Again, the crowd shouted an exuberant, "NO!"

"Where is outrage from the National Rifle Association? Where's the damned NRA?" The crowd boos and chants. 'Where's the NRA?'

The speaker holds out both arms for quiet.

"Why are these faux gun advocates silent in the face of a senseless shooting of a legally armed man who was shot solely because he was a legally armed man?

"Isn't this the NRA's thing? Isn't this an issue they always *scream* about? So, where the hell are they? Why aren't they fired up about this? We *know* why brothers and sisters! This was a legally armed *black* man!

"The NRA claims to believe the Second Amendment of the Constitution of the United States grants all of our citizens the right to survive and protect their families with any gun they want. I guess that's only true when those citizens are *Caucasian*! Does the Second Amendment apply if you're a *black* man driving through a *white* neighborhood?"

Again, the speaker directs the microphone toward the crowd. This time the rowdy crowd not only shouts "NO," they begin to boo. They effectively drown out the speaker. He lays down the microphone and waits for quiet.

"The NRA has found some other constitutional amendments that they roll out for special occasions, like when a black man is holding the gun. When a black man holds the gun, they exercise their Fifth Amendment right against self-incrimination. When a black man is holding the gun, they exercise their right to remain silent. Hell, they sure have maintained silence in this case!"

The crowd erupts with its most prolonged cheer of the morning. The speaker pauses until quiet is restored.

"Brothers and sisters, the beauty of America is that when we see something is broken, we have the power to fix it. All we need is the resolve to do the heavy lifting. One person doesn't need to do all the work himself. In fact, one person is rarely enough. A few people aren't enough. We, the people, all of us, need to mobilize to repair what is wrong in America.

"Why do we need a group called *Black Lives Matter*? Why not 'all lives matter?' The answer is crystal clear if you're willing to come into the light.

"You see, brothers and sisters, in America today, a police officer can pull over a law-abiding citizen for no damn reason, ask for identification, and shoot that citizen when he or she reaches for it.

"Why was Marcus Hayes pulled over? We *know* the answer. He was a black man driving through a white community. He was a black man with an Afro. An officer alleged he resembled a teenaged fast-food restaurant robber.

"His shooting prompted little outrage in Cedar Ridge and other parts of Ronald John's America. We need to address routine injustice to minorities in America."

Protestors begin to chant "*Black Lives Matter*" in unison, followed by less enthusiastic chants of "all lives matter" from counter-protesters.

"*Black Lives Matter* has nothing against good, hard-working police officers. But we are vehemently opposed to corrupt cops, racist cops, cops who shoot innocent men in cold blood in front of their wives and small children. Why is this cop policing citizens on the streets of our cities? Why wasn't he fired long ago? The word on the street is that this cop had a history, but he wasn't fired after the first incident or even the second.

"Would we tolerate a bad doctor? No, we'd fire him and hire someone else. Would we tolerate a bad lawyer? No, we'd fire him and hire someone else. A bad electrician, a bad plumber, or a bad carpenter?"

He holds out the microphone, and the crowd shouts emphatically, "NO, we'd fire them and hire someone else."

"And what should we do with a bad congressman or a bad president?"

The speaker holds out the mic, and the crowd goes wild. 'We should fire them and hire someone else! We should fire them and hire someone else!'

The crowd repeats this mantra until the speaker puts his finger to his lips and whispers for silence.

"We aren't asking for any more rights than anyone else in this country. We're not trying to take anything or anyone's rights away. We're not looking for a handout unless it is a handout in friendship. We *are* looking for our full rights under the Constitution of the United States of America, our full and equal rights to freedom and life, liberty, and the pursuit of happiness."

The counter-protestors shout, "All lives matter, all lives matter." The speaker decides to address that element of the crowd.

"You are absolutely right, brothers and sisters. All lives *do* matter. But when a white person's life is lost, white people almost always get justice for their loss. When a black life is lost, justice is delayed or denied. I am a proud American. I care deeply about this country. And if we truly want to be a great country, the land of the free and the home of the brave, we must rise up together and demand liberty and justice for *all* Americans, regardless of race!"

"Justice, justice, justice," chants the crowd on both sides of the barriers.

Many begin to sing, "We shall overcome."

Amidst the cheers and the singing, protestors climb over barriers to approach their counterparts with hands extended in brotherhood. The stunned law enforcement counter-protestors take their hands and shake them. The two groups begin to pat each other on the back vigorously.

Some embrace, others snap photographs. Different cultures and perspectives do whatever is necessary to immortalize this amazing moment. Two sides of people who never listen to the other's point of view, men and women who are blind and deaf to the others' protest, actually come together for a moment of peace and solidarity. Community progress is made in front of a high-rise in Detroit, Michigan.

Chapter Twelve

Rochelle Lynch is surprised and awed by what she is witnessing. As angry as she is about the leak, Rochelle realizes that she is witnessing a "never before-never again" moment in Detroit's history. A multi-cultural crowd of protesters and counter-protesters, cops and citizens, embraced in brotherhood on the streets of Detroit. *This moment isn't likely to repeat itself in my lifetime.*

Rochelle climbs the front steps of the building, enters the building, and approaches the security screening area.

"Hey Roger," she addresses the head of security.

"And how are you this fine morning?"

She rolls her eyes and glances back at the scene in front of the building.

"I'll be great when this is all over. Who spilled the beans?"

"I don't know, but if I find out that person is going to jail."

Rochelle surrenders her purse, cell phone, and any other objects that might cause an X-ray machine blast. She passes quietly through the machine, collects her belongings, and tells Roger and his assistants to have a nice day.

She takes the elevator to twelve, passes through an empty courtroom, and greets grand jurors in the break room. The jurors have entered through a private entrance arranged by Roger to avoid the crowd.

"Good morning, ladies and gentlemen. Ready to go?" Rochelle scans the room.

"What's going on out there?" A concerned juror wants to know.

"There is a surprisingly peaceful demonstration and exercise of First Amendment rights going on out front."

"Can't say that I'm surprised, given what this case is about," the juror opines.

"Me either," Lynch agrees. "However, our sessions are supposed to be conducted in secret. Your identities aren't supposed to be made public. Someone has leaked the fact that this grand jury is hearing the Hayes case. This is troubling, but not completely surprising."

"So, what do we do?"

"Conduct the people's business as though these protestors aren't here. Hopefully, by the end of the day, the crowd will have dispersed, and you can leave the same way you arrived without being harassed by protesters. If someone does approach you, your response is a firm and consistent "no comment." Does everyone understand? No one is to even know you're a juror."

"Understood," several jurors reply. Others simply nod their heads. The group heads into the courtroom.

***

The second day of grand jury testimony begins in earnest with Marshall Bingham, a crime scene investigator, on the stand. Bingham was the first law enforcement official to access the crime scene after it was secured.

Rochelle Lynch qualifies him as a crime scene investigation expert and begins to examine him about the crime scene.

"Officer Bingham, you permitted Officer Jones to leave the scene, is that correct?

"Yes."

"Typically, in an officer-involved shooting, the officer remains on the scene until you, the crime scene tech, can talk with him and walk the scene with him, correct?"

"Yes."

"Why wasn't that procedure followed in this case?"

"A crowd was gathering, with some hostility toward the officer. I was concerned about the overall safety of the people at the scene."

"How did Officer Jones leave the scene?"

"I believe he left with Officer Brian Jenkins."

"Jones left his vehicle at the scene?"

"Yes, at my instruction."

"Did you process his vehicle?"

"I did."

"Was there any damage to his vehicle, gunshot hole in the

window, a dented fender, anything?"

"No."

"There was no sign of any hostile actions by the deceased or anyone else as it relates to the vehicle. Is that a fair statement?"

"It is."

"Was the car equipped with a dash cam and an audio recorder?"

"It was."

"And you secured those devices?"

"I did."

"Have you viewed and listened to the recordings made by those devices?"

"I have."

"Were you present in the grand jury room, at my request, to view the video and listen to the audio we played here on Monday?"

"I was."

"Were they the same as the ones you reviewed from Officer Jones's vehicle?"

"They were."

"Have you spoken to Officer Jones about this case?"

"Yes."

"Did he give you a statement?"

"It wasn't a formal statement."

"Was it before or after his statement to Internal Affairs?"

"After."

"What were the circumstances of the statement?"

"It wasn't formal. I'm not sure I would even call it a statement. Officer Jones called me on the phone—he wanted to talk. I told him I might be called to testify and that it wasn't a good idea. However, he was upset and wanted to go over the whole thing to see what I thought. I told him that as long as he understood that I might have to tell investigators what we discussed, it was okay with me if it was okay with him."

"What did he tell you?"

"He wondered what I thought after processing the scene. I told him I couldn't discuss that with him."

"Go on."

"He began to cry. He told me the whole story. It wasn't much different from his statement to Internal Affairs. His tone and mood were a bit less confident or upbeat than they were then. He was very conflicted. He kept repeating, "Am I a racist?" I inquired whether he ever saw a gun or signs of instability from the victim. He indicated he hadn't. He claimed he had trouble getting Mr. Hayes to show him his hands."

Bingham could not shake the feeling he was ratting on a brother.

"Did he describe the shooting?"

"He described it as an out-of-body experience."

"Did you ask him to explain that?"

"Yes, I did. Officer Jones was fixated on Mr. Hayes' statement that he had a license to carry and was, indeed, carrying a gun. Hayes offered to show Officer Jones the carry permit. Randy alleges that Hayes reached down when he, Officer Jones, ordered him to put his hands on the dashboard. When Mr. Hayes didn't comply and began to lift his hand upward, Officer Jones shot him."

"Did you observe Mr. Hayes at the scene?"

"I did."

"What was his condition when you first observed him?"

"He was dead. He had four gunshot wounds, one to the stomach, three more to the chest. The one that killed him went through his heart."

"Did you check his hands?"

"I did."

"Was there anything in his hands?"

"Yes."

"What did you find in his hands, Officer Bingham?"

Bingham pauses and sighs.

"His gun permit, driver's license, and vehicle registration."

"How long have you been a police officer, sir?"

"Twenty years."

"And in Cedar Ridge?"

"The whole twenty."

"What would you say is the Cedar Ridge Police Department's experience with African American citizens?"

"I'm not sure how to answer that, ma'am."

"You spent some time on patrol?"

"Yes."

"How many years?"

"Seventeen years, give or take."

"What percentage of your citizen encounters has been with white people as opposed to black people?"

"I'm not sure. Cedar Ridge is predominately white, so I would say something like ninety-ten."

"Would that be typical?"

"I would say so, yes."

"So that would be true of Jones, as well."

"Most likely."

"Has the department ever provided specialized sensitivity training, or the like, regarding officers' treatment of minorities?"

"No."

"How well do you know Officer Jones?"

"Very well."

"Do you recall another encounter Jones had with a black person that ended rather badly?"

"Yes, I do."

Bingham looks down and glares at the floor. He knows where this is going but is powerless to avoid it.

"Did you have a conversation with him about that encounter?"

"I did."

"Please recount the conversation for the jury."

"He told me he had had a similar encounter once before."

"How so?"

"Apparently, he once pulled over another black guy who matched the description of some guy who had committed a B and E."

"What is a 'B and E,' officer, for the jury?"

"Sorry, breaking and entering."

"What did Jones say happened in that incident, if you know?"

Bingham squirms in the witness chair. "He killed a man in an incident similar to the Hayes case."

"Similar how?"

"Like I mentioned earlier, there was a traffic stop of an African American citizen following the B and E. Jones claimed the driver resembled the suspect."

"Did he?"

Bingham looks away.

"I don't know."

"Allow me to show you two photographs, Officer Bingham. Have you seen these two photographs before?"

"Yes, I have."

"In what context, may I ask?"

"As part of this investigation."

"Why? Who are they?"

"The previous Jones victim and the previous B and E suspect."

"The court officer is passing these photos out to our jurors. The photos speak for themselves, but do you see a resemblance between these two men, Officer Bingham?"

"No, I do not."

"When Jones told you the story about the previous incident involving two men who look nothing alike, how did he explain the traffic stop to you? I remind you, sir, that you have been duly sworn and are under oath to tell the truth."

"Randy stated the driver seemed out of place in Cedar Ridge."

"Did he say anything else to justify the stop?"

"N-not really," Bingham stammers.

"Not really or no?"

"I know this will be taken out of context, but I think he was joking."

"What did he say, sir?"

"That the driver seemed out of place in Cedar Ridge, and they all look alike anyway. But, as I'm sure he was joking." Bingham pleads.

His searches faces and eyes in the room for understanding. He finds none.

"Officer Jones killed another citizen for driving while black. This one was unarmed, but it is okay because he was joking?"

"You're putting words in my mouth."

"I have nothing further for this witness."

Chapter Thirteen

"Micah Love Investigations, may I help you?"

"Micah Love, please. Zack Blake calling."

"Hey, Zack, it's Jessica."

"Jessica? Jessica Klein?"

"In the flesh."

"Jessica! How have you been? I've missed you!"

Blake is happy to hear her voice. Micah Love is Blake's private investigator. His work was a significant factor in Blake's success on various high-profile cases. The two men became famous when they blew the lid off the child abuse scandal involving the church and a pedophile priest named Father Gerry Bartholomew in Farmington, Michigan. The investigation and subsequent high-profile trial resulted in a nine-figure verdict and recovery for their clients. Those clients were Jennifer, Kenny, and Jake Tracey, now Blake's wife and adopted kids.

Jessica Klein is from Berea, Ohio. She met Micah while he was investigating the abusive priest's previous placement in Ohio. Micah and Jessica hit it off right away, sparks flew, and they became a couple. Over the years, they have continued an on-again-off-again relationship. *I guess that it's on again, for now, but why is she answering phones in Detroit?*

"Why are you answering Micah's phones?"

"One of Micah's bimbos just quit, and I happened to be in town. So, I'm the bimbo today," she jokes.

"You're gorgeous, but you're no bimbo," Blake quips.

"Aw shucks. What's up, Zack?"

"I've got a new case."

"Great! Let me get Micah on the phone. It's nice to hear your voice, Zack. Micah and I need to get together with you and Jenny."

"Absolutely. We'd love to see you. I'll have Jennifer call you to set it up."

"I'd like that. I'll connect you now."

"Thanks, Jess."

Love soon interrupts the hold music.

"Hey Zack, how's my favorite legal guru?"

"Put me back on hold; I'm listening to Streisand."

"Huh? Okay, hold on," Love kibitzes.

"Wait, Micah! I was kidding man,"

"I know. I was just messing with you. Whaddaya got?"

"You're going to shit when I tell you."

"I love a good shit."

"I've been retained to handle the Hayes case."

"That great Zack, congrats." Love doesn't have a clue. "Uh . . . what's the Hayes case?"

"Where have you been, man? Have you been sleeping under a rock for the last month or so? Marcus Hayes is the man who was shot and killed by the cop in Cedar Ridge," Blake exclaims.

"Holy crap! You've got that one? I love it! When do we begin? Whaddaya need? Full Monty?" Blake now has Love's full attention.

"Yes. I want the full A-to-Z investigation. I don't trust the city or the feds. I can't even assume the cop will get convicted in this case, not in RonJohn's America.

"Start by getting your hands on whatever investigation materials already exist. There are witness statements to obtain, videos and audios, cops, and crime scene techs who came to the scene. The Hayes vehicle is still impounded. But the biggest issue in my mind is the culture. Does the City of Cedar Ridge have a systemic problem with how cops treat people of color? Does this cop or any other cop have previous negative encounters? Has anything like this ever happened before?

"What's this cop's background? What's his mental status? What protocols or training programs are in place? Have those been violated? Do they even have protocols or training programs for cops to deal with cultures and people they don't typically encounter? I want it all, Micah."

Love understands and appreciates Blake's enthusiasm. Cases like Hayes do not come along very often.

"Got it. How much time do I have?" Love inquires.

"Plenty. Mrs. Hayes just signed the retainer agreement. By the way, you also need to get a videographer out to her home and put together day-in-the-life video footage before and after Mr. Hayes's death. If there are any segments of Mr. Hayes's interactions with his family and friends, I want them. I also need candid video on how the wife and kids are dealing with his loss and their grief."

"I've got it, Zack. I heard you—the full Monty."

"That's one way to put it, I guess."

"I'm on it. I *always* enjoy working with the superhero of law."

"Same here, Micah. Working with you is always entertaining. I told Mrs. Hayes to expect a call from you. Anything you need, any extra help, anything, give me a call."

"What's Mrs. Hayes like?"

"She's a nice lady, an eyewitness to the shooting death of her husband, so you need to take a detailed statement from her. Play nice, please. The incident took place directly in front of her and her children. That has tremendous shock value and is a big part of the case. She's got cell phone video on her iPhone."

"That must be one powerful video. Did the cop have a dash cam, too?"

"Yes, he did. The entire incident is captured on the two videos. Maybe we add the dash cam and the iPhone footage to the day-in-the-life video. Can you imagine sitting in the passenger seat and back seat of a car and watching a cop shoot and kill your husband and father?

"Sarah Hayes is college-educated, attractive, and articulate and will make an awesome witness. By all accounts, her husband was a good guy too. About the only negatives I have encountered is that the victim was legally carrying a weapon and may have smoked some pot at some time before the stop."

"Yeah, I might have read something about that somewhere. If it's true, we can deal with it." Micah trails off, reflecting.

"What is it, Micah?"

"I'm just thinking. I guess I'm a little worried about our current political climate. The country, the state, and even the city . . . we are very divided, maybe more divided than any time in recent history. The silent underbelly of racist attitudes has become far more emboldened.

"Our own experiences with the Arya Khan and Jack Dylan cases demonstrate how brazen and active some of these groups are, with POTUS setting an atrocious behavioral example. And the more active these people become, the more active and hostile their counter-protesters become.

"Social justice groups, the ACLU, and other groups like *Black Lives Matter*, are primed for a clash with white supremacist and neo-Nazi elements. And those are only the extreme elements of this racist movement. There are also several President John supporters and closet racists, who will come out of their closets to defend white cops, regardless of how egregious their conduct is."

"You're worried that one small case will trigger some kind of race war?"

Blake hasn't considered this possibility.

"Don't forget you've got a criminal case out there too. Rumor has it that the grand jury is convened in Detroit and looking into the case to determine whether there's enough evidence for an indictment. And, there's a civil rights case germinating in the federal system. If either criminal case fails and the black community doesn't get justice for yet another of their fallen citizens, what do you think will happen? Will we have another Ferguson? And, if we do, how will it affect your case?"

"I read you, brother, loud and clear," Blake shudders. "By the way, between you and me, I have *confirmed* that grand jury rumor with Larry Bialy. The grand jury *is* looking into this case. As to the climate, we'll cross that bridge when we come to it, especially in *voir dire* and jury selection—if the case gets that far.

"For now, we have to look at this like any other case we handle together, high profile or not. We do the work to the best of our ability. We fight the fight that needs to be fought and ignore those outside elements unless or until they begin to affect our client's case. If or when they do, we're smart guys. We'll figure out a way to handle them. At this moment, I've given you a lot of work to do. You have an unlimited budget, and I expect your usual kickass performance."

"Nice pep talk, boss. I especially like the unlimited budget part."

"Yeah? Well, remember, we're talking about the *client's* money. Don't get carried away. The larger message is that I do not want you to cut corners to save money, got it? I want a Mercedes, not a Yugo."

"When do I ever produce a Yugo? My feelings are hurt," Love whines, dolefully.

"Sorry. We good to go?"

"Good to go. Anything else?"

"What's going on with you and Jessica?"

"Nothing, what do you mean?"

"She's answering your phones."

"She was in town, and I'm short a person. Ginger left me."

"Singsong Ginger?" Blake cracks.

"The woman who can sing with her lips *and* with her *hips*? Ginger, the woman that made 'good morning, Micah Love Investigations' sound like an X-rated movie score, *that* Ginger?"

"Alas, she left for greener pastures. Jessica, bless her heart, offered to help out."

"Don't let Jessica get away, Micah," Blake warns.

"What are you suggesting, Zack, not the M-word?"

"Why not?"

"Marriage isn't my style," Love cringes. "I'm reasonably sure it's a dirty word for Jessica, as well."

"That may be true, but you'll never know unless you ask. I didn't believe I would get married again or know the happiness of a loving wife and great kids. But I'm enjoying every minute of it."

"I know you are; you're a very lucky man." Love is truly envious.

"A wife and some kids would look nice on you, Micah. And Jessica is a great lady."

"Yes, she is," Micah admits. "I've never been with anyone like her before. She makes every minute I spend with her exciting. And has she got an appetite in bed, man! I'm telling you Zack; she's fucking exhausting! Is that a pun?

"Anyway, I don't have to go to the gym or jog or anything to get in shape. All I have to do is spend a week or two with Jessica. I don't want to ruin this wonderful relationship with a marriage proposal."

"Marriage is a positive step, Micah, not a negative one. Do you want me to ask her about it? She likes me."

"No, thanks. I realize I'm a wuss, but not so much that I can't handle my own relationship issues."

"Okay, but I love Jessica. Do not let her get away."

"You have made your feelings known, Zack. I've got to cut this short. We've got a lot of shit going on today. I'll assemble a team. We'll get to work on this right away."

"Thanks, Micah. Talk soon. Kiss Jessica for me."

"Will do."

Chapter Fourteen

Sarah Hayes has never seen the inside of a courtroom before. Unfortunately, her virgin courtroom experience will require her to recount the events that led to the death of her husband. On the morning she is to give her grand jury testimony, Zachary Blake picks her up and drives her downtown to breakfast at a restaurant that was too expensive for her taste.

As she scans the menu and observes the prices, she looks up at Blake, aghast.

"You're a client, " he assures her. "Order anything you want."

She relaxes and orders bacon and eggs with a biscuit.

"Sarah, I know you're scared, but Rochelle Lynch is a very nice woman. She will walk you through what happened that night. All you have to do is tell the truth."

"Will you be in the room with me?"

"No, I won't. Everything in front of the grand jury is secret - no television and no reporters. If the criminal case or wrongful death case gets to trial, there will be lots of publicity and media coverage, but not so with the grand jury. The only attorney allowed in the grand jury room is the prosecutor."

"I've never done anything like this before. I'm not sure I can do it," whispers Sarah.

"Sure you can, Sarah. Here's what I want you to do. When you walk into the room, you will see several people. A clerk will swear you in. You must promise to tell the truth, the whole truth, and nothing but the truth. Someone will invite you to be seated in the witness chair.

"Rochelle Lynch will approach you. At that point, I want you to focus only on her and her questions. I want you to pretend no one else is in the room, block out all the other noise and all the other people, and have a simple conversation with Rochelle. Answer her questions as honestly and forthrightly as possible. Can you do that for me?" Blake cajoles.

"I guess so," she concedes. "Where will you be?"

"I will be right outside the door. And here's the good news. If you don't like the way things are going, you need a break for any reason, or you want to talk to me before answering a question, ask for a time out and say you want to confer with your attorney. They are required to allow a witness to do that, understood?"

"I want to confer with my attorney." She moves her arms up and down robotically.

Blake laughs. *This woman will make a fabulous impression on a jury.*

"You can ask to speak to me as often as you want. Too bad if constant interruptions begin to piss off Rochelle or the jurors. I want *you* to be comfortable. That's all I care about."

"Will you be here the whole time?"

"Of course, I'm your chauffeur for the day, remember?"

"That's right, I forgot you picked me up. I'm such a nervous wreck. I'm so glad Larry gave me your name and number."

"So am I."

Sarah Hayes smiles to herself. Zachary Blake is a beacon of light, through the smog of sorrow, fear, and apprehension. They finish breakfast, Blake pays the bill, and attorney and client walk to the building where the grand jury is conducting hearings.

Reporters, as usual, are camped out in front of the building, while a more modest protest group is chanting and waving signs. There is no police presence and no counter-protest. Blake stops Sarah in her tracks.

"Sarah? I have not called a press conference to announce that we are pursuing a civil case against the officer and the city. Reporters are camped out in front of this building. All they're getting from everyone, so far, is a terse, 'no comment.' I want to engage them and get interviewed by as many of these media people as possible. This is big news. What I say will be on television, radio, in newspapers, and on social media. Do you have a problem with that?"

"W-will they ask me anything?" She stammers, unsure of the strategy.

"They might."

"Do you want me to answer?"

"Depends on the question. I'll be right there with you to cut it off if that's what you want."

"Will it help the case?"

"As long as I control the reporters and they need me more than I need them."

"Okay, let's do it, but Zack?"

"Yes, Sarah?"

"Don't let go of my arm."

"I won't. Let's go."

***

As Sarah and Blake approach the building, reporters jump to their feet.

"It's Zachary Blake. He's with the widow," a female reporter cries.

She grabs her microphone and pulls on a cameraman's shirt. Together, they run toward Blake and Sarah. Other news people are slower to react, so they will be forced to follow her lead.

"Zack, Zack, Jillian Zimmer from Seven Action News, remember me? I covered the Khan case."

"I remember you, Jillian, what may I do for you?"

The cameras start rolling as a mass of reporters crowd around Zack and shove microphones in his face.

"What are you doing here, Zack?"

"I represent Mrs. Sarah Hayes and her family. Mrs. Hayes has an appointment in the building. I'm accompanying her for, ahem, moral support."

"Is the grand jury convened today, Zack?"

"No comment, Jillian. Grand jury proceedings are private— not public proceedings. You know that."

"What kind of appointment does your client have, Zack?"

"She needs to meet with someone and answer a few questions."

"What about?"

"I really can't say."

"Well, what can you say?"

"Actually, Jillian, I have a scoop for you," Blake gloats.

"What's that?" Jillian brightens.

"Mrs. Hayes has instructed me to file a police misconduct and civil rights wrongful death lawsuit in Wayne County Circuit Court against the officer who murdered her husband and against the city and police department that hired and trained this officer and turned him loose on an unsuspecting public."

"May I quote you on that?" Jillian is eager for a scoop.

"Absolutely. Police brutality is a heinous act. Police officers work in service to the public. The public should be able to rely on that service and the preservation of their safety. The public should expect that police officer functions and services are even-handed, fair, and appropriate, applied the same way for all citizens, regardless of race, creed, color, or national origin. Police officers must know how to handle many different types of situations.

"For example, should a peaceful protester who shouts slogans that denigrate police officers be beaten? Of course not.

"A police officer must develop a thick skin and the skills to ignore these verbal attacks. If a criminal becomes physically or verbally abusive, force should be only that which is necessary to control or subdue the behavior. *Deadly* force should only be used as an absolute last resort. There are precious few examples where such force might become necessary.

"Now, let's compare these situations to a routine traffic stop where the citizen is lawfully complying with traffic laws. Was he pulled over because of an officer's racial bias, on the absurd premise that he and his wife 'resemble' two black teenaged males who are at least twenty years younger? As the officer reaches the driver's side, the innocent driver informs him that he carries a gun and has a license to do so. According to video evidence and eyewitness accounts, the officer panics and blurts out conflicting instructions.

"'Hands on the dash! License and registration!' The driver hears 'license and registration' and reaches down to retrieve them. The officer shoots him four times, claiming the man was reaching for his gun.

"Why would Marcus Hayes tell the officer he was carrying a gun if he intended to use it? He wouldn't, of course. Did this officer ever see a gun? Was the man belligerent or threatening?

The evidence will show that he wasn't. Yet, this officer shot this man four times and killed him in cold blood. Crime scene technicians who examined Mr. Hayes' body found his license and registration balled up in his clenched fist. His family watched the whole thing unfold before their eyes. The murder of their loved one is forever etched on their memories.

"Being a police officer is a tough job. These brave men and women deal every day with a criminal element that most private citizens never wish to encounter. Police officers put their lives on the line for us. They should be honored for their service. Most are careful, honest, and good cops. However, in every precinct, there are a small number of careless, negligent, dangerous, even *crooked* cops.

"I haven't met Officer Randy Jones, but here's what I know about his behavior on the night in question. He pulled over Marcus Hayes because two young black teenagers had committed a robbery in the predominately white community of Cedar Ridge. I hope to prove this stop was premised upon Jones's belief that 'all black men look alike,' a myth racists have perpetuated for years.

"Officer Jones might have approached the window and *apologized* once he observed a forty-year-old man instead of a teenager. 'Sorry, sir. I have made a mistake. Have a nice day.' Make more sense? Clearly, this family wasn't the Burger King robbery suspects. Yet, Jones persisted.

"Jones requests the driver's license and registration. According to Mrs. Hayes, when her husband attempts to produce the requested paperwork, the officer shoots him, not once, but *four times,* once through the heart.

"Whether this was murder or criminal negligence is up to a criminal jury. Whatever the jury decides, this was certainly *not* the preservation of safety or service to the public."

Are potential jurors watching on television? Blake carefully chooses his words. He doesn't want a change in venue, but he does want to plant seeds in the minds of his future jury.

"You certainly make a compelling argument, Zack. We haven't heard much from the city. They've been pretty tight-lipped about this case. Do you know why?"

"I presume it's because the incident is still under investigation and they operate under stricter rules and protocols than I do. I'm certain they are doing their due diligence and seeking to get to the truth, same as me."

"You're bringing suit against the department *and* the City of Cedar Ridge. Would you care to comment on those lawsuits?"

"Not at this time—we are still developing the case and our legal theories. I *will* say that this officer is a product of the Cedar Ridge Police Department's system, training, and culture. We will be looking into whether there is a systemic problem with how people of color are typically treated on the streets of Cedar Ridge."

Zimmer turns and looks to Sarah Hayes. "Is this Mrs. Hayes?" She turns from Sarah back to Blake.

"It is." Blake looks toward Sarah and nods.

"May I ask her a couple of questions?"

"As long as you are willing to take 'no comment' for an answer and you don't badger her. She has been extremely traumatized."

Blake plays to the camera and all future *civil* jurors.

Zimmer turns back to Sarah and sticks a microphone in her face. Sarah tilts her head back.

"Mrs. Hayes, I am so sorry for your loss. What you are doing here today?"

"No comment, Jillian. I told you earlier, off-camera, that question is out of bounds," Blake interrupts, usurping Sarah's answer.

"I forgot. Mrs. Hayes, can you describe that night for us?"

"It was terrible. The officer would not listen to reason. He shot my husband four times in front of my children and me. But that wasn't enough. Another police officer arrested and handcuffed me for no reason while my terrified kids looked on. I wasn't released until the following morning. I wasn't permitted to see my kids until much later after my release. I had to retrieve them from social services. It is the worst night of my life. I will never forget it."

Sarah sniffles. Blake hands her a handkerchief.

"I'm so sorry you had to go through that. Please, tell me, how do you feel about this proposed lawsuit?"

"She has no comment about that, Jillian," Blake interrupts again.

Sarah pulls away and dabs her eyes with the hanky.

"Actually, Zack, I do. I want to see justice done for my husband, for me, and for my kids. Whether I get that justice in criminal court, civil court, or both is up to the prosecutor and a jury," she challenges.

Blake is not happy. Sarah ignored his instructions, but he is extremely pleased with her response to the question. He was impressed, not only with her answers but her demeanor in delivering them. Both were perfect. However, he could risk no further questioning or a potential rogue comment. He takes her arm and gently pulls her along, away from the microphones and cameras.

"That's it for now, Jillian. We'll be in touch if we have anything else for you."

He whisks Sarah away, with reporters and cameramen scrambling behind, shouting questions and filming.

Chapter Fifteen

Randy Jones is suspended and depressed. He sits on the living room couch and watches television. A breaking news update interrupts his program. There, in 4K Ultra HD, are Sarah Hayes and Zachary Blake discussing a civil suit they plan to file against him, the department and the city.

Randy is quite familiar with Zachary Blake. He remembers how Blake got that Dearborn cop acquitted on a murder charge. The whole thing was dismissed. The cop was hailed as a hero. That Dearborn guy must be the kind of cop Blake is now talking about, someone who deserves to be honored for his service.

Randy does not harbor ill feelings toward Sarah Hayes.

Her husband's dead. She's got a right to be pissed. Watches her husband die, then gets arrested and handcuffed in front of her kids. Who can blame her for being pissed?

And me? I'm the careless cop, the bad cop, the criminal cop that Blake's talking about. Maybe I am a RACIST cop.

But it wasn't like that, dammit! I saw extreme danger. I saw a suspect with a gun. Why can't anyone see what I saw? People are right about one thing. Looking back, Mr. and Mrs. Hayes don't look anything like the BK robbers. Why wasn't it obvious that night? I know why I pulled them over, but why didn't I let them go when I saw they were an older couple with kids?

Was it because they were black? Why didn't I let them go? Why? Am I a racist? Am I a murderer? What am I going to do? Help me, please God, what am I going to do?

Chapter Sixteen

The grand jury reconvenes on Tuesday of the following week. A use-of-force expert is called to testify. Rochelle Lynch isn't much of a fan of expert testimony in these types of cases. Experts tend to be long-winded, opinionated, and cocksure. They fashion themselves to be, well . . . *experts.*

In *this* case, however, Rochelle believes that this expert's testimony, if delivered cogently, will be the final puzzle piece that secures an indictment against Officer Randy Jones.

She swears and qualifies Brian Dunn as an expert in use of force. Dunn has been a police officer for nearly thirty years until he retired in June 2016 as the Deputy Chief of Police for Coldwater, Michigan. As deputy chief, he was directly responsible for all police operations, including patrol, traffic, investigations, emergency management, crime prevention, and SWAT.

Post-retirement, Dunn was retained by the City of Albion, temporarily, and assigned to review all department policies, including internal affairs. During tenures in Coldwater and Albion, he acted as a special investigator on officer-involved shooting incidents for various police organizations.

He now acts as a liaison to Albion City Council, assisting in investigations into the criminal activities of officers. One particular investigation led to indictments and improvements in officer training programs and monitoring protocols for the department.

Unlike most police officers, Dunn did not attend the police academy. He obtained a bachelor's degree in criminal justice from Kalamazoo College and a law degree from Western Michigan Cooley Law School.

He has extensive background and training in internal investigations, use of force, and officer misconduct investigations. He is a distinguished fellow at the Carnegie Institute of Peace Think Tank. Dunn has testified in well over one hundred use-of-force cases, for both defense and prosecution. His dissertation focused on police officer use of force in developing countries. Brian Dunn clearly qualifies as a use-of-force expert.

Rochelle begins questioning the witness.

"Chief Dunn, have you reviewed the Jones-Hayes matter at my request?"

"Yes, Ma'am, I have."

"And have you prepared a summary report of the incident?"

"I have."

"Please recount your summary for the grand jury."

"Sure. On the evening of the incident, Marcus Hayes is driving with his family west on Cedar Avenue in Cedar Ridge. Officer Randy Jones observes Mr. Hayes's vehicle as it crosses Pennsylvania Avenue. A neighborhood Burger King had been robbed earlier by two black men—Officer Jones decides that the driver resembles one of the suspects and radios Officer Alexander Mickler for assistance. Mickler, however, is otherwise engaged. Mickler advises Jones that he cannot dispatch immediately but will do so soon.

"Jones decides to stop the Hayes vehicle without waiting for Mickler to arrive. Because of the Burger King issue, I am willing to give Officer Jones the benefit of the doubt in pulling over the Hayes vehicle. Maybe it's a case of better safe than sorry.

"However, Jones never notifies central that he intends to stop the Hayes vehicle on his own, and he does not conduct a high-risk stop.

"The vehicle is pulled over and comes to a stop. Jones exits his squad car and approaches the driver's side door of the Hayes vehicle with his gun holstered. He immediately notices that Mr. Hayes is many years older than the Burger King suspects. He also sees Mr. Hayes's wife and two young children are present in the vehicle. The wife is seated in the passenger front seat, and the kids are in car seats in the two back seat positions.

"Rather than telling Mr. Hayes the stop was made in error, Jones proceeds. He claims he smells marijuana and asks Mr. Hayes for his license and registration. Mr. Hayes begins to reach for the information and casually tells Jones that he has a firearm in the vehicle and a license to carry.

"Jones panics and begins to shout conflicting orders: 'License and registration,' 'show me your hands,' 'license and registration,' 'hands on the dash,' and, finally, 'don't reach for it,' after which Jones shoots Hayes four times.

"A driver's license and registration are found in Mr. Hayes's hand as the crime scene is processed. Jones's various explanations for the shooting are that 'suspect appeared to be going for the gun,' 'I couldn't see his hand,' and 'Hayes was non-compliant.'

"The shooting and conversations are recorded on Officer Jones's dash cam system. Significant portions of events are also recorded on Mrs. Hayes's cellphone. Ambulances and crime scene technicians arrive at the scene, and sometime later, investigators discover a handgun in the center glove box of the vehicle. My conclusions are as follows: One—Officer Jones did not know Mr. Hayes' identity at the time of the shooting but must have concluded that Hayes and his wife were not the Burger King suspects. Two—no reasonable police officer would have believed that Mr. Hayes matched the description of the Burger King suspects. Three—the car stop was inconsistent with generally accepted police practices and procedures. If Officer Jones truly believed that Mr. Hayes was a robbery suspect, a reasonable officer would have conducted a high-risk stop. Four—the weight of the evidence indicates that the handgun was in the vehicle glove box. Officer Jones's use of deadly force was objectively unreasonable and inconsistent with generally accepted police procedures."

"Thank you for that, Chief Dunn." Lynch turns to the jury and back to the witness.

"We have your full report. I will need you to identify and qualify it for the record. That way, we won't require hours of testimony about its contents, and the grand jury may read the report. Sound good to everyone?" Lynch scans the jurors, most of whom are nodding their heads.

Dunn skims through the report and declares it to be complete and accurate. Lynch moves for its admission and requests that the clerk hand out copies to every juror.

"Chief Dunn, your report is now in evidence, which will

shorten our time today, " Lynch declares.

"Thank you, I appreciate it," Dunn smiles.

"Let me ask you this, Chief: What were the key pieces of information you used to reach your conclusions?"

"The dash cam video and audio, the cellphone video, Officer Jones's statement to Internal Affairs, and the statements of all of the officers who responded to the incident."

"What do you believe to be the reason Mr. Hayes was pulled over, Chief Dunn?"

"In my professional opinion, Mr. Hayes was pulled over because he was a black male. The Burger King robbery was a thinly veiled attempt to justify the stop."

Lynch knew this answer was coming, but the grand jurors did not. Several members visibly flinch at the blunt response. Lynch pounces on the moment. "Why do you feel race was the reason for the stop?"

"The robbery happened much earlier. Mr. Hayes's presence near the scene of the earlier crime may have been remotely consistent with his possible involvement. However, his age and his family's presence in the vehicle renders his potential involvement nonsensical."

"Anything else?"

"Yes. There is no other explanation for the detention of the vehicle. Mr. Hayes had no equipment problems. He was not speeding. In fact, he did not violate a single traffic law. Once Officer Jones determines that Hayes is a middle-aged family man, the stop becomes inconsistent with generally accepted police practices."

"Any other observations you wish to share?"

"Yes, Officer Jones's decision to proceed alone and not wait for Officer Mickler is inconsistent with police procedure."

"How do you mean?"

"Police officers are trained to evaluate potentially dangerous situations. The officer's goal must always focus on minimizing the risk of danger. In this case, Jones radios Mickler to advise that he suspects these people of the Burger King robbery. Because the Burger King crime is quite serious, the two officers decide Jones should wait for backup. For reasons known only to

Jones, he decides to pull them over anyway and proceeds alone. This suggests two distinct possibilities, neither favorable to Officer Jones."

"What are those, Chief?

"Jones was extremely careless for pursuing two robbers on his own, without backup. Or he knew these people weren't the suspects and he just wanted to hassle them. Either way, this is inferior police work and decision-making," Dunn concluded.

"Why do you come to that conclusion?"

"Because there is no evidence Jones conducted a high-risk stop. You have to understand that cops are trained on how to stop a suspect who might be armed. We *work* on this. There are *drills*. The officer uses the cover of his car door and calls to the driver and the passengers to exit and assume a prone position on the ground. Only then does the officer approach and cuff. He detains them until he confirms whether he has the correct suspects. This is basic training stuff.

"If Jones thought Hayes was the Burger King suspect, that's the procedure to follow when conducting the stop. Had Officer Jones employed these tactics rather than approaching the window, Mr. Hayes would have stepped out of the vehicle, obeyed orders to assume a prone position, and permitted Officer Jones to handcuff him. Following protocol avoids tragedy."

"So, Chief, just to confirm, your expert opinion on the use of deadly force in this case is?"

"In Michigan, use of deadly force is only permissible to prevent death or great bodily harm. The Supreme Court of the United States, in *Graham v. Conner*, held that a balance test must be made between the rights of the individual and the government's interests. This is a test of reasonableness. Factors to consider are the severity of the crime the person is suspected of, whether the person poses an immediate threat to safety, or whether the person is resisting. Age and demeanor of the victim are also potential factors.

"These tests do not lend support to Officer Jones's conduct. Mr. Hayes broke no laws at the time of the stop. He was traveling with his wife and kids. He was candid and forthright in letting Jones know he had a gun. He took no evasive or threatening action. His 'crime' was to be male, black, and driving near the site of a previous robbery committed by a couple of young black guys. Had Jones actually believed Hayes to be one of the suspects, he would have engaged in the high-risk stop tactics I described earlier."

"What about the marijuana allegation by Officer Jones?"

"In my humble opinion, the possibility that Mr. Hayes smoked marijuana at some point is a 'so what?' factor," Dunn scoffs.

"Even if an investigator gives credence to the allegation, it isn't enough to justify Officer Jones' actions that evening. Possession of marijuana is no longer a crime in Michigan, and there is nothing to suggest that Mr. Hayes was driving under the influence. No evidence was present to cause any reasonable police officer to use deadly force. Mr. Hayes doesn't resist. He doesn't try to flee the scene. He's respectful to the officer throughout and attempts to comply with the officer's inconsistent commands."

"Thanks, Chief. Any questions from the grand jury?"

"Yes, I have a question." Juror Number Three raises her hand.

"Juror Three, what is your question?"

"Officer Jones claimed he couldn't see the gun, and Mr. Hayes was reaching for something despite the officer's contrary orders. Why couldn't those factors be interpreted as actions justifying the use of deadly force?"

"Good question. The problem is Officer Jones gives Mr. Hayes multiple inconsistent commands. 'License and registration' is requested several times. 'Hands on the dashboard' is ordered several times. Mr. Hayes has reason to be confused. Furthermore, this man is sitting in a car with his *family,* and Officer Jones shoots him without ever catching a *glimpse* of a gun.

"Mr. Hayes is seat belted and doesn't remotely match the description of either robbery suspect. He's cooperative and pulls over as ordered. He doesn't try to flee or resist in any way and volunteers information. There is no one factor here, but if we look at every factor together, especially Jones's failure to employ high-risk techniques, it is evident deadly force is unnecessary and inconsistent with generally accepted police practices."

Juror Three sits back in her chair, entirely placated.

"Anyone else have a question?" Lynch scans the grand jury. No takers.

"Let's take a break."

Chapter Seventeen

Lawrence Bialy and Rochelle Lynch are seated to the left and right of a podium hastily set up for a news conference in the lobby of the Wayne County Prosecutor's Office. The two prosecutors are stone-faced, discreetly watching various media members float in and locate seats.

Soon, all seats are occupied—it is standing room only. The purpose of the news conference is to announce the findings of the grand jury investigating the Jones-Hayes shooting. Five minutes late, Bialy steps to the podium.

"Ladies and gentlemen. We are assembled here today to announce the grand jury impaneled to investigate the shooting death of Marcus Hayes has published its findings. The grand jury's principal focus was to determine whether Officer Randy Jones has criminal culpability for the shooting.

"There are many different types of potential charges considered when one causes another's death. First and Second Degree Murder and Voluntary or Involuntary Manslaughter are all considerations. Charges depend on the degree of planning or provocation, as well as the actions and state of mind of the perpetrator.

"When we apply these standards to this case, we ask whether Officer Jones believed he needed to defend his life that evening. Was this belief reasonable or unreasonable? Assistant District Attorney Rochelle Lynch will now publish the findings of the grand jury. Ms. Lynch?"

Bialy sits as Rochelle Lynch rises and approaches the podium.

"Thank you, Mr. Bialy. Ladies and gentlemen, the grand jury has issued an indictment charging Cedar Ridge Police Officer Randy Jones with one count of voluntary manslaughter in the shooting death of Marcus Hayes of Detroit. The grand jury has determined Officer Jones was unreasonable in stopping Mr. Hayes and for not releasing him when it became obvious Mr.

Hayes bore no resemblance to the so-called 'Burger King Suspect.'"

"Furthermore, the grand jury has determined Officer Jones acted unreasonably in giving the suspect multiple, inconsistent orders and expecting compliance with those orders.

"The grand jury finds Officer Jones acted out of fear for his life and the lives of others in the immediate vicinity. However, the grand jury also finds those fears were unjustified under the existing circumstances. I quote from the indictment."

Lynch dons a pair of reading glasses and begins to read directly from a document.

"'Officer Randy Jones unreasonably pulled Mr. Hayes over. Mr. Hayes complied fully with the traffic stop even though he had done nothing wrong. When Officer Jones approached the driver's side window, Mr. Hayes immediately informed Officer Jones he was lawfully carrying a permitted gun. That information caused unjustified or unwarranted panic in Officer Jones, a trained police officer, and that panic was a direct cause of Mr. Hayes's death. Mr. Hayes complied with the stop, did not act in a threatening manner, and complied, as best he could, with the officer's inconsistent orders and commands. After Officer Jones approached Mr. Hayes' vehicle, it was obvious Hayes was with his young family and bore no resemblance to the robbery suspects. Therefore, we, the Grand Jury, do hereby indict and charge Officer Randy Jones with the crime of Voluntary Manslaughter.'

"We will take your questions . . ."

***

Officer Randy Jones is glued to the television. While he expected the indictment, he is still shocked, not only by the indictment but the harshness of the prosecutors' rhetoric.

He watches the press conference. The prosecutors and the press attack his behavior. Question upon question and comment upon comment attack his integrity, judgment, training, and ability. He feels like a tired, beaten, and bloodied boxer backed into the corner, taking blow after blow from his opponent, helpless to weather the assault.

I panicked. Was Hayes compliant? Did he do anything wrong? Did I allow my prejudice to control my actions? This wasn't the first time. I've done this before. Am I a racist? Maybe I am. I deserve whatever I get. I am unfit to be a police officer— unfit to be Brenda's husband . . .

Brenda is at work, so Randy is home alone. He walks to the computer and begins to type. When he finishes, he hits 'print' and hears the printer awake, whir, and begin to spit out pages. He rises and walks to the closet, opens the door, reaches in and punches buttons on a digital wall safe. The lock clicks. Randy grabs the handle and pulls the door open. Inside are important papers and a gun box.

Randy removes a file folder. Everything is in order. Brenda gets everything. He checks his term life policy. It's been in force long enough to avoid the suicide clause. Brenda will receive the five hundred thousand dollar death benefit.

A framed photo of Brenda sits on his desk. Randy glances at the photograph and smiles. *God, she's beautiful. Thank you, Lord, for the love of my life. Brenda, you're a great woman, and you deserve better. I know this will be painful for you, but soon you will forget all the pain I caused. Find love with someone smarter and better, someone who has better judgment, a man who deserves you. You are free to live a happy life, my darling.*

Tears fill his eyes and slowly cascade into his lap as he removes the gun box and opens it to reveal his secondary weapon, a Sig P226. He takes the gun and cradles it in his hands. He kneels and begins to pray in silence. He completes his prayer, takes the gun in his right hand, and directs it to his temple.

"Forgive me, Brenda. Forgive me, Mr. and Mrs. Hayes. I am so sorry for the pain I have caused," he cries aloud.

Randy Jones pulls the trigger. A loud pop echoes through the empty house. A soft breeze blows a single printed page from the printer cradle. The weightless paper floats in the air until it finally reaches the floor, landing softly and soundlessly over the outstretched hand of the late Officer Randy Jones.

Chapter Eighteen

The grand jury indictment is big news around the office. According to various news reports, Randy's been indicted and charged with a single count of voluntary manslaughter. Prosecutors are asking him to surrender voluntarily. Brenda's bosses and coworkers sneak peeks at her while mumbling back and forth. It's impossible to concentrate on her work, so Brenda leaves early.

She drives the short distance home and wonders if Randy will be immediately bonded out. *Perhaps he'll get released on his own recognizance. After all, he's a police officer. Maybe there's a plea bargain to be worked out. Randy's a good man, a kind man. He's protected and served the public. Surely those things will count for something.*

She pulls her Ford Focus into the garage next to Randy's Ford Edge and enters the house.

"Honey, I'm home. Where are you?" No answer. She turns the corner. "Honey?" No answer. She peers into the office and stands at the door, *horrified*. Randy is sprawled on the floor, a large pool of blood oozing from a head wound. Brenda staggers, pulls out her cellphone, and dials 9-1-1.

***

The Cedar Ridge Police Department responds to the scene. The paper and gun still lay on the floor in their original positions. Brenda knows police procedures. She's touched nothing to avoid crime scene contamination.

A crime scene technician escorts her out of the office and into the living room. Chief Warren Brooks is standing at the front door.

"Brenda, I am so sorry for your loss. Are you up to answering a few questions?"

"Thank you, Chief. What questions do you have?"

"You came home and found him like this?" Brooks queries.

"Yes, it was *awful.* I knew Randy was depressed and angry. I told him to talk to someone. But I never expected him to do anything like this," she cries. *Did I miss the signs?*

"He felt terrible about what happened and questioned his ability to be a police officer. I thought he was going to resign. He decided he made a terrible mistake with Mr. Hayes. The guilt he felt over that man's death was overwhelming. It was all he talked about.

"'He would say: Am I a murderer? A racist? Did I really pull an innocent man over for driving while black?' He was upset, yes, but did I think he was capable of suicide? Never," she ruminates.

"Is this exactly how you found the body?" Brooks startles Brenda out of her thoughts.

Brenda wipes her eyes. "Yes, Chief. I know the rules; touch nothing, call 9-1-1."

"You didn't touch the note?"

"What note? I didn't notice a note. Where is it?"

"There," he points. "Next to the body."

"May I see it?"

"It hasn't been processed yet," Brooks advises.

"I need to read my husband's note. This is obviously a suicide. These are *his . . . last . . . words*," she wails.

She's right. It's open and shut. Jones did all of us a huge favor. The city and the department won't have to be dragged through the mud in Wayne Circuit. What the hell . . .

"Sure, Brenda, let's get the crime scene boys in here. It shouldn't take long to process," Brooks concedes.

Brenda Jones fights hard to compose herself. She wipes tears from her eyes and face.

"Thanks, Chief," she sniffles. "I really appreciate this and everything else you tried to do for Randy."

"I haven't done shit, Brenda. You don't owe me a thing," Brooks grumbles.

"Chief, this was an impossible situation, and Randy understood that. He didn't blame you for a thing," she lies.

"Brenda, you're a terrific liar."

Brooks looks over to the office, the room where the Wayne

County coroner is now working on the body. A crime scene tech bags and tags the note and hands it to Brooks.

"It looks like there is only one set of prints, Chief. I'll match them ASAP."

"Thanks, Otto."

Brooks turns to Brenda.

"Here's the note, Brenda." He hands her the plastic baggie covered note without reading it.

Brenda tries to focus and begins to read the note aloud.

"My dearest Brenda: I've loved you for all of my adult life, and I thank God Almighty for every day we spent together. My will is inside the safe. Everything belongs to you. I know you're hurting, but please try to move on with your life. You deserve happiness and a rich, fulfilling life. I love you, my darling.

"To the Hayes family: What made me pull Mr. Hayes over that night? I don't quite know. There had been an earlier robbery that weighed heavily on my mind. I tried to be a fair officer who worked for justice. I should have caught myself as soon as I saw your family. Mr. Hayes was innocent. I've thought about that night a great deal lately. I must have prejudices I was previously unaware of. Still, that doesn't justify having them or acting upon them. I cannot explain or justify my actions, but I am truly sorry for the pain I have caused you.

"To my fellow police officers and the Cedar Ridge Police Department: Thanks for always having my back. I'm sorry my actions have caused you pain and embarrassment. I've let all of you down. Learn from my mistakes. Enforce the law but do so even-handedly with a clear conscience. Go with God, my brothers and sisters. Hopefully, I am with Him now.

"Peace and love to all, Randy."

Chief Warren Brooks retrieves the note from Brenda Jones and hands it back to the evidence tech—the tech secures it with other crime scene evidence. Seconds later, the coroner emerges from the office and announces that the body was being taken to the morgue for autopsy.

Behind him, two men push a gurney carrying a zippered blue tarp-like wrap that contains the body of Randy Jones. The men carry the body out the front door and load it into a van labeled

'Wayne County Medical Examiner.'

Brenda turns to Chief Brooks. "Are you guys going to be much longer? I need to make dinner, take a shower, and get some sleep. I have a funeral to plan," she mutters.

"Nonsense, Brenda. You can't stay here. This is a crime scene, and you are obviously in shock," Brooks orders.

"We'll arrange for a hotel at department expense. Please pack a bag and I'll take you downtown."

"Or, you can stay at our house," Alex Mickler offers. "Jill and I would be happy to have you."

"That's a nice offer, Alex. How about it, Brenda? Is it Jill and Alex or a hotel on the department?" Brooks inquires.

"Alex, thank you, but I think I'll take Chief Brooks up on his hotel offer. I'd rather be alone tonight."

***

Two hours later, Brenda Jones lay in a hot bubble bath in her downtown hotel room. She closes her eyes and pictures her husband, Randy—all smiles on their wedding day.

When did you stop being that guy? When did your job claim the man I once knew? Oh, Randy, how could you do this? We used to be able to talk about things. When did you start internalizing, burying things so far under the surface that they ate at you from the inside out? Why couldn't you let me in, let me help you? I love you, but I don't know how I can ever forgive you.

Brenda Jones slips under the water.

Chapter Nineteen

Word of Randy Jones's suicide spreads quickly through the metropolitan Detroit area. Cedar Ridge mayor, the Honorable George Mendoza, offers his deepest condolences to the widow. Police Chief Warren Brooks issues a statement saying the Cedar Ridge Police community has lost one of its brothers and sons, and the entire law enforcement community is officially in mourning. City flags will fly at half-mast.

A flock of reporters gathers on the sidewalk and street in front of Sarah Hayes's home in Detroit, hoping for a comment. Instead of accommodating them, Sarah calls Zack Blake.

Blake hops into his BMW and drives to her house. When he arrives, he observes a swarm of reporters and camera crews milling about, waiting to catch a glimpse of or a word from Sarah Hayes.

Jillian Zimmer approaches Blake and requests a comment or statement.

"Sure, Jillian. Do you have a microphone I can borrow?"

"Can I have an exclusive?"

"I can borrow the microphone from someone else, Jillian. You're invading my client's privacy and scaring the hell out of her kids."

Jillian pouts and hands Blake a microphone, as reporters and cameramen cram into each other in a quest to position themselves as close to Zack Blake as possible.

"Ladies and gentlemen of the press. This is a sad day for the Detroit area law enforcement community. They have lost one of their own. When a fallen officer is from the Detroit area, the entire Southeastern Lower Michigan brotherhood in blue feels that loss. I'm sorry the tragedy of Marcus Hayes has expanded to include the tragedy of Officer Randy Jones.

"My client is distraught and unwilling to comment about these events. She knows the pain of losing a husband and wishes to extend her deepest condolences to Officer Jones's wife, Brenda.

"However, this tragic event will not deter our pursuit of justice in this case. I will take no questions and ask all of you to vacate these premises. Thank you in advance for respecting my client's privacy."

Blake hands the microphone back to Jillian. She and others begin shouting questions. Blake ignores them and moves toward the house. Reporters begin to vacate the property, reporting live as they do so. Blake knocks gently on the front door and announces himself. Sarah answers and Blake quickly enters the home and closes the front door

"Zack, my kids, and I can't live like this. A couple of these guys followed them to school and tried to ask *them* questions—kids as young as they are—can you believe that?" Sarah is distraught.

"Sarah, I'm so sorry. I will put a stop to this harassment. I promise."

"Thank you. I know you're doing your best. How's Mrs. Jones doing? What's her name, Brenda? She's joined an exclusive club."

"This is a tragic mess all the way around, Sarah. As for the press, though, we knew when we started our journey together that it would be a media circus. Would you like to stop? We don't have to continue. We can drop the civil case. Just say the word."

"No, Zack. I'll be okay. You told me this lawsuit would help to prevent these types of occurrences in the future, and I think Marcus would want me to continue. I hope the press will respect boundaries when it comes to my kids and our privacy."

"I'll do my best, Sarah. Hang in there."

"Thank you, Zack. Thanks for coming all the way out here on such short notice."

"My pleasure."

Chapter Twenty

Chief Warren Brooks grimaces as he watches Zachary Blake's impromptu press conference. He takes special note of Blake's "flawed system," "root cause," "gross negligence," and "pursuit of justice" comments.

If systemic racism and gross negligence can be proven, punitive and compensatory damages are available. Punitive damages, those which *punish* a defendant for egregious behavior, are a wildcard and may drastically increase a jury award, even result in the type of nine-figure award that made Zachary Blake the Detroit area's most famous lawyer.

Brooks wants to hate Zachary Blake. He'd also like to talk some sense into Sarah Hayes. *Pulling multiple millions out of the law enforcement treasury will not make our citizens safer. It will make us less safe.*

But he could not detest Blake for doing his job or being good at it. Sarah Hayes had an absolute right to seek justice for her husband's death. Blake and his client are absolutely correct, both factually and politically. They're fully justified in their pursuit of this case. Jones *was* a product of the Cedar Ridge law enforcement system, and that system *is* to blame for this nightmare, even though Jones's actions that evening were abhorrent to Brooks.

If this type of behavior is endemic to my police force, I need to clean house.

Unfortunately, his position as Cedar Ridge Chief of Police is very much a political one. As such, Brooks' private feelings on these subjects are, by necessity, quite different than his public ones. In public, his role is to defend the department and the brave young men and women who protect and serve the community. In private, however, he's inclined to root for Zack Blake and Sarah Hayes.

***

Michael Kendell is executive director of the Midwest Region

of *Black Lives Matter*. He watches Zachary Blake's news conference in his home office and is intrigued by the news that Randy Jones has taken his own life. In his mind, there are two possible explanations for suicide.

Suicide was often the coward's way out. Either Jones was a coward and unwilling to face criminal or civil juries, or he was genuinely remorseful and despondent. Perhaps his death resulted from a lethal combination of the two.

Whatever the reason, Jones' death could now be used to advance BLM's cause and its quest for equal and humane treatment by police officers.

Kendell is a historian of racism at a time when President Ronald John's open bigotry has created a national debate. Kendell is concerned that John's rhetoric and events like Cedar Ridge will eventually converge, if they haven't already, to create an atmosphere of unrest and racial violence.

As an activist, his positions sit somewhere between King and Farrakhan. Kendell doesn't condone or encourage violence, and his writings and speeches reflect that. But he is also keenly aware that the sword is sometimes mightier than the pen.

His ultimate goal is to drive racism out of America and American culture. He believes systemic discriminatory policies are the cause of racism and that dismantling those policies will concurrently curb racist ideas and ideology.

A full professor at Wayne State University in Detroit, Kendell holds a Ph.D. in African American studies from that very same university. He currently teaches a popular course called *Systemic Racism in African American History* and a more generalized, less controversial African American history class. He's a well-known authority on television and head of a privately funded think tank, which conducts volumes of research into root causes of racist activity and attitudes.

While many of his contemporaries feel education, political power, and assimilation into the dominant white infrastructure of America are keys to the decline of racist attitudes, Kendell believes these things actually *perpetuate* those attitudes.

If a black man is educated and earns a good income, for example, his insecure white contemporaries now view him as a threat, someone who is "uppity" and a challenge to the status quo. Therefore, this insecurity or threat to the white man's self-interest is a root cause of racism in America. An educated and assimilated black man might, in fact, be a cause of racial tension and not a solution.

Michael Kendell possesses a burning desire to make a difference. He wants the justice system to continue to pursue the Jones-Hayes case, pedal to the metal. He believes such pursuit might lead to meaningful change in training, social education, hiring practices, and attitudes in police departments in the Detroit area and beyond. He is concerned Jones's death might have a chilling effect on that effort.

Jones's death has killed the criminal case. Will it claim the civil case as well?

Kendell is quite concerned about that possible outcome.

Michael wants Zachary Blake to put systemic racism and the Cedar Ridge Police Department on trial, along with the racist actions and attitudes of Randy Jones. The civil case might be as compelling as the criminal case would have been, especially if it has a substantial economic impact on the Cedar Ridge Police Department. He is confident of one thing: Zachary Blake is the absolute right man for the job.

Blake's a powerful guy who's successfully taken on and taken down powerful institutions in the past.

Kendell is an expert at researching and flushing out racist attitudes and policies at the institutional level. He's been at the forefront of change in many colleges and universities around the country. He's assembled teams of activists and students to conduct research projects into the racial history of Cedar Ridge and the Cedar Ridge Police Department. He plans to present that research to Zachary Blake and Sarah Hayes.

The key to success for his movement, though, is to prevent the City of Cedar Ridge from resolving the case before evidence of the police department's racist actions and attitudes are exposed or before they blame the shooting on the actions of one rogue cop. He silently hopes that one day soon, Zachary Blake and Sarah Hayes will consider partnering with him and his followers in a quest for progress and meaningful change.

Chapter Twenty-One

Blake changes his mind about filing the case in Wayne County Circuit Court. The Estate of Marcus Hayes files a four-count complaint in the Federal District Court in Detroit. The complaint alleges violations of the First, Fourth, and Fourteenth Amendments of the United States Constitution, 42 USC Sections 1983 and 1988, and related sections of the Michigan Constitution and State of Michigan common law.

Since the alleged acts were committed in the Eastern District of Michigan and a federal question has been raised, venue is proper in federal district court.

Wayne County Circuit Court is a far better venue than any federal district court, but Blake knows the defense would have moved the case to federal court when filing its formal answer.

Why fuck around?

Count one, the plaintiff's first cause of action in the formal complaint, is a so-called *1983* cause of action. Virtually all police misconduct or police brutality cases allege this violation because 42 USC Section 1983 and the First, Fourth, and Fourteenth Amendments of the United States Constitution provide guarantees that a citizen must be free from gratuitous and excessive force. This is the reason that legal insiders refer to these as *1983 lawsuits.*

Sarcastically, Blake decides to add that there is no force more excessive than the unnecessary force that takes the life of a citizen. Further, Blake alleges that Marcus Hayes's death was a direct and proximate cause of this gratuitous and excessive force.

Count two is a straightforward and simple assault and battery with a deadly weapon allegation. As straightforward as it is, however, this is an allegation that, if proven against all defendants, is likely to reach the deep pockets of the City of Cedar Ridge. Blake alleges Officer Randy Jones intentionally assaulted and battered Marcus Hayes in violation of Michigan law. Furthermore, Blake argues Jones committed these willful, wrongful, and unlawful acts of assault, battery, and threatening behavior against the entire Hayes family while acting with the scope of his employment as a Cedar Ridge police officer.

Under the legal doctrine of *respondeat superior,* Jones's employers—the Cedar Ridge Police Department and the City of Cedar Ridge are equally responsible for his wrongdoing. This count repeats that Marcus Hayes's death and damages to the Hayes family are directly and proximately caused by these alleged wrongful acts.

Counts three and four are also counts designed to pick deep pockets. They are directed at the City of Cedar Ridge and its' police department. *Count Three* alleges the city and police department both committed Section 1983 and constitutional violations similar to those alleged in count one. In essence, Blake is arguing both caused or contributed to Hayes's death and his family's horror because they tolerated these types of traffic stops against people of color in Cedar Ridge and also tolerated serial practices of excessive use of force by its officers.

Count four alleges the City of Cedar Ridge and the police department failed to properly train and discipline police officers in connection with the use of injurious and excessive force. Blake decides to add a controversial racial profiling allegation to this count.

He alleges negligent training and discipline protocols have failed to provide officers in this virtually all-white community with sensitivity and tolerance training. Proper training and discipline might have prevented cultural and ethnic misunderstandings. In this case, Officer Jones was incapable of communicating with his minority subject.

Counts three and four aver these negligent behaviors and failures are a direct and proximate result of Marcus Hayes's death and his family's pain and suffering.

Blake decides to notify the press of the lawsuit filing and the fact that he will make a statement on the courthouse steps. After formally filing the lawsuit with the clerk of the court, Blake steps outside the courthouse on Fort Street and is greeted by a modest but growing crowd of reporters.

"Ladies and gentlemen, the Detroit metropolitan area is an American community with a unique heritage. It is a true melting pot of many races, creeds, and religions. As I look out at you today, I notice the vast majority of you are white. As a white person, it is often difficult to comprehend that your black neighbor, coworker, or friend is living a completely different life from you, simply because of the color of their skin.

"Stopping a black couple in a predominately white city like Cedar Ridge, when no traffic laws have been broken, is a serious example of this phenomenon. Perhaps you are the only black hire at a company, the only black couple at a party, or seated in a restaurant. Maybe you're the token black person on a committee because it needs to demonstrate diversity. These are less serious examples.

"Talking frankly about race may make white people uncomfortable. Taking a stand to demonstrate the impact of race on law enforcement is difficult.

"Look what happened when a National Football League star, protesting discrimination, decided to kneel during the national anthem. Some understood the protest and the right to peacefully demonstrate under the First Amendment to our Constitution. Others have used the protest to divide us further and rally the white supremacist elements of their constituency. Yes, I am speaking to *you*, Mr. President, the principal antagonist of racial harmony.

"Talking about race causes some to shake their heads in disgust, others to nod understandingly and still others to bristle and rant. The message from white America to black America is clear. We don't want to listen to your bitching. Get an education. Get a job. Do what the rest of us do. But when they do precisely that, they are accused of being 'uppity.'

"So, black people, despite how much racism may hurt, bottle up their feelings. They ignore hate speech, off-color jokes, and nasty emails because they don't want to appear too sensitive. Imagine, if you can, how destructive these bottled-up emotions are to one's self-esteem. Extend these types of examples to authority figures with guns.

"A racist cop pulls over a black driver for little reason other than his skin color, and a recent robbery was committed by a couple of young black guys in a white community. The cop quickly realizes the driver is *not* one of the robbery suspects when he sees a man with a wife and two small children. They are not a couple of young punks. Still, he persists. Why?

"He asks to see the driver's license and registration. While locating the appropriate documents, the black driver respectfully volunteers he is legally carrying a handgun. The cop panics—is it the image of a black man with a gun? He barks out conflicting orders and then shoots the man to death in front of his family. Why?

"Is it because the cop is an insensitive racist? Maybe he wasn't trained or taught any better? Perhaps he lived a completely different life in a completely different world than that of the black man. In this cop's world, were all black men potential criminals, people to be watched, people to be feared?

"It is not fun to be pulled over by a police officer. We're upset or anxious when we're pulled over by the police. We often know what we did wrong and await the penalty, or we wonder what we did wrong and await the explanation.

"But, do we expect to be manhandled or abused by the officer? Do we fear he might kill us? For black people, especially black men, those fears are too frequently an unfortunate reality.

"Did Marcus Hayes feel this way the evening of his death? Why should *any* law-abiding citizen feel this way when an officer who is sworn to protect and serve approaches his or her vehicle? Yet, we can all watch the video and see the stop is suspicious, the officer overreacts, and this lethal combination results in an innocent man's death. This incident makes clear to all of us the extreme danger of being pulled over for 'driving while black.'

"If the defense stays true to the police abuse case playbook, its attorneys will make a great deal of noise about Mr. Hayes's lack of cooperation. We have all been taught, regardless of skin color, to be respectful and cooperative with officers of the law. And maybe someone, I don't see how, but *someone* could view the video and conclude that Mr. Hayes was less than respectful or cooperative.

"If you tend to feel this way, *please,* give me a break! How does being slow to respond to conflicting commands justify being shot four times? The Hayes-Jones video is a textbook case study on how a police officer may stop a citizen without probable cause and provoke an unnecessary and deadly escalation.

"How can anyone view this video and not be outraged by the officer's behavior? The video is shocking and heart-wrenching. My client is slumped over, covered in blood, while his wife prays for his life and his children watch in horror. And, what does the Cedar Ridge police officer do? Gun still drawn, he peers into the window and then trains the weapon on the victim's family members, instead of calling paramedics.

"Ladies and gentlemen, something is societally wrong. The deliberate social distance between the races creates a lack of understanding and appreciation, as well as suspicion, segregation, and isolation. We must learn to live together and improve our understanding of each other. We need equality and inclusion.

"Instead, we have cops who don't understand the Fourth and Fourteenth Amendments. We have elected officials who don't understand the First. Worse, neither these cops nor these elected officials understand that *we the people*, regardless of race, creed, religion, or national origin, employ all of them.

"We must try to see the world through a black person's eyes, see hard truths, and not unfairly judge those who deliver them. We need to see people—*real people*—not the stereotypes handed down by previous generations.

"We must support those who speak out against injustice and inequality while harshly standing in judgment of those who perpetrate them. We must embrace our cultural differences, learn to understand them, and stop fighting over them.

"While white people may never completely understand or fully grasp the experience of being black in America, together, *We The People* must try to bridge the racial divide. And the result will be a stronger nation.

"The unwarranted and inexplicable shooting death of Marcus Hayes has ripped open the scabs of racial wounds that never seem to get a fighting chance to heal. Day after day, week after week, month after month, year after year, these events of bigotry and hatred rear their ugly heads and prevent healing, laying bare the ugly specters, the seemingly endless cycles of racism.

"We should call out the bigots, those who bathe themselves in patriotism and wrap themselves in the American flag but have no idea what that flag stands for. For us to indeed be a nation of immigrants where all people are created equal, the flag cannot only be a symbol of patriotism but must also be a symbol of protest. Understanding, celebrating, and teaching our First Amendment rights are our true tickets to understanding the fundamental freedoms that make this country great. A great leader realizes he or she represents both the flag-wavers *and* the flag burners.

"This lawsuit seeks to do more than call out racist cops. It aims to call out racist policies and racist systems. It seeks to call out and, hopefully, improve the education, training, and sensitivity of the police. The rhetoric in Washington and in states and cities across America is creating us versus them conflicts. If we embrace this philosophy, all of us will be losers.

"Whether we speak of small communities or large cities, states, or an entire nation, we succeed together. Separately, we fail. Sarah Hayes and her family want us to succeed.

"Blackness cannot be hidden. Whether one is stopped by the police or applying for a loan, one's race or blackness is the first noticeable piece of information. And with that information comes multiple judgments or pre-judgments, conscious or unconscious.

"*Thank God* there's a video in this case—otherwise, we'd face cries of 'he must have done *something* to provoke the shooting.' This is the prevailing attitude in white America, the America where the worst thing that happens to a white person in a traffic stop is that he or she gets a traffic citation.

"This is the Twenty-First Century. Much progress has been made. Schools and neighborhoods are integrated. People of different cultures and races live together, work together, even love one another. But we're at a crossroads.

"I don't want to see anyone, ever again, mourn the loss of a loved one under these types of circumstances. We can use this tragedy as a teachable moment, or we can continue to hide behind our politics and our religious, social, or cultural isolation. We can embrace our past but learn from experience to shape a better future for all Americans, regardless of their race, creed, or color. I'll take your questions—"

"Zack, do you intend to try this case?" A reporter shouts.

"I prepare every case I file for trial. This is an excellent case to take to a jury. Plaintiff attorneys don't usually choose trials. Defendants make those choices by failing to make reasonable settlement offers. If the defendants, in this case, are reasonable, there's a strong possibility the case resolves short of trial. If they aren't, we know where the courthouse is. We'll be prepared."

"How is Mrs. Hayes holding up, Zack?"

"Thanks for that question and your concern. Sarah Hayes is doing as well as can be expected under these circumstances. She's strong and determined to see justice done."

"How does Officer Jones's suicide affect the case, Zack? Does it hurt your chances?"

"Not at all. We have dash cam video and audio. We have the officer's interview with Internal Affairs. We have mountains of collateral evidence. Would we have preferred Officer Jones to be alive and able to testify? Absolutely. His death is one more tragedy, and Brenda Jones is one more grieving widow, yet another tragic circumstance caused by this officer's actions. How the tragedy of his death affects our case is the least of my concerns."

"What is Judge Berg's record or experience with these types of cases? Are you happy with the draw?"

"Judge Berg is an excellent judge, a fair judge. We are pleased with the draw as, I'm sure, are our opponents."

"Wasn't he appointed by Bush Two?"

"I have no idea. It doesn't matter who appointed him. I don't know his politics and I don't care. I've had numerous cases in his courtroom. He always exhibits great wisdom. He treats attorneys and clients with courtesy and respect and issues fair and reasonable rulings from the bench. That's all any trial lawyer can ask. I'm out of time. Have a good one."

Hopefully, Judge Berg will see this interview sometime very soon. Zachary Blake terminates the impromptu press conference and scurries down the courthouse steps trailed by a mob of reporters shouting out more questions. He hops into a waiting car, waves to reporters, and zooms off up Fort Street.

Chapter Twenty-Two

Three weeks later, Blake walks into his conference room for the deposition of Lieutenant Douglas Kelly.

For the purpose of the hearing, Ven Jackson represents the Cedar Ridge Police Association and Kelly. Steven Adler is the attorney of record for all other defendants in the case. Adler's a no-show. His silk-stocking law firm sends a rookie, Kyle Murray, in his place.

Not important enough? Blake wonders. He's pissed at Adler's no-show. The two men have locked horns on numerous occasions, and Blake was successful each time. Zack's quite confident about the Hayes case and is looking forward to laying another ass-kicking on Adler and his firm. Kelly's deposition is the first of many in the case. One deposition, especially of a deponent who has written a detailed report, is not critically important.

Murray is all decked out in a three-piece suit and carries a handsome leather briefcase, which he opens upon his arrival. He removes a Mont Blanc pen and three legal pads and stands when Blake enters the room.

The rookie is shocked to see Blake arrive wearing blue jeans and a sport shirt. Blake ignores the young man, greets Kelly, and then turns to Jackson. The two men shake hands and then chat a bit. Finally, he addresses Murray,

"First deposition?" Blake smirks.

"Is it that obvious? Murray squirms.

"Well, it's not a video or court appearance. Most of us dress down, when possible."

"I prefer to dress this way, and my firm requires it," Murray rebuts. He won't let the hotshot plaintiff lawyer intimidate him.

"You prefer it, or the firm requires it, which is it?"

The rookie opens his mouth and closes it again. He decides not to respond.

"No skin off my nose," Blake scoffs, dismissing the rookie. The kid's rattled. *Mission accomplished.* Blake turns to the court reporter.

"All set, Merrill?"

"Ready when you are, Zack," advises Merrill Bass, one of Blake's favorite, long-time reporters. Blake begins the interrogation.

"Let the record reflect this is the date and time set for the deposition of Lieutenant Douglas Kelly, taken pursuant to a subpoena to be used for any and all purposes contemplated by the Federal Rules of Civil Procedure and the Michigan Court Rules.

"Present today are attorneys Ven Jackson, representing the witness and the Cedar Ridge Police Association, and Kyle Murray, representing the remaining defendants.

"Lieutenant Kelly, my name is Zachary Blake. I represent the Estate of Marcus Hayes in a lawsuit filed against Officer Randy Jones, the City of Cedar Ridge, and the Cedar Ridge Police Department. I'm going to ask you a few questions. I need you to respond verbally.

"Our court reporter is the fabulous Merrill Bass. She is going to transcribe everything you say. She cannot transcribe a positive or negative head nod or a shoulder shrug. 'Uh-huh' and 'unh unh' are also difficult to transcribe, so if the question calls for a 'yes' or a 'no,' please answer accordingly. If I ask a question and you answer it, I will presume you understood the question. If you don't understand a question, please say so and I'll rephrase it. Fair?"

"Fair."

"Now, you are in charge of Internal Affairs for the Cedar Ridge Police Department, is that correct?"

"Uh-huh."

"Is that a 'yes?' Please answer 'yes' or 'no.' No negative or positive grunting allowed. Okay?" *Never fails, regardless of instructions or smarts.*

"You warned me, yet I still did it!" Kelly exclaims, embarrassed. "Sorry. The answer is yes."

"Everyone does the same thing," Blake smiles. "Now, you conducted an Internal Affairs investigation into Officer Randy Jones's conduct in the shooting death of Marcus Hayes, correct?"

"Objection, leading the witness," Murray screeches.

"Kyle, this is cross-examination, not direct. I can lead on cross." Blake schools the rookie.

"He's your witness. You can't lead." Murray postures.

"He's not my witness. He's an adverse party. He works for a defendant in the case. This is cross. If you'd like, we can stop and ask the judge. I'll seek sanctions. Want to call your boss? Maybe he can help. But don't waste my time." Jackson suppresses a chuckle.

Murray backs off. "N-no, that's okay. G-go ahead," he stammers.

"Thank you, Mr. Murray," Blake sneers and turns back to Kelly.

"Please answer the question, Lieutenant Kelly,"

"I don't remember the question," Kelly chuckles.

"You conducted an investigation into Officer Jones's shooting of Marcus Hayes, correct?" Blake repeats.

Murray starts to object again but holds his tongue.

"Correct."

"Lieutenant Kelly, please sum up your career and experience with the Cedar Ridge Police Department."

"I was originally a patrol officer, started in 1984 when the Tigers won the World Series, which is why I'll never forget my first year. I was promoted to sergeant in 1992 and lieutenant in 2005. I was assigned to Internal Affairs in 2010. I've been heading the unit since 2013."

"And when did the name 'Randy Jones' first hit your radar screen?"

When Murray starts to object, Blake waves at him like a bothersome fly. Murray backs off, intimidated.

"Soon after, I became the head of Internal Affairs, around 2013 or 2014, maybe."

"And how was the name brought to your attention?"

"Cedar Ridge is not very racially diverse, so our officers do not often interact with black citizens. During my time at Internal Affairs, Jones was an officer that minorities complained about more frequently than others. It wasn't a contest, mind you, but he was the clear frontrunner for minority complaints."

"Please elaborate, lieutenant. Give us some sense of the

complaints."

"May I refer to my files?"

"Absolutely."

"Frivolous stops of vehicles driven by African Americans, citizens and non-citizens, stopped and detained by Jones for little or no reason. Some charged harassment during the stops."

"Harassment in what form?"

"Snide remarks. 'What are you doing this far south?' 'What's your business in Cedar Ridge?' 'After I let you go, keep driving past the next city limits sign,' that sort of thing.'"

"Did he face disciplinary action or receive additional training in response to these complaints?"

"Well, these matters were turned over to Internal Affairs, and we did talk to Jones and interview victims. As you can imagine, the victims didn't trust anyone who represented the Cedar Ridge police. Most wouldn't talk to us. We referred Jones for psychological workup and sensitivity training."

"How many incidents were reported?"

"Objection, hearsay," cries Murray.

"Noted. Please answer the question, lieutenant."

"But I objected," Murray spouts. He crosses his arms in front of his chest for effect.

"And your objection has been noted, Murray. This is a deposition. I ask the questions and he answers them. If you don't like the question, you can object. If this testimony or your objections require a judicial ruling, the judge will rule, but this will happen later in the case, much later.

"What you can't do now is prevent the witness from answering my questions. Are you suggesting we discontinue questioning this witness every time you object, stop the deposition, and then go to the judge for a ruling? If so, let's terminate the deposition and visit the judge. It won't be pretty. I'm trying to be nice, but you're starting to piss me off. What's it going to be, Murray?"

"Uh . . . ah . . ." Murray stutters and hesitates, uncertain how to proceed. He looks to Jackson, who chuckles and turns away.

"Uh . . . Proceed, Mr. Blake. I'll bring this to the judge's attention at a later date," Murray concedes.

"Thank you," Blake taunts. "Please answer the question, lieutenant."

"What was the question?"

Blake laughs.

"How many such incidents?"

Kelly rifles through his file and counts under his breath. "There were, uh, three—no—*four* similar incidents."

"And you reached a conclusion?"

"I did."

"And what was that conclusion?"

'That Officer Jones needed help dealing with black people."

"And did you report this conclusion to anyone?"

"I did."

"To whom did you report?"

"To Chief Warren Brooks of the Cedar Ridge PD."

"To your knowledge, what did Chief Brooks do with the information?"

"I don't know."

"There was a more serious incident, similar to the one that is the subject of this lawsuit, correct?"

"Yes."

"Tell us about that incident."

"Jones pulled over a black man he thought resembled a criminal suspect. Sometime during the stop, Jones shot the man."

"That sounds familiar."

"Is there a question here, Mr. Blake?" Jackson challenges.

"Yes, I have in my possession two photographs. Could you identify these, Lieutenant Kelly?"

Kelly studies the pictures, hands them back to Blake, and signals he is ready.

"Lieutenant Kelly?"

"One photo is the man Jones pulled over and shot. The other is the criminal suspect Jones claimed the man resembled."

"Do they look anything alike?"

"Objection, Murray interjects. "Whether two people look alike is a very subjective issue. That this witness believes they are dissimilar is not proof that Officer Jones's belief that they looked alike was unreasonable." Murray looks pleased with himself.

"I move to admit the two photos and let a judge or jury decide. Any idiot can see these two look nothing alike," Blake chides. Murray grimaces but remains silent.

"Lieutenant Kelly," Blake continues, "after that particular shooting, was there an Internal Affairs investigation of Officer Jones?"

"There was."

"Were you in charge of that investigation?"

"I was."

"What was the result of the investigation?"

"Officer Jones was suspended for six months. Against my recommendation, the suspension was commuted to thirty days."

"Why?"

"This was Jones's first serious offense. The brass could not determine the officer's actions were unreasonable because identification is subjective, and the suspect acted with belligerence."

"What did you think of that determination?"

"Objection, relevance!" Murray cries.

"Let's just say I disagreed with my superiors."

"Why?"

"Well, Mr. Blake, it's kind of like you mentioned earlier."

"What did I mention earlier?"

"Any idiot can see these two look nothing alike."

"Objection!" Murray screeches.

"On what grounds?" Blake is yanking his chain.

"Inflammatory?"

"There is no such objection in the rules of civil procedure or evidence, Mr. Murray," Blake lectures.

"My objection stands, for the record," Murray manages.

"Okay, young man," Blake rolls his eyes. "Your objection is noted. Lieutenant Kelly's response is a matter of record. Let's move on, shall we? Lieutenant Kelly, you are present here today under subpoena, is that correct?"

"Correct."

"And the subpoena was *duces tecum*, was it not?"

"Yes"

"You brought the entire file on Jones?"

"Yes."

He picks up the file and presents it to Blake.

"This file contains everything that Internal Affairs has on Jones?"

"It does."

"Is it kept in the ordinary course of business?"

"It is."

"I move for the admission of the Internal Affairs office file as plaintiff's deposition exhibit three. We will copy the file in the presence of the witness and attach the copy to the file, returning the original to the lieutenant. Lieutenant, will you please maintain the original, please?"

"Will do."

"Thanks. That's all I have for now, subject to recall rights." Blake stands. The deposition is apparently over.

Murray hesitates and locks eyes with Blake. *Should I object? Should I ask questions? I was told to sit here and shut up.*

"Murray?" Blake gestures.

"I have a few questions."

"Murray, I am paying for this deposition. If you want to ask questions, I can instruct Merrill here to restart the meter, run a tab, and bill you and your firm for the additional cost of your questions. What would you like to do?"

Murray has no idea what to do. He is entitled to examine the witness, but Blake has him completely confused. Murray questions why he decided to go to law school.

"Nothing further," Murray squeaks.

"Ven?"

"No questions."

"Merrill, that's a wrap," Blake smiles.

The battle has begun.

Chapter Twenty-Three

Sarah Hayes' home telephone rings. *Hardly anyone calls the landline. It's probably a solicitor.* She checks the small Caller ID text screen, which reads 'unknown number.' She ignores the call, and it disconnects after several rings. The phone rings a second time. Again the text screen reads 'unknown number.' She decides to answer.

"Hello?"

"Sarah Hayes?"

White male? "Speaking."

"Nigger bitch, whose dead husband caused the death of a good cop?"

Definitely a white male! "Who is this?"

"Nigger bitch suing the Cedar Ridge Police Department?"

"Who the hell is this?"

"Drop the case if you care about your children, bitch."

"I'm calling the police." Sarah's terrified. This man is threatening her children!

"Please do. Call the police. Call any department you want. See who comes running and how soon. Do you think the police will help you? Do you think good cops will come running to help the bitch who's *suing* the cops?"

The caller taunts and laughs. The man's menacing laugh scares the hell out of Sarah. She slams down the receiver and trembles with fear and anger. *Is it true? Is this guy right? Would cops really ignore her cry for help because of the lawsuit?*

The phone rings again. *Unknown number.*

Staring at the phone, she lets it ring and ring. *Will he ever stop?*

The phone finally goes silent. Sarah picks up the receiver and dials Zachary Blake's office.

"Zachary Blake and Associates, Kristin speaking. How may I direct your call?"

"This is urgent. I need to speak to Zachary Blake immediately." Sarah is frantic.

"I will connect you immediately," Kristin assures. "Who may I say is calling?"

"This is Sarah Hayes. Hurry, please."

"Please hold, Mrs. Hayes." The line disconnects. Within seconds, the receiver clicks.

"Sarah, what's wrong?" Zack wonders.

Sarah bursts into tears. "Oh, Zack, I just received a terrifying telephone call."

She recounts the caller's threat, word for word.

Zack doesn't hesitate. "Sarah. Stay where you are. I'm calling the Detroit police and my private investigator. Security will be at your house before you know it! And I'm on my way, too. Sarah, where are the children?"

"They're visiting with my mother at her house."

"Give me that address. I'll send someone over there, too."

Sarah gives him her mother's address and telephone number.

"Sit tight. Don't answer the door for anyone except the Detroit police or me. If a cop shows up, make sure it's a *Detroit* cop."

"Hurry, Zack. I'm scared."

"On my way!"

Less than an hour later, Sarah Hayes sits on her living room couch, hugging her two daughters, recounting the telephone call with her mother, two Detroit police officers, Micah Love, and Zachary Blake.

The officers are more robotic than sympathetic.

Just the facts, ma'am, Love muses.

"What time did the call come in, Mrs. Hayes?" A uniformed officer asks.

His uniform tag reads, 'Collins.'

"About an hour ago."

"Was there only one call?"

"He called multiple times from an unknown number. I only picked it up the one time."

"When was the last time you heard the phone ring?"

"About ten minutes before you arrived. I took it off the hook after that."

"Would you mind if we put a tap on your phone? We might

be able to capture a number or a general location."

"No, not at all. Do whatever you need to do to track this guy down. He scares the hell out of me!"

"Can you tell me what the man—it was a man, right?"

"Yes, a white man—he called me the *N-word*."

"What else did he say?" Collins prods.

Sarah repeats the conversation for a second time. Like she has already done for Blake, she restates it, word for word.

"Did you recognize his voice?"

"He was a white guy. Other than that, I did not recognize it."

"Would you recognize his voice if you heard it again?"

"I will never forget it. Deep, very white, accent I can't place."

"Have you received any other threats of any kind?"

"No, I haven't."

"It's probably nothing. Some jerk trying to yank your chain, trying to get you to drop the case. You might want to consider settling this as soon as possible," Collins coaxes.

"She takes her legal advice from me, Officer Collins, " Blake interrupts, tersely. "You advise she should allow this guy to intimidate her into settling a legitimate case too early for too little compensation? Her husband was killed. She has small children. Do you know the case?"

"Everyone in law enforcement knows this case, Mr. Blake. There are two sides to every story," Collins sneers.

"True. Officer Collins and I look forward to hearing Cedar Ridge's side of the story. But we won't get that side if we settle the case, now will we? You would agree that intimidation of a witness in litigation is not appropriate, regardless of the type of case, would you not?" Blake is in the officer's face, almost nose-to-nose.

"Of course, I agree. I wasn't suggesting—"

"We understand, Collins. Will there be anything else?" Blake not only interrupts Collins, he *dismisses* the officer as well. He motions to the front door.

Collins strolls to the door.

"We'll station a car out front for the night and monitor all incoming calls for a while. Hopefully, we'll catch a break."

"But don't count on it, right?" Blake bristles.

"You never know," Collins shrugs. "Let us know if anything else occurs to you, Mrs. Hayes. I'm sorry for your loss and the hassle today."

"Thank you, officer," Sarah groans.

The two officers let themselves out the front door.

"They don't have the manpower to watch this house long-term," Love warns. "We will put one of our guys on you after they pull surveillance."

"Thank you, Mr. Love."

"Collins was right about one thing, Sarah," Blake suggests. "You can drop this case anytime you want."

"Would you drop the case if you were me, Zack?"

"Hell no, Sarah," he exclaims.

"Can you protect my children, Mr. Love? I don't care about me, but nothing can happen to my babies," Sarah moans.

"I will protect you *and* your children, Sarah. You can count on me," Love promises.

"Okay, then. Onward and upward," she rallies, gathering strength.

"Onward and upward," Blake repeats.

Chapter Twenty-Four

Cedar Ridge Police Chief Warren Brooks assembles every police officer in the city in a local auditorium.

"I believe that all of you know the name 'Sarah Hayes.' On the off chance that someone in this room has been in a coma for the past several weeks, Mrs. Hayes is the woman whose husband was shot and killed by Officer Randy Jones, a Cedar Ridge police officer who took his own life following the shooting incident. Many of you knew and liked Officer Jones. I understand that. Hell, *I liked* Randy Jones. I feel terrible for his widow and his family.

"However, the circumstances surrounding Marcus Hayes's death are troubling. The Wayne County grand jury and our internal investigation found Officer Jones culpable.

"We are troubled that Jones's stop of Mr. Hayes appears to have been racially motivated. He's engaged in similar conduct in the past. Even more troubling, is the fact this most recent incident appears to have escalated because Officer Jones, despite his training, racially targeted and profiled Mr. Hayes. He feared him, simply because he was an African American male.

"It should surprise no one in this room his widow is pursuing a civil rights lawsuit against the deceased officer's estate and the Cedar Ridge Police Department. No one in a supervisory position is surprised by this development.

"Recently, Mrs. Hayes received an anonymous and threatening telephone call from someone who has been identified only as a 'white male' with, perhaps, a touch of an accent. The caller told Mrs. Hayes harm would come to her or her children unless she drops her lawsuit.

"I am not accusing anyone in this room of placing that telephone call. I am not suggesting anyone in this room even knows the call was made or has any idea who made the call. However, if anyone in this room *does* know anything at all about this call or caller, that person is urged to report what they know, directly to me. Your call or visit will be kept strictly confidential.

"We will be reviewing our training and re-training procedures from top to bottom. Continuing law enforcement education will focus on race and how we as a police department deal with minorities or people of color present in our community, whether they are citizens or visitors.

"Our police force must not only enforce the law; it must obey the law. In America, that applies to all citizens, regardless of race, creed, or ethnic origin. Our goal as a department, as a community, hell, as a society, is total colorblindness when it comes to law enforcement.

"Does everyone understand me? That is all I have to say on the subject. Anyone have any questions or comments?"

"Yes, sir, I have a comment."

A young white policewoman rises. The room falls silent. Chief Brooks does not recognize her.

"What is your name, officer?" Brooks inquires.

"Simpson, sir. Officer Erica Simpson."

"What is your comment, Officer Simpson?"

"Sir, I haven't been in Cedar Ridge very long. Hell, I haven't been a police officer for very long."

The audience chuckles, and Brooks calls for order. "Go on, Officer Simpson. Make your point."

"Sir, I only want to say that I am encouraged by your words. I believe racism is a serious problem in America, not only in Cedar Ridge but everywhere. Not just in how cops relate to citizens of color, but in how citizens of one race or religion relate to citizens of another race or religion. Too many of us, including, may I say, our current president, see racial diversity as a threat to our country rather than the source of our strength as a country. Racism, whether it is deliberate and overt or unconscious and covert, is hurtful, not just to the individual who is the immediate target, but to our local and national communities. It undermines the values our country stands for.

"Hopefully, this gathering is the start of meaningful change. If so, other communities can look to Cedar Ridge as a community that gets it, a community that treats all of its citizens justly and fairly, sharing our experiences and speaking openly and honestly about these issues. Our conduct cannot be governed by fear and misunderstanding. We must celebrate the things that unite us, not our differences or the things that divide us.

"Just a short time removed from electing our first African American President, we have become polarized and segregated. I see more examples of racial and ethnic divides in our streets than I see examples of tolerance and unity. As cops, I believe it is our civic duty to shine a light on this problem and act as positive examples to our citizens.

"I don't have any immediate solutions to offer here tonight, but I am offering to volunteer to be a part of any task force or training program that seeks solutions to this very serious problem that plagues our department and our country."

"A compelling speech, Officer Simpson. We will, indeed, contact you when we decide how we are going to move forward on these issues." Chief Brooks is impressed with the rookie. "Anyone else?"

"Yes, sir," comes a voice from the back of the room.

A middle-aged, white officer stands.

"Your name, officer?" Brooks prompts.

"Shannon, sir. Rick Shannon. I have been a cop for more than twenty years. I have seen a lot of things and met a lot of people. Some were bad, some good. Some were white. Others were people of color. Color does not determine a person's decision to do good or evil.

"Many people thought racism was officially over with when we elected a black man to be President of the United States. However, not long after that election, we received numerous complaints police officers were killing black men with little or no justification. These complaints resulted in the *Black Lives Matter* movement.

"The fact police officers have also been killed has been virtually ignored. I believe white Americans, especially white police officers, are very uncomfortable talking about race in America. So, this is an essential conversation.

"No one wants to be accused of racism, but it is alive and well. We have to discuss it, get to the root of why these deaths are occurring, and take steps to prevent them from happening in the future. We also have to protect our officers from harm. It is a delicate balance. Perhaps those discussions can begin tonight, right here, right now."

"Thanks, Shannon. Anyone else have anything to say?" Brooks is encouraged by these remarks.

"Sir?"

The voice belongs to a young officer in the first few rows. He stands and turns backward and forward to acknowledge fellow officers in all directions.

"My name is Ryan Jenson, sir, and as I understand things, Sir, you believe the threat to Mrs. Hayes might have come from someone in the Cedar Ridge Police Department or a friend or family member of one of us. Is that what you are thinking?"

"I'm glad you raised that issue, Jenson. Everyone in this room is an officer of the law. We must uphold the law, not break the law. If any of us are sympathetic to this caller or, worse, if anyone in this room *is* the caller or knows the caller, I urge you to do your duty."

"Sir?" A young black officer stands. He is one of only three black men on the Cedar Ridge police force.

"My name is Alton Greenfield. Most police officers I know are color blind, but it only takes one or a few to give all of us a bad name. When police brutality claims the life of a young, innocent black man, we can call that an anomaly, a bad act committed by a bad cop.

"But when we see multiple instances of young unarmed black kids gunned down by police officers, not only here in Cedar Ridge, but all over the country, we have a responsibility to do something about it, to set a better example. We must stand up and say '*Black Lives Matter*, young lives matter, all lives matter.' This gathering is a good start.

"How we treat Sarah Hayes is important. But we must follow up on this meeting with a call to action. I do not want to see any innocent citizen, white or black, killed unnecessarily by a police officer. When something like this happens to a black kid, my natural instinct is to say, 'Thank God it's not my kid' or to ask, 'What if that were my kid?' Wouldn't any officer feel the same way if a person of their race was killed? I agree with Simpson, sir. Sign me up."

The audience breaks out in spontaneous applause. Several officers offer comments and suggestions. Many more volunteer to be part of a task force. It appears the group is appalled by the behavior of the person who telephoned Sarah Hayes. Chief Warren Brooks can only smile and be proud of this display of unity and courage.

Chapter Twenty-Five

Sarah Hayes is more determined than ever to pursue justice for her slain husband. If the threatening caller intended to scare her into dismissing the case, his attempt is a dismal failure.

Instead, the call inspires her, invigorates her, and makes her more eager than ever to move the case forward. Zachary Blake shares Sarah's enthusiasm, but his pace is deliberate. His strategy must be calculated.

Cedar Ridge is an overwhelmingly white city, yet, in the two years leading up to the death of Marcus Hayes, more than thirty percent of the city's traffic stops and forty-five percent of the arrests were of blacks, both citizens and visitors.

In cases where an officer has discretion, like jaywalking, statistics reveal blacks were cited at more than twice the rate of whites. In Blake's judgment, the statistics lead to only one conclusion: The Cedar Ridge Police Department is systemically racist. Consciously or unconsciously, its officers are routinely violating the constitutional rights of black people. Armed with this knowledge and these statistics, Blake takes the deposition of Officer Alexander Mickler, the first officer to arrive at the scene of Marcus Hayes's death.

Steve Adler appears as the city's representative. Apparently, Kyle Murray's performance did not impress his superiors. Blake qualifies Mickler as an experienced Cedar Ridge police officer and bores in on the substantive issues in the case.

"Officer Mickler, you are still with the Cedar Ridge Police Department, are you not?"

"Yes, I am."

"And were you so employed on the night of Marcus Hayes's death?"

"I was."

"What was your rank at the time of the incident that led to this litigation?"

"I was a patrol officer."

"And your rank today?"

"The same."

"You work the evening shift, correct? The same shift as Officer Randy Jones?"

"Yes."

"Were you on duty on the night Officer Jones pulled over the vehicle driven by Marcus Hayes?"

"Yes, I was."

He's been coached. He's keeping his answers to my specific questions. Let's see if I can shake him. "I assume that means that you were in the city that night, somewhere, on patrol."

"That's correct."

"And while you were on patrol, a call came in from Officer Randy Jones, is that correct?"

"Yes."

"Where were you and what were you doing at the time of Officer Jones's call?"

"I was at Vinewood and Ninth in the City of Cedar Ridge waiting for the owner of a building to arrive to open the door. The building was the site of a possible breaking and entering."

"How far was that from where Officer Jones pulled over Marcus Hayes?"

"Not far. Minutes away."

"When Jones called you, what did he say?"

"He was pulling over a vehicle and read me the plate number."

Pulling teeth. "Did he say anything else?" Blake presses.

"He thought the driver and passenger looked like the Burger King robbers. He agreed to wait for me before approaching the vehicle."

"Jones also mentioned he didn't get a good look, didn't he?"

"He might have mentioned that."

"But he was going to pull them over anyway, wasn't he?"

"Yes."

"Did Jones suggest the driver had done anything to warrant being pulled over?"

"I don't know what you mean."

"Had the driver broken any traffic laws? Was he speeding? Did he make an illegal turn? Did his vehicle have any defective equipment?"

"Not that Officer Jones made me aware of."

"So, Jones had no legal basis to pull the vehicle over, correct?"

"I wouldn't say that. Jones claimed he had a reasonable suspicion the driver and passenger resembled the Burger King robbers."

"Reasonable?"

"That was the word Jones used."

"And was it?"

"Was it what?"

"Reasonable."

"Was what reasonable?"

"Jones's suspicion that the occupants resembled the Burger King robbers."

"How would I know? I'm not Jones." Mickler squirms in his seat.

I'm getting under his skin. "How would you know? You went to the scene, true, Officer Mickler?"

"I did."

"And what did you find when you got there?"

"Officer Jones was standing outside of his vehicle to the side of what I presumed was the vehicle he pulled over. I approached the vehicle and looked inside. The driver was slumped over, bleeding, and appeared to be unconscious. I turned to Jones. He looked . . . agitated, dejected, confused. He had a 'what do I do now?' look on his face. A female passenger in the front seat of the suspect vehicle was screaming."

"What did *you* do?"

"I inquired whether Jones called an ambulance."

"Did he?"

"No. I immediately called central dispatch and ordered an ambulance to the scene, stat."

"What does 'stat' mean?"

"Right away."

"Did Jones say anything to you at that point?"

"He suggested I remove the female from the vehicle."

"What did you do next?"

"I told Jones to go sit on the curb and ordered the female to exit the vehicle with her hands in the air."

"Officer Mickler, what was the race of the driver and the front seat passenger of the 'suspect' vehicle, as you have referred to it."

"African American."

"Were you surprised at their race, officer?"

"I don't understand what you are getting at, Mr. Blake."

"It's a simple question. Yes or no, were you surprised at the race of the two people?"

Adler has had enough. "Objection! Inflammatory! Badgering the witness!"

"I'll take the answer over the objection unless you are instructing him not to answer, Mr. Adler. This is a simple question, and it deserves an answer," Blake snarled.

Adler turns to Mickler. "Answer, if you can."

"No, I wasn't surprised," Mickler admits.

"Was that because most of the people Officer Jones pulled over were African American?"

"Objection! The question is inflammatory and calls for speculation. Further, it assumes facts not in evidence. I instruct the witness not to answer."

"No, Mr. Adler. I'd like to answer if you don't mind," Mickler insists.

Adler glares at Mickler. *Is he trying to sabotage the defense? Whose side is he on?*

"The Burger King suspects were black," Mickler explains. "It stands to reason this driver and passenger were also black.."

"I withdraw my previous objection," Adler interjects with relief.

Blake bores in. "Officer Mickler, are you personally familiar with the facts and circumstances of the Burger King robbery?"

"I am."

"Are you familiar with the composite drawing of the suspects?"

"I am."

"Are you also familiar with the department's profile of the suspects?"

"I'm not sure what you mean," Mickler hesitates.

"Do the suspects profile as male and female?" Blake demands.

"No."

"Do the suspects profile as adults with small children, or do they profile as teenagers?"

Blake leans in toward the witness. His eyes meet Mickler's. He's *daring* him to lie. Adler is powerless to prevent an answer.

"Teenagers," Mickler concedes.

"They were profiled as *male* teenagers, correct?"

"Yes."

"Were the driver and passenger in the suspect vehicle both male?"

"No, one was female, as I have already indicated."

"Were driver or passenger teenagers?"

"No, they weren't." Mickler breaks eye contact and stares at the floor. He wants desperately to assist the defense, but the truth is standing in his way.

"In your opinion, did the people Officer Randy Jones pulled over that evening look anything like the composite drawing of the Burger King suspects?"

Mickler winces. "One had an Afro; the other had dreads, like the suspects."

"Please answer my question, Officer Mickler," Blake insists.

"Did the two people Jones pulled over look anything like the drawing?"

"No, they didn't," Mickler blurts.

"In your opinion, Officer Mickler, do all blacks look alike?"

"Objection. Inflammatory," Adler shouts.

"Of course not," Mickler grouses.

"There were two minor children in the back seat of the 'suspect' vehicle, were there not?"

"There were."

"To your knowledge, were infant children present during the commission of the Burger King robberies?"

"No." *Smartass.*

"Do the suspects profile as having children?"

"Objection! Calls for speculation." Adler erupts.

"No," Mickler concedes.

Did he deliberately ignore Adler? "Officer Mickler," Blake continues, "did you subsequently learn what happened to the driver? The man you referred to as being in 'bad shape?'"

"Yes, he'd been shot. He was DOA at Cedar Ridge General."

"And so to clarify for everyone who reads or hears this testimony, what does 'DOA' refer to?"

"Dead on arrival."

"He had been shot?"

"Yes."

"How many times was he shot?"

"Four times." Mickler again squirms in his chair.

"Did you determine who shot him?"

"Yes, I did."

"Who shot him, Officer Mickler?"

"According to both the female passenger and Officer Jones, Officer Jones shot the victim."

'Victim?' I love that choice of words. "Did you try to investigate the motive behind the shooting, Officer Mickler?"

"Jones claimed the victim had a gun in his possession."

"How did Jones discover the victim had a gun?"

"Mr. Hayes told Officer Jones that he was carrying and had a license to carry."

"In your vast experience as a law enforcement officer, does a person who intends to shoot a cop usually tell that cop that he is carrying?"

"Objection! Calls for speculation!" Adler screeches.

"I'll take the answer," Blake snaps.

"No, he does not," Mickler admits. *This is not going the way I hoped it would.*

"Did you discover why Jones decided to shoot Marcus Hayes?"

"According to Randy, uh, Officer Jones, the victim was not obeying commands. After the victim indicated he was carrying, Jones demanded that he show his hands. Instead, the victim reached for something, and Jones could not see his hands."

"Is that when he shot him?"

"That is my understanding."

"Did a subsequent investigation determine what Mr. Hayes was reaching for?"

"Yes, his wallet to access his license, registration, and gun permit."

"Which Officer Jones had requested he produce, correct?"

"Correct."

"Would you say Officer Jones issued inconsistent commands to Mr. Hayes?"

"I don't understand the question."

Mickler understands the question perfectly. Blake presses for an answer. *I will get the answer, one way or another.*

"I'll ask this question another way, Officer Mickler. During the stop, did Officer Jones ask to see Mr. Hayes' license and registration?"

"Yes."

"That's routine procedure for a traffic stop, is it not?"

"Yes."

"And did a subsequent investigation determine where the gun was kept at the time of the stop?"

"Yes, sir. It was in the glove box."

"And what was in Mr. Hayes' wallet that he had reached for in his left-hand pocket?"

"Among other things, his gun permit and his driver's license and registration."

"And so the record is clear, Officer Jones ordered Mr. Hayes to produce a license and registration, did he not, Officer Mickler?"

"The investigation and common sense reveals that he did." Mickler feels terrible, helpless.

"A command to produce license and registration is inconsistent with a command to 'show me your hands,' is it not?"

"I suppose it is."

"You suppose?"

"It is." Mickler concedes.

"It is what?"

"Inconsistent."

"When Jones called you to report that he was going to pull this vehicle over, did you give him any cautionary advice?"

"Yes, I told him to wait until I got there before he approached the vehicle."

"Did he wait for you to get there?"

"No, he didn't."

"Why did you ask him to wait?"

"He indicated he might be pulling over the Burger King robbery suspects. I was concerned for his safety."

"Did Jones say anything else about the victims?"

"He indicated they seemed 'out of place' for the area."

"What did you take that to mean?"

"I don't know."

"You testified earlier, Officer Mickler, that at the time of this incident, you and Officer Jones were both patrol officers, is that correct?"

"Correct."

"To your knowledge, had you both been trained in how to conduct traffic stops?"

"I don't know about Jones, specifically, but I was trained, yes."

"Where were you trained?"

"I started my training at Ferris State College. And both of us did in-house training at the department, through the CRLETC."

"What does CRLETC stand for?"

"Sorry. It stands for 'Cedar Ridge Law Enforcement Training Council.' It is the formal training arm of the department. All continuing law enforcement training in Cedar Ridge is offered through the council."

"Did Jones complete that training?"

"I don't know where he received his education and training before Cedar Ridge, but I do know that he received CRLETC training because we trained together."

"Do you know whether or not he completed the training, Officer Mickler?"

"I don't recall."

"And when someone is pulled over by a police officer, there is always a risk that they will run, drive away, or do something bad, right?"

"Right."

"Those are only a few examples of the many contingencies that you are trained to handle, correct?"

"Correct."

"And what are you trained to do in those circumstances?"

"I need more information. Why did I pull them over?"

"Let's assume a simple traffic stop. The driver is speeding. The officer tries to pull the guy over, but let's say, he speeds away. What should the officer do? Pull his or her gun?"

"It depends on the circumstances. What's going on? If he simply leaves the scene, protocol requires us to call out and, perhaps, give chase, either on foot or in the squad car."

"Does Cedar Ridge have any specific policies and procedures for traffic stops? Anything in writing?"

"Not that I am aware of."

"Have you received any training on dealing with people of different races or religious backgrounds?"

"No."

"The rules are applied the same way for everyone, correct?"

"You could put it that way. There is no training that I am aware of that tells us to treat different types of people in different ways."

"And that would be true of Jones as well, correct?"

"I would presume so, yes."

"You were the first officer on the scene after the shooting, correct?"

"Correct."

"How long after the shooting did you arrive?"

"Within minutes."

"And Mr. Hayes was slumped over and bleeding, correct?"

"Correct."

"From obvious gunshot wounds?"

"Correct."

"And according to your previous testimony, Jones had not called for an ambulance or EMS by the time you arrived?"

"Objection! Asked and answered," Adler exclaims.

"I'll take the answer."

"He had not, Mickler concedes. "I had to make the call."

"Did you review any materials to prepare for today's deposition?"

"I reviewed the file and the dash cam video."

"We'll get to the dash cam. What was in the file that you are referring to?"

"Officer Jones's report and my original report."

"We have marked those as exhibits one and two. Do you recognize these as the reports you reviewed?"

"Yes, I do."

"And is your testimony today and your actions at the time consistent with what is contained in those reports?"

"Yes."

"You secured the scene for the arriving supervisors and evidence technicians, did you not?"

"I did."

"The scene they arrived at was preserved as you saw it when you arrived and acted to preserve it, correct?"

"Correct."

"Was your report based on contemporaneous notes you took at the scene?"

"Yes."

"So, if your testimony conflicts with your notes or your report, we should assume the notes or report are more accurate, correct?"

"I suppose so. I don't believe you will find inconsistencies."

"For example, everything Jones did and said is contained in your report, right?"

"I believe so. Don't forget the entire incident is recorded on the dash cam."

"True. And that is the most accurate reflection of what happened, correct, Officer Mickler?"

"Yes."

"We can absolutely rely on the dash cam, right?"

"Right."

"Let's mark the dash cam DVD as an exhibit and play it for the record. Afterward, please comment on its accuracy as it compares to your report and your testimony. Sound good?"

"Sure."

"No objection," Adler comments, for the record.

After the intense video is replayed, Blake resumes his cross-examination. Mickler is discomforted by the video.

"For the record, Officer Mickler, is this recording the same one you reviewed?"

"Yes."

"And you reviewed it with Officer Jones before his death, correct?"

"Correct."

"And Jones indicated at that time it was an accurate representation of the events of that evening?"

"Yes."

"I'm going to object at this point," Steven Adler interrupts. "I've listened closely to this officer's testimony. Several words being bandied about are subject to misinterpretation or transcription error. We need an expert to make certain everyone understands the words."

"Nice speech, Mr. Adler, but you aren't the witness. The witness has testified the DVD video was an accurate representation. That is all I asked—he answered. That's all there is to it. Your objection is noted."

Blake turns back to Mickler. "By the way, Officer Mickler, for the record, the audio of the DVD is provided via a wireless microphone Officer Jones wears on his person, correct?"

"Correct."

"And the video and the audio are made simultaneous with and recorded during the events of the shooting, correct?"

"Correct."

"After watching and listening to the DVD, would you agree Officer Jones did, indeed, make inconsistent commands to Mr. Hayes? Specifically, Officer Mickler, Jones ordered Hayes to show him his hands at the same time he ordered him to produce his license and registration."

"He did."

"Is that protocol?"

"No."

"Would you have done things differently?"

"I'd like to think so."

"How so?"

"That's a very broad question. I'll have to give you a very long answer."

"Go ahead. Knock yourself out," Blake prompts. A cardinal rule of cross-examination is that the examining attorney asks only those questions that call for a "yes" or "no" answer. Plaintiff attorneys don't want defense witnesses rambling or providing long-winded explanations. Blake decides to gamble, confident Mickler, despite his cordial relationship with Jones, disagrees with Jones's behavior during the Hayes traffic stop.

"First of all, statistically, a traffic stop is one of the most dangerous things that a police officer does," Mickler begins.

"Why is that?"

"Because the officer never knows who they are approaching. They don't know whether they're law-abiding citizens or criminals, whether they're on drugs, drinking, or whether they're armed or otherwise dangerous. So, with a traffic stop, there is already a heightened state of awareness."

"Understood. Please continue, Officer Mickler."

"In this case, Officer Jones had to couple that heightened awareness with the discovery the driver was armed. This new fact exacerbated an already tense situation, especially when added to the fact that Jones pulled the vehicle over because he was suspicious of criminality—rightly or wrongly."

"Wrongly, in this case."

"True, but that doesn't change Officer Jones's state of mind as he approaches the vehicle," Mickler explains.

"Understood. Continue, please."

"This is where, unfortunately, I fail to understand Jones's conduct that night. If you follow the dash cam video, it is clear Jones gave inconsistent commands and apparently shot Mr. Hayes for doing what he was told to do. Jones requested his license and registration. When Hayes told Officer Jones he was carrying, Jones panicked and failed to provide clear direction. He should not have demanded the carry permit. He should have positioned himself behind rather than in front of Hayes, for his own safety and the safety of the children in the back seat. The officer's positioning put the children in the direct line of fire.

"From a position behind Hayes, Jones should have directed Hayes to raise his hands. At that point, Jones could have opened the driver's side door with his gun trained on the driver, ordered him out of the vehicle with his hands raised, and waited for backup. He was advised not to approach before backup arrived, but he ignored that advice and approached anyway."

Bingo! Blake is pumped. *Why stop him now?* "Anything else, Officer Mickler?"

"Yes. Officer Jones was afraid for his life. He thought he was dealing with a robber. He smelled marijuana, and the driver told him he had a gun. This was a tough situation."

Shit! Well, that's what I get for letting him ramble on. Time to gamble a bit. "Did the fact Hayes was carrying automatically make the stop more dangerous?"

"I'm not sure I understand."

"Mr. Hayes told the officer he was carrying, right?"

"Right."

"And I believe you have already testified it would be unusual for someone about to pull a gun and shoot you to advise you he or she is carrying?"

"Yes, that would be unusual."

"So, the fact Mr. Hayes informed Officer Jones he was carrying should have reassured the officer, not panicked him, correct?"

"I don't know about reassured, but it should not have automatically panicked Jones, as it seems to have done in this case. Concealed weapons carriers are among the most law-abiding demographics in this country.

"Jones saw the age of the driver and the sex and ages of the passengers. He saw the children. Why didn't the presence of children diffuse the situation? Was this driver a teenaged robber or a law-abiding adult citizen? Marijuana and race are the wild cards here, but I question whether these people should have been pulled over in the first place."

Wow! "Have you or any other officers you know of been through any special training on dealing with drivers who are legally carrying?"

"Training, yes. *Special* training, no."

"Jones?"

"Not to my knowledge. Cedar Ridge has never offered *special* training in this area. If Jones was trained, he was trained elsewhere."

"Do you know whether or not other departments offer special training or are more proactive in how officers deal with this issue?"

"I do not."

"As more and more people carry guns, you would agree this education should be offered, since cops are going to encounter a responsibly armed citizen and that fact should not, by itself, place an officer in fear, correct?"

"Absolutely."

"What do you believe, as an experienced officer of the law, happened to cause Officer Jones to shoot Mr. Hayes that night?"

"Objection, calls for speculation. Mr. Hayes was dead when Officer Mickler arrived at the scene," Adler grumbles.

"I'll take the answer."

"Officer Jones is dead. Only *he* knew whether Hayes made a threatening move. I do not see one on dash cam video. On the other hand, shooting someone is a last resort activity by *any* cop. We take our training, tactics, and performance to avoid having to discharge our weapons very seriously. No cop wants to shoot someone."

"There's an imminent peril requirement to use lethal force, isn't there?"

"Yes."

"Did you see imminent peril here?"

"Objection. Asked and answered. This is becoming very redundant overkill, Mr. Blake," Adler declares in frustration.

"Interesting choice of words, 'overkill.' I'll take the answer over the objection."

"No," Mickler concedes.

"Any threat of death or serious bodily harm?"

"Same objection," Adler blusters.

"No," Mickler sighs. "I did not."

"Your superiors have reviewed the dash cam video, have they not?"

"Some of them have."

"Chief Brooks?"

"Yes."

"What was his conclusion?"

"Objection!"

"I'll ask the Chief," Blake snickers.

"By the way, a use-of-force report is required in every officer-involved shooting, is it not?"

"Yes."

"Who completes that?"

"The officer involved."

"Jones, in this case?"

"Yes."

"Was one completed for this case?"

"Not to my knowledge."

"Why not?"

"I don't know. That's above my pay grade."

"Do you know what a high-risk stop is, Officer Mickler?"

"I do."

"Based on his perception of the danger, Officer Mickler, should Officer Jones have handled the Marcus Hayes traffic stop as a high-risk stop?"

"Based on his perception? Yes."

"And did he?"

"Did he what?"

"Handle this as a high-risk stop?"

"No, he did not."

"The rules say that firearms shall not be discharged when it appears likely that innocents may be injured, correct?"

"Yes."

"You've already testified that there were children in the back seat?"

"Yes."

"And that they were in the direct line of fire?"

"I'm not—"

"Objection! This witness does not know the exact positioning and would be testifying to a presumption. There is no foundation," cries Adler.

"Steven, Steven," Blake mocks. He turns his back to his adversary and faces the witness.

"Officer Mickler? Would you like me to have the court reporter read Mr. Adler's objection back to you? After all, his words are exactly the ones he wants you to utilize in answering my question. Mr. Adler was *prompting* you," Blake posits.

"Objection! Adler shrieks. "Editorializing! My objection stands for the record."

"If the bullets missed Mr. Hayes, where would they have gone?"

"Objection! Calls for speculation."

"I'll take the answer. Where would they have gone, Officer Mickler?"

"Back seat," Mickler admits. He looks away.

"And who was in the back seat?"

"The children."

"How old?"

"Toddlers."

"Nothing further."

"No questions," Adler fumes.

"No questions," Jackson chuckles.

Chapter Twenty-Six

Chief Warren Brooks was dead serious about changing the culture and practices of the Cedar Ridge Police Department. His blue-ribbon community task force included multicultural civic leaders, politicians, attorneys, police executives, retired police and federal officers, and, most importantly, ordinary citizens. One of the task force members was Michael Kendell of *Black Lives Matter.*

Cedar Ridge mayor Mendoza and other city officials and dignitaries were on board as long as the work and findings of the task force remained confidential. The mayor was concerned committee criticisms might be used against the city in present and future civil rights litigation.

Professor Kendell promised himself that he would research and help flush out any institutional racism problem in the Cedar Ridge Police Department. Initially, he pledged to share that research with Zachary Blake and Sarah Hayes for use in their civil rights litigation against the city.

Appointment to the task force required Kendell to sign an NDA and a confidentiality agreement. If he followed through with his pledge to share committee findings with Blake and Sarah, he'd be in violation of his oath. He was seriously conflicted and almost declined the appointment.

In the end, Kendell decided the appointment served the greater good. Sister Sarah was in good hands with Zack Blake and would get the justice she deserves.

At the first meeting of the task force, Chief Brooks reinforced Cedar Ridge's commitment to racial justice in the city. His goal was a completely colorblind police force. He acknowledged policing reforms must come, not only from the cops but also from a range of constituencies, like the "people in this room."

He encouraged innovative ideas and declared these ideas could come from the most distinguished and decorated officer or from John Q Citizen. Brooks didn't care. He just wanted as many as possible.

Cedar Ridge shared its cultural problems with other American communities, large and small, but Brooks determined Cedar Ridge would be a leader in developing solutions rather than allowing its department to be part of the problem. A police shooting takes a terrible toll on a community. Marcus Hayes was not the sole victim in this case. A criminal indictment was issued, a young officer took his own life, two widows and young children were left behind, and a city and its police force were in turmoil.

The committee listened intently and absorbed every word. Each member then rolled up their sleeves and went to work. Like a Fortune 500 company searching for the ultimate competitive advantage, Chief Brooks was looking to become a leader, an innovator who changed the rules and the culture of the game.

He desired to reinvent community policing, to drastically reduce— eliminate was probably too lofty a goal—the likelihood people of different races and creeds were treated differently than their white neighbors. Privately, he was determined that an incident like the Marcus Hayes shooting would never be repeated in his beloved city.

***

Chief Warren Brooks sits in his dimly lit office at the end of a long day and begins to leaf through a multi-page bound document. It has been nine months since he assembled the blue ribbon task force. The committee has finally submitted its report to Brooks and Mayor Mendoza. The report is entitled "PROPOSALS FOR COLORBLIND POLICE PROCEDURES." Some proposals were updates to older policies and procedures. Others were refreshing and innovative.

Brooks leans back in his executive chair and places shoeless feet up on his desk. With reading glasses perched at the end of his nose, he begins to study the comprehensive report. He's very pleased with what he's reading.

The committee has provided a list of procedural proposals that include improved transparency, use of non-lethal weapons, scaling down purchases of military hardware from the federal government, increasing educational standards for recruitment of police officers, warnings training, data collections and reporting by involved officers, increased civilian and internal affairs oversight, and recruiting a more diversified workforce.

Cedar Ridge is actually ahead of the curve.

Brooks is pleased to discover his city has already implemented many of the task force proposals. For example, suggestions for improved transparency include body microphones, body cameras, and dash cams. These devices are already affixed to all Cedar Ridge Officers and patrol cars. Brooks is acutely aware these microphones and cameras assist in evidence collection and help control behavior.

People behave better when they know they are on camera. That goes for both cops and citizens.

Cedar Ridge does not purchase or employ military-style equipment on its streets, even for use by its elite SWAT unit. The unit does own a spiffy Hummer vehicle, but that's the only 'military-style' equipment that the city owns.

President Obama once banned the use of certain military-style hardware to local police, but President John rescinded Obama's executive order when he became president. Brooks and other Cedar Ridge officials firmly believe Obama was correct. Military equipment and weaponry intimidate and alienate members of the community. Citizens are made to feel their police department is some sort of occupying force, which negatively impacts trust between cops and citizens.

Nobody wants that.

Brooks skims the pages and comes to the task force's recommendations on so-called non-lethal weapons. The use of Tasers or stun guns rather than guns is a tricky subject. Brooks recalls certain studies that demonstrate these weapons decrease incidents of officer and citizen injuries and deaths. However, he also knows officers tend to overuse them to obtain compliance from people who aren't necessarily a threat.

Tasers or stun guns may cause death and serious injuries from falls, or the electric pulses emitted that override the brain's control of the body. They do not necessarily prevent the use of lethal force. He believes the issue requires more thought and more study.

Brooks likes the idea of recruiting and training highly educated officers. He believes this will raise the level of officer performance. The obvious problem with this proposal is cost. It's difficult to recruit college and postgraduate level officers when the pay is substandard as compared to private sector law enforcement.

How do you pay new recruits, regardless of academic prowess, more than officers with years of experience, but no college degree? The proposal would result in an increase in pay levels across the board.

Can the city afford this? Can it afford not to consider it?

Chief Brooks studies the proposals regarding improved and increased training for officers in employing the use of verbal warnings and warning shots. According to the committee, the goal is for an officer to refrain from using deadly force unless such force is absolutely necessary. The committee report states that a reasonable belief or a suspicion the suspect has a gun, does not meet that standard. Brooks is not convinced this is realistic or consistent with 'real world' policing.

It's easy to 'Monday morning quarterback' these incidents or find shades of grey from an armchair. On the streets, decisions are made in split seconds, with officers and innocent citizens' lives on the line. Is this realistic?

He reads on. The panel suggests Marcus Hayes and Randy Jones would still be alive if Jones had better communicated and issued appropriate verbal warnings to Hayes. This is the only category in which the committee refers to the case directly. The committee indicates that Jones should have remained calm and waited for back up. Failing that, however, he still could have issued consistent verbal warnings, followed protocol, fired a warning shot, or shot at a non-vital body part.

The committee is not convinced Hayes posed any threat to Jones even though Hayes was legally armed. There was no evidence the suspect was dangerous, high on drugs, mentally ill or desperate. However, studies have shown that specific restrictions on police behavior and quality training, communication, and counseling for officers in dealing with disturbed or distraught suspects reduce the number of serious injuries and deaths.

This training would include what it called 'inherent bias' training. Studies have demonstrated many officers subconsciously associate young black men with criminality, and these inherent biases shape whom an officer will stop and whether he or she will presume the potential for criminal behavior.

Brooks ponders the various recommendations. He's dubious that a person with some type of inherent bias can be trained to ignore that bias. However, he's on board with the general concept that de-escalation of deadly altercations is the ultimate goal of all of the task force's recommendations.

Chief Brooks is less-than-enthusiastic about the committee's recommendations for data reporting and civilian oversight. The report suggests officers collect and report data for all people they stop. Report details would include the race or ethnicity of the person stopped, the reason for the stop, and the ultimate disposition of the stop. This would consist of all officer-involved altercations and shootings, whether they are fatal or not.

According to the committee, collecting this data would help in determining the scope of the problem, creating a best practices model, and holding a bad officer accountable for his or her actions. The goal of this recommendation, like many of the others, was to improve community trust in law enforcement professionals.

As to civilian oversight, the committee recommends that those overseeing these types of occurrences be consistent with the make-up of the committee itself. In other words, civilians would be part of a blue-ribbon panel that consisted of city officials, police officers, politicians, attorneys, and prominent citizens. Brooks is fine with the idea and with increasing or improving the diversity of the police force and strengthening Internal Affairs. In his opinion, these measures are long overdue.

Brooks is surprised to learn the committee has included criminal prosecution and civil litigation as potential deterrents to officer-involved violence. While communities often demanded criminal prosecutions for the involved officers, police and internal affairs units often disagree with those demands. Further, Internal Affairs tends to exonerate officers more often than not.

The committee believes these statistics lead the community to distrust police and Internal Affairs when it comes to cop-on-citizen criminality. Diversifying Internal Affairs and including civilian fact-finders are recommended. When the quest for a criminal indictment fails, the committee believes, the potentially high cost of a civil lawsuit may act as a deterrent to bad officer behavior.

The committee cites the *Hayes vs. Jones, et al* lawsuit as an example of a civil lawsuit prompting a community to act. In fact, the committee's own existence was prompted by Sara Hayes' decision to sue Officer Jones and the City of Cedar Ridge. Fear of substantial verdicts and public humiliations in court are serious deterrents to appalling police behavior, and these lawsuits must be encouraged, not discouraged, by police hierarchy.

Brooks chuckles. *This could bankrupt a city—I can see myself sitting down at a meeting with Mayor Mendoza and City Council, advising them I encouraged the widow of a citizen to pursue a lawsuit against the city for civil rights violations by the Cedar Ridge Police. How long would I continue to be employed as Chief?*

While it may sound like a good idea in theory, Brooks does not think any city official, anywhere in the world, would *encourage* civil litigation. As he reflects on the proposal, he is positive Michael Kendell had a hand in its drafting.

Little does Brooks know it was *Bialy,* not Kendell, who encouraged Sarah Hayes to pursue this litigation. The top prosecutor even handpicked Zachary Blake to be Sarah's attorney.

Whether or not Brooks is willing to admit the truth, statistics demonstrate civil suits *do* have a positive effect on a city or a police department dealing with a police misconduct scandal. Lawsuits often cause a city to review its police practices or discuss prevention of similar incidents. *Hayes v. Jones, et al* is a perfect example of this simple truth. The offended community constituency is often assuaged by these commitments to alter future policies and procedures.

Chief Warren Brooks finishes his reading, leans forward, and places the report on his desk. He again leans back in his executive chair, hands clasped behind his head, and spends the next twenty minutes or so staring at the ceiling.

Interesting reading, but is it doable? To move forward, we must put this case behind us, put the money together, and be done with this thing. It's going to cost a shitload of money! This tragedy resulted in the formation of the task force, its findings, and recommendations. If our city implements some or all of these proposals, some good may come from this, after all. Will Blake be reasonable?

Chapter Twenty-Seven

1983 lawsuits haven't always been an effective deterrent to police brutality or misconduct. However, under recent case law, it is now possible for misconduct victims to sue police *departments*, imposing liability on the department itself for the misconduct of its' officers. This more global liability might result from a lack of or a complete failure to train or supervise. It is this type of potential liability that leads a community to establish a committee like the one created by Chief Warren Brooks in Cedar Ridge.

The downside is that when private information is published in the digital age, good lawyers and private investigators may discover its existence. While after-incident safety measures cannot be used in court (on the theory that they would discourage such safety measures from being implemented), they can certainly be used for value assumptions and settlement leverage.

Why would a municipality assemble a blue-ribbon committee if no serious systemic problems caused or contributed to the Hayes tragedy?

The telephone rang in Zachary Blake's office.

"Yes, Kristin?"

"Micah Love is calling for you, Mr. Blake."

"Put him through, thank you."

"Micah?"

"Zack, buddy, I've got interesting news."

Micah's pumped.

"What news is that, Micah?"

"The City of Cedar Ridge has assembled a blue-ribbon committee to study police misconduct and make recommendations."

"That *is* interesting . . ."

"It gets better. The committee has recently presented city officials with its preliminary findings."

"That seems quick; when was this committee assembled?"

"About nine months ago."

"Why am I just hearing about this?"

"Because the committee's existence was a well-kept secret, even after it published its recommendations. Apparently, everyone involved signed non-disclosure and confidentiality agreements. Surprisingly, they all kept silent about it for a long time."

"It's impressive they were able to keep the committee secret for that long, No leaks, huh? If that's true, how did you come by the information?"

"Because I am a miracle worker. I also have a source with a conscience and a strong desire to see justice done."

"And your source?"

"If I told you I would have to kill you."

"I'm not asking for a name. I'm asking about reliability."

"Extremely reliable."

"Any juicy stuff?"

"Absolutely. Lots of issues the task force feels need correcting and lots of solutions to correct them. The group was assembled by the Chief of Police and includes a broad cross-section of city officials, former law enforcement types, municipal, state and federal, as well as prominent and ordinary citizens."

"Examples?"

"The main recommendations are improved transparency and communication with the public regarding stops, increased use of Tasers or stun guns rather than firearms, reducing the use of military-style equipment, increased educational standards and more diversity for police recruits, better warnings and alternate weapons training, and an increase in civilian and internal affairs oversight."

"What does 'improved transparency and communication' look like?"

"Body microphones and cameras on all officers, dash cams on all vehicles. My source advises Cedar Ridge had all of that *before* the Hayes shooting."

"None of which helped Marcus Hayes."

"True, but better warnings and Taser use might have."

"How does 'better warnings' work?"

"An officer is trained to use verbal warnings and warning shots and refrain from the use of deadly force until absolutely necessary. Applying the standard to the Hayes case, for instance, my source claims the fact the suspect tells the officer he's legally armed is not enough justification to even consider lethal force. Some overt threat or action is required to justify that type of force. Appropriate verbal warnings or a warning shot prevents the death of Marcus Hayes.

"The committee recommends a cooler head and a call for back up. They are very critical of Jones's use of inconsistent verbal commands. They feel this tragedy would have been prevented if Jones had received proper training. If an officer has no choice but to shoot, the recommendation is to shoot at a non-vital body part. This is all good stuff, Zack."

"It sure is. Anything else to report?" Zack urges.

He's piqued about the panel and its' report.

"Let me read my notes…"

Zack hears Micah ruffling through note pages.

"They recommend training to improve recognition when a suspect is under duress or under the influence of alcohol or drugs. And, get this; they recommend something called inherent bias training."

"What does that look like?"

"A bigot will pull over a black guy before he will pull over a white guy. Furthermore, he will presume the black guy is a criminal because of inherent bias. The training focuses on ignoring the bias even if you have it and concentrating on whether someone did something to merit a stop."

"Again—*good stuff*. We need to find a way to get this in, somehow, through the back door."

"You're the legal wiz. I'm your lowly and humble servant. I'm sure you'll find a way."

"Good work, Micah. Just knowing Chief Brooks and other city officials have been given these recommendations and criticisms makes our case stronger. They are getting these critiques from people with no skin in the game, not from attorneys or clients with secondary gain issues."

Micah continues to review his notes.

"Oh . . ." he starts . . ." I almost forgot! You're going to love this one! The committee feels the threat of criminal prosecution and civil litigation are important deterrents to bad officer behavior. Police officials should *embrace* litigation as a deterrent rather than *discourage* litigation. How about them apples?"

"Seriously?"

"As a heart attack. The committee believes large verdicts and public humiliations are serious deterrents."

"Wow. These findings may be inadmissible, but they certainly create a great political environment for us to pursue this case."

"I thought you'd be pleased."

Chapter Twenty-Eight

Sarah Hayes is leaving work to pick up her kids at an after-school daycare center located in the Fisher Building. She's just completed her third day as a tour guide at the *Charles H. Wright Museum of African American History* on East Warren in Detroit's Cultural Center.

This is a plum job for Sarah. African American history is a passion of hers. She majored in History at Wayne State and took every Black history course the school offers. Ironically, her favorite class was *Systemic Racism in African American History*, taught by Professor Michael Kendell.

As she approaches her car, she's thinking about history and the sacrifices made by those who came before her. Sarah's not old enough to remember separate but equal, colored and white drinking fountains, separate lunch counters, school busing, Rosa Parks, or Martin Luther King, Jr., but as a student of black history, she reads everything she can get her hands on.

Sarah knows, firsthand, what it's like to feel inferior, something less valuable. She grew up reading books about white people, watching white television shows, playing with white dolls, and going to movies that starred or featured white actors and actresses. Sarah isn't surprised there are still white supremacists or nationalists in America.

America, with white and black societal differences in education, media portrayal, neighborhoods, and opportunities, is, in many ways, a white supremacist country. Even black people are conditioned to believe in the superiority of the white race.

In the early 1600s, my people were hunted and captured in Africa, jammed into slave ships and brought to America in chains, where they were sold into slavery. Finally freed during civil war times, they spent another one hundred years or so facing segregation, lynching, and Jim Crow laws.

Civil rights legislation in America, the crowning achievement of Martin and others, is only fifty years old. Every time we take two steps forward, we take a step back. The election of a black president should have been a source of pride, honor, and unity. Instead, many use Barak Obama's victory as a divisive tool. Why should anyone in America be shocked when a white cop murders my husband?

Sarah starts the car and eases out of her parking space. Her cell phone rings, startling her out of her thoughts. She slides the bar on the screen to answer.

"Hello?"

"Sarah?"

The voice is female, familiar.

"Yes?"

"Oh, my God, Sarah!"

The woman is frantic.

"She's gone! She's wandered away . . . worse . . . someone's taken her."

"Taken who?"

Sarah is confused.

Who is this?

"Who is this?"

"Dalia at *KidCare*. Aisha is missing."

Sarah's heart leaves her chest.

"Missing? What the hell, Dalia—what the hell does that *mean?*"

Aisha is her six-year-old daughter.

"Oh God, oh dear God . . . can't breathe . . . can't think . . . what the hell, *Dalia!*"

Sarah frantically checks her rear and side-view mirrors and quickly pulls over.

"What to do, what to do . . . oh God . . . how did this happen? On my way . . . will be there in ten . . . Shit! Wait . . . Tasia . . . Where is *Tasia*? Is s-*she* okay?"

"She's fine, Sarah. I-I'm *holding* her. I won't let her out of my sight until you get here," Dalia cries.

Sarah shoots out into traffic and speeds up Woodward Avenue. Angry drivers lay on their horns.

"The police have been called Sarah. They're coming! I hear the sirens!" Dalia is hysterical. "It was naptime! When the kids woke up, Aisha was gone!

"Where is she? How could she just . . . *disappear?" Sarah was near hysteria.*

"We don't know. The aides were all here. Maybe they turned their backs for a minute or two. Who knows? I'm so . . . so . . . s-*sorry*! The police will . . . *find* her!" Dalia sobs.

Sarah steps on the gas.

Chapter Twenty-Nine

There are multiple police vehicles at the Fisher Building lining Grand Boulevard, Second Avenue and Lothrop, bubble gum flashing. Sarah double-parks her car and tries to run into the building, She's stopped by a police officer standing at the door.

"Whoa, whoa. Where do you think you're going? This is a *crime scene.*"

"My daughter is missing—get the hell out of my way," Sarah bellows, completely ignoring the uniform.

"S-sorry ma'am . . . come with me . . . right this way."

"I know the damned way!" Sarah shrieks.

They run through the lobby to *KidCare* where Dalia is standing, holding Tasia and talking with a dark-skinned African American man in a business suit. Dalia sees Sarah approach and immediately breaks into tears.

"Oh, Sarah . . . Sarah . . . I'm so sorry . . . this is terrible . . . I'm so sorry!" Dalia screeches.

"Nothing like this has ever happened here before. I can't believe this. "You will find her, won't you?"

Dalia pleads with the man in the suit. Her head bobs back and forth from Sarah to the man and back again.

"Shut the hell up, Dalia. Where is Aisha? Where is my *daughter,* damn you!"

"Are you the mother?" The man inquires.

"Of *course,* I'm the mother. Who the hell are you?"

Sarah grabs Tasia out of Dalia's arms and holds on for dear life.

Where is my Aisha? We have to *find* her! Dalia, where are the police, for God's sake?"

"Sarah," Dalia manages, motioning to the man in the suit.

"This is Detective Ellington. He *is* the police."

"Ma'am..."

Ellington holds up a cell phone picture of Aisha.

"Is this a current picture of your daughter?"

"Yes . . . Yes! Where is she?" Sarah howls.

"We were notified shortly after the incident, Ma'am. We've set up roadblocks in every direction, put out an Amber Alert and an APB. We've started a door-by-door sweep of the area. If she's nearby, we'll find her."

"Of course she's nearby! How long has she been gone?"

Dalia buries her head in her hands.

"Are you okay to answer some questions, ma'am? The more information we have, the easier it will be to find her."

Ellington turns to Dalia.

"Are there video cameras in these hallways, especially near the entrance to your daycare center?"

"Not sure," Dalia mumbles.

"Not to worry. My officers are talking to building security right now. He turns back to Sarah.

"Ma'am? Can you think of anybody who would take your daughter? Any reason why anyone would want to? Wealthy? Famous? Anyone pissed off at you? Family member? Ex-boyfriend? Ex-husband? Child's father in the picture?"

Sarah opens her mouth to speak, but can't talk. She bursts into tears.

Ellington ignores this and continues.

"A kidnapping, if that's what this is, happens for a lot of reasons. Money is one reason—revenge is another.

"I've got no frigging money, damn it!" I'm sure as hell not wealthy." I'm a widow-just started working again . . . Marcus was killed . . . revenge? Who the hell would do something like this? Can't think . . . family member . . . revenge?"

"I'm sorry for your loss. What happened to your husband?" The two lock eyes.

"Shot and killed for no damn reason by a Cedar Ridge *cop*."

"Y-you're Sarah *Hayes*?" Ellington stammers.

"I am."

"Excuse me."

Ellington turns and addresses a group of uniforms standing close by. He is angry and animated, barking orders in all directions. When he finishes, the cops take off in different directions, and Ellington turns back to Sarah and Dalia.

"Sarah. I am quite familiar with Cedar Ridge . . . A terrible tragedy. You filed a civil rights case, right?"

"What the hell's the difference?"

"Has anyone threatened you in any way since you filed?"

The lawsuit! The damn lawsuit!

"Aisha was taken by a Cedar Ridge cop! The phone call! The white guy! Called me the N-word for suing the police and causing the death of a cop. Drop the case, he demanded . . . threatened my kids . . . the cops would never help anyone who is suing a cop . . . Where's Zack? He promised he'd take care of this . . . he'd protect my kids . . . Where the hell is *Zack*? Sarah screams.

"Zack, who? Blake?"

"He promised me that Micah Love was watching my kids."

"Focus, Mrs. Hayes. Let's go back to the call. Was there only one call or more?"

"The phone would ring and ring after the first one, but I wouldn't answer. He finally stopped."

"When was the last time?"

"A few months ago, maybe. They put in a tap. Maybe he knew."

"Who tapped your phones?"

"You guys did. I live in Detroit. Nearby. That's why I chose this place for daycare. I'll never forget. A cop named Collins came to the house. Not a nice guy."

"I think I know who 'Collins' is. Why do you say he's not a nice guy?"

"Because he treated me like shit for suing a cop. He got into it with Zack."

"Your attorney was there when you spoke with Collins?"

"Yes, and his investigator, Micah Love. They promised to protect us."

"I've butted head with Love. He's not my favorite person, but he's a terrific P I. It's hard to prevent a crime you don't know will happen. I'll reach out to Collins. Anything else come to mind?"

"The caller was a white guy. I'd know his voice if I heard it again. He warned me the cops wouldn't care. He sure was right. No one cares. I should've listened. I should've dropped the case.

I lost my husband, now I've lost my daughter. What good is a lawsuit? Won't bring my family back."

"I care, Mrs. Hayes. And Aisha is *missing*, not *gone*. We'll find her. Trust me."

"Trust a *cop*? That's a laugh. You cops have made a mess of my life. How am I supposed to trust a cop?"

"You have no choice. I'll do everything in my power to find her and bring her home to you."

"You're damn sure right about one thing, *Detective*. I have no choice. Find her! Find my baby!"

Chapter Thirty

It is pitch black when Aisha Hayes awakens. She hears a humming sound in the darkness.

Where am I? Where's my Mama?!

"Where's my Mama? "I want my mama!"

Aisha cries aloud in the dark.

Where's Miss Dalia? Is Tasia okay? Is she here too?

Aisha lies face down on a cold tile floor. Her face is numb. There are no blankets, pillows, or mattress. She tries to turn onto her back and push herself up, but she's tired, dizzy, her legs hurt, and she's terrified. She feels, even *hears,* her heart thumping in her chest.

Are my eyes open?

She blinks several times and tries to focus.

Where am I?

She's disoriented. She struggles to her feet and reaches her hands out into the darkness. She feels only bare walls, no shelves, no furniture, and no bed. She locates a door and tries the handle— *locked.*

So small—is it a closet? What happened? I'm asleep at KidCare . . . a *hand covers my nose and mouth. I can't breathe!*

Aisha is dressed in black spandex active pants and a pink 'I'm a Princess' sweatshirt, the same clothes she was wearing at *KidCare.*

As cobwebs clear, she remembers. She trembles as she recalls a large white man who scoops her up and covers her mouth and nose. It's hard to breathe . . . she passes out . . .

I remember . . .

She screams in horror at the memory, pees her pants, and hugs herself in a corner.

"Hello?" She screams.

Her face registers the horror she's feeling.

"Mama? I want my mama!"

She continues to sob. She's hungry, thirsty and . . . terrified.

"Quit your yapping, kid," comes a voice from outside the

room.

Aisha is strangely comforted by the fact that she is not alone. *Six-year-olds aren't supposed to be alone!*

"I'm here Mama . . . Mama? Where's Mama? I want Mama." She recoils in horror.

"You are someplace where no one can see you, no one can hear you, and no one will find you. What happens to you is up to your mother."

"Who are you? Why am I here?"

"Your mama did a bad thing, and I'm punishing her."

"*Mommies* don't do bad things. I'm hungry. I wet my pants." A cold chill runs down her spine.

This man is mean! He took me away.

Aisha remembers the 'stranger danger' talk with Mama.

Is this the guy?

The door opens. A ray of light blasts through the opening and momentarily blinds her. The mean man grabs her with one arm and sits her back down on the cold floor. Drops of water splash against her face. She screams bloody murder. A plate with a sandwich and a glass of water are placed on the floor. She tries to focus, but all she sees are two huge legs. She looks up to see a face, but the door slams. She is plunged into darkness once again.

Chapter Thirty-One

Detective Billy Ellington hears a slight knock on his open door and sets down a file. Captain Wanda Ellis is standing at the door with an attractive white woman.

She's vaguely familiar . . .

"Detective Billy Ellington, meet Michelle Delany from *WWJ News Radio 950.* You may remember her from her reporting on that Vandenberg kidnapping case we worked with the FBI."

Billy stands and offers his hand to Delany. He's an imposing, well-dressed man in his late thirties.

"Detective Ellington, it's nice to see you again," Delany flirts.

He's very nice looking, well built. Wonder if he works out. When I have more time . . .

"Nice to see you, too, Michelle."

Ellington shrugs and ignores her playfulness. He's focused on one thing only: Sarah Hayes and her missing daughter.

"What can I do for you?"

"I'm wondering if I can ask you some questions about the Gilbert case. It is beginning to look like a cold case. The parents are prominent members of our community. They're looking for us to run a story about their missing teenager.

I know you've pegged this is as a runaway situation, but have you ruled out foul play? Could it be a kidnapping? Has the FBI been notified?"

"I'm a little busy right now, Michelle. I've got this new case, tons of calls to return, leads to follow up, and I am late for an interview with a potential witness."

"The child abduction in Detroit?"

"That's the one, Michelle."

"We can talk about that one at some point, Detective, but I've got a few questions about this other matter. Please? A moment of your time?" She purrs.

"About the Gilbert case?"

"Yes."

"Why, the Gilbert case? Because a nice white girl from the suburbs goes missing and the public feels terrible? How about a six-year-old girl goes missing from a daycare center in broad daylight, right under the noses of three caregivers? How does that float your boat? She's black and from the big city. That's a deal-breaker, right?"

He glares at her. She stands her ground.

"Come on, Detective. Give me a minute, would you? I don't choose assignments. I follow orders."

"This young girl is the daughter of Sarah Hayes, who is suing the city of Cedar Ridge for the cop-on-black shooting. It should be big news. Zack Blake's involved. What's the deal, Delany, *Black Lives Matter*, but not to the media? Even the fact that she's Zack Blake's client doesn't float your boat? How's this? If we can't talk about *both* cases, then get the hell out of my face."

"Those are *your* words, not mine, Detective. I'm happy to talk to my producer about this new case and that poor child. It's a great story, considering the lawsuit and the Blake angle, but that's not my assignment today. Fair enough?"

"No! God damn it!" Ellington explodes. "It is not even close to fair enough. A teenaged white girl goes missing and the whole world stops. The media frenzy begins in earnest, and everyone drops everything they're doing to assist with the investigation.

"A beautiful six-year-old *black* kid goes missing and what? Is she just one more missing kid from the hood? What's the big deal? Have I missed anything?"

"I'll talk to my boss and get back to you on that one."

Delany continues her cajoles, but Ellington's rants and raves about racial injustice in news reporting finally sends her out the door.

I'm wasting my damn time.

Captain Ellis watches her leave and calls Billy into her office. She's heard every word uttered between Billy and Delaney.

"Play nice, would you please, Billy? We need the press to help us in these situations. You can't treat her like that. She didn't choose one story over the other. She's doing her damn job. You know this. Besides, Gilbert *is* an important case, too, right?"

Ellington knows his boss is right, but he is beyond frustrated with the double standard.

"News services want to cover stories that involve white people with a lot of money. Who cares about a little six-year-old from the hood? We both know that when a child disappears, the more media coverage the child gets, the more and better tips we get. The better chance we have to solve the case.

"When a little black kid disappears and the media ignores it, so does the public. I *know* you know this. Not only that, but how much media coverage a case gets has a direct relationship to how much manpower the brass assigns to solving that case. It also impacts whether or not the feds get involved. I know you know this, too, dammit!"

"What you say may be true, Billy, but our department needs the media, and I still need you to play nice."

"Gilbert is a *cold* case, probably a *runaway!* Hayes is a *hot* case. The media should be reporting the hell out of the Hayes case! They damn sure thought the *lawsuit* was big news. They reported the hell out of that. Why isn't *WWJ* interested in reporting on both cases, Cap? *Why?*"

"I don't know, Billy. I don't dictate these things."

"I know, but it's not only Delany and *WWJ*. Why does Detroit PD want me to discuss Gilbert and not Hayes? Hayes is *piping* hot. It's a developing situation. It's the *priority* right now. Delany is only following orders, but she had to get clearance. How does this make any sense coming from our top brass?"

"Don't play the race card with me, Billy Ellington! You're crossing the line!"

"Since when is child abduction a racial issue? Both of these kids are *innocent* for Christ's sake!"

"This is not about race, Billy. It is about taking advantage of what is offered and when it is offered, regardless of why."

"We both know exactly what this is about, don't we Cap?"

"So, let me see if I understand. You want me to get all high and mighty, play the angry black woman and tell media to fuck off. And this will get us exactly what? *Two* dead kids! Is that what you want?"

"Of course not, and you damn well know that! But what I *do* want is a fair and equal distribution of media and manpower based on circumstances, not race. I want to talk to Michelle Delany when she wants to talk about and report on *both* cases.

"I've got no problem with the press helping us, Captain. But this Hayes case is an immediate pressure cooker. There's a strong *motive* here. We have a chance to solve this case here and now. The first twenty-four to forty-eight hours are vital. How is this not the priority right now, even if the victim is black?"

"That's disgustingly cynical, Billy. *Every* child abduction case is important to us. We allocate manpower based on the circumstances and needs of the case at the moment."

"I know that Cap, but I stand by my previous statement. I want permission to talk to Delany. She will report on both cases or not at all."

"I can't do that, Billy."

"May I assume that Chief Balfour is on board with this bullshit?"

"That's above your pay grade, Detective. Now, make a deal with Delany, or I'll do it myself. Lobby her on the other case at the same time, knock yourself out, but grant her an interview on Gilbert. Is that understood?"

"Loud and clear, boss. After all, we can't let a little thing like institutional racism get in our way, now, can we?"

Chapter Thirty-Two

The following day, Billy Ellington sits in Sarah Hayes' living room. He's concerned. She's distraught.

"Any leads, Detective?"

"Nothing yet, Sarah. We're getting tons of tips. Do you have another picture of Aisha?"

"Yes, I do. Hang on a second."

Sarah rises and walks into the back of the house. She returns holding a small photograph; a beautiful picture of a smiling, happy six-year-old girl.

"Man-o-man, Sarah. She sure is a beautiful child. She looks like her mother."

Ellington glances back and forth from Sarah to the photo and back to Sarah.

"Thank you. *Find* Aisha," demands Sarah, oblivious of the compliment and Ellington's apparent interest in her.

"We're doing our best."

"We've reached out to all of the local newspapers, radio and television stations. Still waiting to hear something,"

Sarah tries to remain optimistic.

"Yeah, good luck with that," Billy growls, fresh from meetings with Michelle Delany and his captain.

He is immediately sorry he vented his frustration with the media in front of the grieving parent of a missing child.

"What does that mean, Detective?"

"I'm Billy—please call me Billy," he insists.

"Okay. What does that mean, *Billy?*"

"You didn't hear this from me, but the media is more focused on a different investigation, and I am pissed as hell because it distracts focus from *your* case. I'm trying to make Aisha front-page news. Let's just say that I've encountered some difficulty with the brass."

"Why?" Sarah is nonplussed.

"Because the other case involves a teenaged *white* kid."

"Seriously? In this day and age, whether a child is white or black is an issue? That's hard to believe."

"Believe it."

"What's the other case?"

"Gilbert case."

"I saw that on the news."

"Exactly!"

"I watch the news all the time. There's some talk about Aisha's case. If they mention her, they pronounce her name wrong. But what can I do?"

"I'm doing everything I can to find your daughter. *Believe* me. I will not rest until she is home with you. Want some advice?"

"Sure."

"If this were *my* daughter, I'd march myself into Captain Ellis' office. I'd make her very aware that I know what is going on and that I won't stand for it."

"If Aisha was yours?"

"You bet."

Billy Ellington is a good man to have in our corner

***

The phone in Captain Wanda Ellis' office rings. The captain answers the phone on the third ring.

"Captain Ellis speaking, how may I help you?"

"Captain Ellis? This is Sarah Hayes. Do you know who I am?"

"Why yes, Ms. Hayes, I do. I want you to know we are doing everything we can to find your daughter. We have our best people on the case. What can I do for you today?"

"Your people promised me the media would be contacted, and I would be interviewed about my daughter. What happened to that interview?"

"We haven't been able to make it happen yet."

"Haven't been able to make that happen yet, why?"

"Look, Ms. Hayes . . . I try to throw my weight around when I can, but I don't control what stories the media feels are important and how much time they devote to a particular story, even when I know what they're doing is wrong,"

Ellis is defensive. Sarah cuts her no slack.

"You mean like the fact the media is covering the Gilbert girl like a blanket, but there's little mention of Aisha? Like that?" Sarah snaps.

"Yes, like that," Captain Ellis concedes.

"I don't know. You're a captain. You control investigations around here, don't you? You've pulled some people off my daughter's case because the media likes the other story better, haven't you?"

Has she been talking to Ellington?

"We follow the leads that come in. If we get leads, we need more people to follow them up."

"It's a vicious circle. Is that what you're telling me? More media results in more leads. More cops are assigned. And that case gets solved while this one's ignored. So, tell me, *Captain*, who's running this place, you or the media?"

"Ms. Hayes. We are doing everything we can to find your daughter."

Sarah explodes. "Then maybe *I* need to do something! Should I grab something, start crying and screaming, or punch you or one of your detectives? Would that get your attention? Maybe the media would come running! I punch you—you arrest me! The media would be all over that! 'Crazy black mother punches police captain! Details at eleven!' I'll do that if it'll help me find my daughter! How's that sound to you?"

"I'm willing if you are," Ellis sighs.

"The bottom line is a black girl's life isn't worth as much as a white girl's life to cops, even in *Detroit*.

"My husband's life wasn't worth a dime to the cops in Cedar Ridge, and my daughter's life isn't worth a dime to the cops in Detroit. You know what, *Captain?*"

"What?" Ellis cringes.

"All you cops should be *ashamed* of yourselves!"

Sarah Hayes slams down the receiver.

Chapter Thirty-Three

After three days in captivity, Aisha Hayes is learning that screaming and crying produces results.

"I have to go potty!" She screams. "I am going to pee in my pants! Hello? Hello! I have to go! Hurry!"

The door opens, and, as always, a blast of light blinds her. The big arm is back. It grabs her again, this time, more gruffly than before. This person is getting tired of hauling Aisha to and from the bathroom all the time.

All Aisha can think about is being locked in a room alone is tough on the bladder. She's becoming accustomed to being carried down a hallway and into a bathroom, a place similar to the small bare room she spends her days in now. The only real difference between the two is one has a toilet and the other doesn't.

Her eyes begin to adjust to the light. In the past, she's been hesitant to look up at her captor. This time she decides to be brave. She looks up and sees the face of a large white man in a blue uniform. He's motioning her toward the toilet.

"I told you," she insists. "I can't pee in front of you." She starts to cry.

"I'm really getting tired of this shit!" The man roars. He cocks his head, huffs, rolls his eyes, and leaves the room. He slams the door behind him. Aisha hears an audible click as he locks the door behind him.

She takes down her pants and climbs onto the commode. As she relieves herself, her eyes continue to adjust to the light. She's trying to a big girl like Mama taught her. After all, she *is* the big sister, six going on seven and Daddy's in heaven. She's trying to be brave.

It's important to see that man's face so I can remember and tell Mama. I've seen that blue suit before. Those men who came to our house that time when Mama got so angry. Those men wore those blue suits. I remember. The man who shot Daddy wore the blue suit. When I see Mama, I'll tell her what I remember.

When she finishes in the bathroom, she flushes the toilet. Almost instantly, the door opens. The man in the blue uniform hoists her up, takes her back down the hall, and deposits her back on the floor. She brazenly gazes up and takes another good look at his face. *This is what stranger danger looks like.*

The man leaves in a huff and slams the door behind him. Aisha is, once again, enveloped in darkness. This time, however, she notices there is no audible click like she usually hears when the bad man takes her back from the potty.

She feels around in the dark and finds the sandwich. It's the usual peanut butter and jelly with a glass of water. She takes a bite. It's fine. She is tired of eating the same thing all the time, but she's *starving.* She drinks the water and finishes the sandwich. Then, she listens intently for a sound, any sound that suggests someone is nearby. After what seems to Aisha to be hours, she walks to the door and turns the handle. *The door's not locked!*

Aisha cracks the door open, and light pours into the room. As usual, it blinds her. She's afraid to breathe. She blinks over and over and tries to adjust her eyes to the light. Finally, she decides she can see well enough and cracks the door a bit more. She sticks out her head and peers down the hall. *Where am I? Where is the bad man?*

She eases, shoeless, through the door. She's terrified the bad man or someone with the bad man will return and grab her again. She wants to scream. She feels sick. But she continues on, bravely, one foot in front of the other, slowly, surely, traversing down the well-lit hall, passing several rooms.

Some rooms have open doors; others are closed. Aisha is buoyed by the fact she hears nothing. She's determined not to make a sound.

At the end of the hall is a door. She tries the handle and is surprised to discover *this* door isn't locked either. She turns the handle—frightened the door might creak. The door opens and expels a slight creak.

This scares her and causes her to utter an audible gasp. She stops, terrified, and waits in silence, holding her breath, until she's satisfied neither the sound of the door nor her audible gasp has caused anyone to come running.

Aisha puts her head through the open door and sees it leads to an alley, outside of her captive building. The sun is very bright, but she isn't sure what time it is, or whether the stark brightness has anything to do with the comparative darkness of the room where she has spent her last few days. Stepping outside of the captive building, Aisha is relieved there is no sign of the bad man. *It's not too cold outside.*

She eases through the opening and peeks around the door. She looks both ways. She sees streets on both sides of the alley with traffic cruising down both of them.

She bolts through the door and, for no reason at all, chooses to turn right. She runs as hard as she can down the alley, arriving at a city sidewalk running perpendicular to the alley and parallel with a street. She isn't old enough to cross the street by herself. *Right or left?*

Aisha has no idea where she is. She's terrified, but nowhere near as she was in that room with the bad man in the blue suit. For no particular reason, Aisha again decides to turn right. She runs until she reaches the next corner. Reaching another street, Aisha again turns right.

As she runs, she sees another man in that familiar blue suit. She pretends he isn't there and continues to run. She tries not to look as frightened as she feels. The man in the blue suit doesn't pay any attention to her. However, Aisha cannot comprehend that if she continues to make right turns, she'll wind up back where her journey began.

Chapter Thirty-Four

Before Aisha completes her run around the block, she stops in front of a small, well-lit diner and peers through the large front window. As Aisha observes a few customers enjoying their meals, she notices there are no men in blue suits.

Aisha pushes open the door, walks in, and looks around. People are staring at her. A man behind the counter smiles and comes through a counter swing door. He walks up to Aisha and crouches to his knees in front of her.

"Is everything okay, sweetheart? Are you lost?" He wonders.

Aisha bursts out crying. The man tries to pick her up to comfort her, which causes her to shriek. She remembers the bad man in the blue suit who picked her up at the daycare center. *Just like that! He put his hands over my nose and mouth and took me to the dark room!*

The man shoots his arms and hands up in the air in surrender and smiles.

"Okay, sweet girl, okay. Calm down. I won't pick you up. Are you hungry? Do you want something to eat?"

"Shouldn't we call 9-1-1?" A customer suggests.

"Or maybe the Cedar Ridge Police," offers another.

Police? Isn't that where the men in blue suits are? Aisha wills herself to calm.

"C-could s-someone please get Mama on the phone?" She manages to ask.

"Sure, honey. What's your mama's number?" The nice man still crouched on his knees, pulls a cellphone out of his pocket. He's ready to dial.

"313-555-2574," Aisha recites from memory.

"What's Mama's name, little one?"

"Sarah."

"And what's your name, sweetheart?"

"Aisha."

"Aisha, that is such a beautiful name! Let's call your mother."

Aisha's calming down. The nice man pokes the phone with his finger several times and puts the phone to his ear. Everyone in the restaurant is watching and waiting. A man answers the phone on the first ring.

"Hayes residence."

"I'm looking for Sarah."

"Who's calling?"

"My name is Steve. I own a restaurant, Nana's, in downtown Cedar Ridge."

The man on the other side of the line is silent, waiting. Steve continues.

"A little girl just walked off the street and into my diner. She's looking for her mother. Her name is Aisha."

The man's voice turns away from the phone.

"Oh, my God! Sarah! It's Aisha! I think we've found her, Sarah! I think we've found her!" Steve hears him say.

The voice turns back to the phone. "Sir, thank you for calling. This is Detective Billy Ellington speaking. The child who walked into your restaurant is most likely a six-year-old girl named Aisha Hayes. She was abducted from a daycare center. How does she seem to you? Is she okay? Hurt in any way?"

Steve is shocked. "Abducted? Why haven't we heard anything about this? She seems fine. Scared. She needs a bath, but otherwise, she's fine. She won't let anyone touch her. How old is she again?"

"Aisha is six. Hang on. I'm putting her mother on the line."

"H-hello?"

"Hi."

"This is Sarah Hayes. You've found my daughter?"

"Apparently," Steve advises.

"May I speak with her?"

"Sure."

Steve holds his phone out to Aisha.

"Aisha? Is your last name, Hayes?"

"Yes," Aisha whispers.

Well, honey, your mama is on the telephone."

Aisha takes the phone and puts it up to her ear. "Mama?" Aisha coos.

"Oh, sweet Jesus!" Sarah bursts into tears. "Yes, sweet baby, this is Mama! Are you okay, honey?"

"I think so, Mama. The bad man in the blue suit took me away. L-locked me in a dark room."

"I know honey . . . You are so brave. Stay with the nice man in the restaurant. We're coming to get you. I'm so happy to hear your voice, sweetness!"

Sarah Hayes continues to cry tears of joy.

"May I talk to . . . what's his name?"

"Mister Steve."

"May I talk to Mister Steve?"

Aisha hands the phone to Steve.

"This is Steve."

"Steve, oh, Steve. Thank you so much! My daughter was kidnapped. Oh, I forgot, Detective Ellington already told you that."

"I understand, Sarah. And I appreciate the thanks and all of that, but I really didn't do very much. Aisha just wandered into my diner and asked me to call you. I'm so happy she did! She seems fine to all of us here in the restaurant."

"Steve, Detective Ellington would like to speak to you again. He's from the Detroit Police Department."

"Detroit?"

"Yes, Aisha was taken from Detroit."

"How did she wind up in Cedar Ridge?"

"I'm not exactly sure, but you are my new best friend. Here's Detective Ellington."

Sarah hands the receiver to Ellington. "Steve, listen to me very carefully. Aisha mentioned a man in blue, right?"

"Right."

"We believe this man is a Cedar Ridge police officer or is impersonating a Cedar Ridge police officer. Please don't call the local police. Just keep Aisha there until her mother and I arrive. Will you do that for us, Steve?"

"A cop did this? In Cedar Ridge? The local police come into my restaurant all the time. They're terrific people."

"Well, he might not be an *actual* cop. He might be someone impersonating a cop. We have to be careful, though, especially in

Cedar Ridge. For now, please understand if we hand Aisha over to the Cedar Ridge Police, we might be handing her back to the man who abducted her."

"I understand completely. I'm surprised, that's all. I'll set her up in the back by the kitchen, away from the window and out of sight. I'll give her something to eat, too."

"That would be great. We should be there in half an hour. What's the address?"

Steve recites the address.

"Thanks," Billy acknowledges.

"No problem. She's a terrific kid."

With red and blue lights flashing from Ellington's unmarked police car, Sarah and Billy are soon speeding south down I-75 toward Cedar Ridge. Ellington, from time to time, glances at the vehicle's navigation screen.

"She was abducted by a Cedar Ridge cop! It's all about the lawsuit, Billy! I knew it, dammit. I knew it! Racist scumbags, all of them! They won't intimidate me. They've crossed the line. A cop kidnaps a kid? This is insane!"

"Calm down, Sarah. Aisha's been found. She's safe, and that's our number one priority. We don't know if he's a cop or someone *pretending* to be a cop. If he's a cop, we don't know for sure he's a *Cedar Ridge* cop. We only know that Cedar Ridge is where he took her."

"He's a *Cedar Ridge* cop. I feel it in my bones. How did he pull this off? Wasn't the whole area on lockdown? How'd he get through the roadblocks?"

"Things *were* locked down, Sarah. This guy looks like a *cop*! Would officers stop a *police vehicle* or someone who identifies himself as a police officer?"

"You're right about one thing. My baby is safe, and that's all that matters. I'll pick her up, hold her tight, and never let her out of my sight. We can figure out who did this later after I get her home where she belongs."

"We'll do our best, Sarah. I'm just happy this whole mess has a happy ending."

"This *isn't* the end. This isn't over, not by a long shot. I'm going to make these people pay. One way or another, they're going to pay."

"As long as you're not talking about doing anything illegal. You aren't, are you? I'm a sworn officer of the law, you know."

"This guy can't be permitted to get away with this bullshit."

"He won't get away with it, Sarah. I'll make damn sure of that."

"Thanks for staying with this Detective."

"Just doing my job."

"A cop who does his job and does it the right way is rare, in my experience."

"That's not fair, Sarah. Cops are people too. Most cops are honest, hardworking, and caring. Good people. A couple of bad eggs can't spoil the whole box now, can they?"

"Until cops stop treating blacks differently than whites, we're going to have problems."

"Police departments are working on solutions. I know for a fact Chief Brooks is working on solutions in Cedar Ridge. He's a good man."

"I'll have to take your word for it. I don't know the man. We'll see how he handles this lawsuit."

"You're still going through with it?"

"Are you kidding me? After this, I'm more determined than ever. My husband's memory has to count for something. I will not be deterred or intimidated. But we *will* need protection."

"I'll talk to Blake and Love. We'll all do our best to protect your family."

"Thanks, Detective."

"Billy. I told you to call me Billy."

"Thank you, *Billy*," Sarah blushes.

Chapter Thirty-Five

The unmarked squad car arrives at Nana's Restaurant. Sarah and Billy jump out of the car and dash inside. A hostess greets Ellington as Steve emerges from the back room with Aisha.

"Mama!" Aisha shouts as soon as she sees Sarah.

The little girl runs, joyfully, to her mother. They hug each other tightly, sobbing. Restaurant patrons, who have refused to leave, stand and applaud the scene.

Sarah looks up and thanks them for their kindness. When Sarah and Aisha finally terminate their embrace, Sarah turns to Steve.

"I presume you are Mr. Steve?"

Aisha walks up to Steve and presents him to her mother.

"Mama? This is Mr. Steve. Mr. Steve? This is Mama."

"It is very nice to meet you, *Mr.* Steve. From the bottom of my heart, thank you so much for the unbelievable goodness and kindness you have extended to my daughter."

"I am so pleased to meet you, Sarah. Your 'thank you' is appreciated, but not necessary. He smiles down at Aisha, who smiles right back at him.

"She's a brave, young lady; very grown-up for her age."

"Yes, she is." Sarah scoops up her daughter. She hugs her again, a big squeeze. "Thank you for taking such good care of her."

"I didn't do anything. She chose to walk into my place. It could've been anyone. She just happened to choose me."

"Because you have a warm and welcoming place. She chose you for a reason. Right, Aisha?"

Aisha nods her head up and down and smiles at Mr. Steve.

"Okay, okay, I won't argue. I'm a hero!" Steve laughs. The entire restaurant breaks out in spontaneous laughter. "I'm happy she chose me. Glad I could help. Would you guys like something to eat?"

"I'm starving," Ellington gasps, glancing around the restaurant. They're the only black people in the place.

"I could eat," Sarah agrees.

Sarah wants to get Aisha to a hospital and have her checked out. Ellington wants to first find out what happened, how Aisha got to the restaurant, where she'd been held, and how far she walked. Both of them want to locate and arrest the bastard who abducted her. Aisha needs nourishment but, otherwise, seems to be okay. They decide Billy can question her in the restaurant. Sarah is also very grateful to Steve and does not wish to seem rude.

Ellington pulls out his cell phone and barks out orders to his fellow cops. After he hangs up, the three visitors sit down amidst staring restaurant patrons. Sarah introduces Aisha to Ellington. Ellington asks Sarah if he can talk to Aisha while things are still fresh in her mind. Sarah leaves it up to Aisha. Both adults turn to Aisha, who gives her nod of approval. Ellington sets his phone on record and places it on the table.

"Aisha, do you remember what happened at KidCare?"

"Yes, the bad man in blue came during nap time and took me away to the dark room. He put his hands on my nose and mouth. I couldn't breathe."

Sarah gags. *Aisha must have been terrified! My baby, my precious baby!*

Ellington continues, undaunted. "Where were the people who were supposed to be watching you?"

"I don't know." Aisha frowns. "Are they in trouble?"

"No, honey. They're not in any trouble. Did the bad man hurt you? Did you bump your head or anything? Are you having any problems at all?"

"I couldn't breathe with his hand on my mouth. I think I fell asleep and woke up in the dark room. He didn't hurt me after that, but he wouldn't let me go potty." She turned to her mother and whispered. "Mama, I peed my pants."

"That's okay, sweetness. It's not your fault. We'll get you checked out and cleaned up soon."

"Anything else you remember, Aisha?"

"He was big and strong and . . . and *mean*, Mama. He locked me in the dark room. The floor was cold. He gave me peanut butter and jelly and water. It's dark and cold in there. Did I say that? When he took me to pee, I saw his face." She scowls.

"You saw his face?" Ellington is buoyed by the revelation.

"Yes. He was white."

"Aisha, this is very important," Ellington coaxes. "Do you think you would remember the bad man's face if you saw it again?"

"Yes, I th-think so." Aisha appears to be trying to reconstruct his face in her mind.

"Wonderful." Ellington turns to Sarah.

"Sarah, is it okay if I set Aisha up with a sketch artist? I can probably get pictures of the entire Cedar Ridge police force, too, but we have to start somewhere."

"If you think this artist can coax a good sketch out of a six-year-old, knock yourself out. Not today, though. She's been through enough for today."

"No, we'll get you guys out of here, do it later. S*oon,* though, while it's fresh in her mind, alright?"

"That's fine, Billy."

Ellington turned back to Aisha. "Aisha, is there anything else you remember? Did the bad man tell you why he took you?"

"He told me Mama did a bad thing, so he was punishing her. That's so silly!" She grinned.

"Why is it silly, precious?"

"*Mommies* don't get punished; little kids do!" Aisha folds both arms across her chest.

Ellington stifles a smile. Sarah giggles.

Aisha looks confused. *What did I say?*

"That *is* silly honey, but sometimes, adults do bad things and are punished by other adults," Sarah explains. "When we find this bad man, we're going to punish him. Do you understand?"

"I guess so."

"Aisha? How did you get away from the bad man?" Ellington wonders.

"I had to go, like *all* the time. The bad man in blue got real mad 'cause I had to go too much, but I was so scared. He carried me to the potty. He wanted to *watch* while I peed. Mama says that it's not 'propriate.'

"I told him. He left and locked the door every time. When I

was done, he came back in and picked me up and took me back to the dark room. It was cold and scary. He locked the door—I heard the click.

"The last time I had to go, he was very mad. He took me back after I peed and slammed the door. I didn't hear the click! I waited and waited. I didn't hear anything. I went to the door and it wasn't locked! I guess the bad man got so mad at me he forgot to lock it.

"I opened the door and looked out. I didn't see anyone. I went down the hall and saw other doors. One of the doors took me outside. When I opened it, it made a loud squeak. I was *soooooo* scared, but no one heard, I guess. I went outside and ran here and met Mr. Steve."

Aisha again nods and folds her arms across her chest in triumph.

"Wow, Aisha! What a story! What a brave little girl you are! Say, do you think that you could take me back there and show me the dark room?"

"I don't know."

She's thinking about it.

"Could we try?"

"I-I guess," she stammers.

"We need to get her to a hospital," Sarah whispers to Ellington.

"I know, Sarah. I'll take her to Children's myself, but it'll be dark soon. This is too important to delay."

"Mama? Is that okay?"

"Whatever you want to do honey. You won't be too scared?"

"Will Mr. Billy be with me?"

"Every step of the way, precious," Ellington promises.

Aisha's mood lightens. "Okay. After I eat."

Chapter Thirty-Six

Steve's special guests finish their meals and thank their host for everything. Aisha gives him a big hug. She pulls back her head, then looks up at him and smiles.

"Thank you so much, Mr. Steve."

"You are so welcome, sweetheart," he beams.

Sarah is pleased to see Aisha isn't avoiding contact with adults who demonstrate goodness. Sarah silently prays that Aisha is vigilant and selective in the future. Aisha has shown guts and moxie well beyond her years.

Steve and Ellington walk Sarah and Aisha out the door. Steve's customers observed Aisha coming from east to west. They begin to walk east on Cedar until they come to First Street. Ellington asks Aisha whether she crossed a street; the child shakes her head 'no.'

"I'm not allowed to cross the street without Mama or Grandma," she explains.

Sarah puts her hand to her mouth and stifles a smile.

The group makes a left turn on First. When they reach the alley, Aisha stops. She recoils into her mother's arms and buries her head in Sarah's chest. Ellington orders all to stay where they are.

He calls his backup team. The correct protocol is to contact the local police department, but in this case, one or more of the locals may be the perp. Backup is minutes away.

The team, made up of mostly black Detroit cops, arrives. The men walk into the alley with guns drawn, a strange scene in Cedar Ridge. Ellington looks back to Aisha, who motions him to keep going.

About halfway down, the officers come upon a door. It's unlocked. Two officers venture inside. A few minutes later, they return with an all-clear sign. Ellington returns to Sarah and Aisha and asks if Aisha is up to going back into what appears to be an abandoned janitorial suite to confirm this is the place of her captivity.

Sarah shrugs. Looking at Aisha, she nods her head toward the door. *Are you willing to go in, sweetness?*

Part of her hopes Aisha will decline. She's afraid to expose her to additional trauma. But Aisha isn't the average six-year-old. She's scared to enter her former prison but agrees, only if her mom and Mr. Billy go with her. The officers have cleared the place. There is no immediate danger.

Ellington leads them inside. Sarah carries her daughter. They're in an old maintenance area. Aisha points to the hall and tells them this is where she made her escape. She tells Sarah to put her down. The minute her feet hit the ground, this brave little girl walks down the hallway. She ignores several empty rooms and arrives at the last door on the left.

"Here," she peeps.

"You sure? Billy probes.

"Yes."

"This is where he kept you?"

"Yes."

"Where's the potty, honey?"

She looks past him and back into the hallway. She begins to walk down the hall again. She looks into a few rooms, but they don't have a toilet. She makes a right, passes two more doors, and points to a tiny bathroom on the other side of the hall.

Billy instructs the officers to seal off the room and calls in a tech team. He's looking for DNA belonging to Aisha and anyone other than Aisha. One officer opens a case, retrieves a DNA evidence collection kit. He asks Aisha to spit into a tube.

"That's gross!" Aisha cries. "Mama says not to spit."

"It's okay, precious. This one time, it is important," Sarah assures.

"Okay, Mama." She spits into the tube and observes the saliva running down the sides. She crinkles her nose and utters, "Eeww."

Ellington instructs Sarah and Aisha to wait in the police cruiser with another officer. Sarah protests, but Ellington explains he wants to explore the building beyond these old maintenance offices. He wants to determine whether there are other means of entry and exit. Ellington feels this part of the investigation *is* too dangerous for civilians.

Sarah immediately drops her protest, and she and Aisha return to the car with a uniformed officer. Ellington and the others return to the back of the hallway and try the last door, the one directly opposite and about twenty feet away from the alley door. The door opens and the hall continues.

They follow it to its end at an old steel door. They push the door open and find themselves in a large, ornate, multilevel atrium, surrounded by retail stores on the bottom floor and professional offices on the upper floors. The building appears to be three stories high. Doctors, dentists, lawyers, accountants, architects, and one private investigator's office populate the upper floors. A florist, diner, UPS store, and tailor shop occupy the first floor.

Ellington huddles with the team. He instructs them to question and clear from wrongdoing anyone they can find. He orders them to pay special attention to the law offices and the private investigator's office. He wants to know if any of these people have any connection to the Cedar Ridge Police or the Hayes litigation. Understanding their charge and respecting their boss, the men go to work.

Ellington returns to his unmarked police cruiser for the ride home. There is no car seat, so Mr. Billy and Sarah must endure an Aisha lecture about six-year-olds being required to sit *only* in the back seat, *only* in a car seat, and *only* with appropriate safety belts tightly fastened.

Sarah assures Aisha that Mr. Billy is a great driver, the flashing lights will be on the whole time, and all other cars will be forced to get out of their way. They assure Aisha that it's just this one time. Reluctantly, Aisha consents to the trip.

With flashing lights on and siren blaring, they soon head north on I-75 toward Detroit. Aisha falls asleep, and Sarah is immediately concerned about the possibility of a head injury. *Perhaps she's more traumatized than any of us know.*

Sarah gently shakes the child awake and asks Ellington how far they are from Children's Hospital.

"Not far, Sarah. I've called and prearranged our visit as a special favor to the Detroit Police. No muss, no fuss, no waiting.

How does that sound?"

"It sounds wonderful, Billy. I appreciate it."

Aisha is not pleased about going to a *hospital*. She pouts, moans, pleads, and even cries. But none of it has any effect on Sarah. *Mama's much tougher than the big bad man in the blue suit.*

Because the visit to Children's is prearranged, they're in and out of the hospital in less than two hours. Aisha's clothes are bagged and tagged for foreign DNA testing, with a note to swab Ellington, Sarah, Steve, and others for elimination purposes. Aisha endures a thorough examination. All test results were negative except for a slight bladder infection. Fortunately, there were no signs of head trauma or physical abuse.

Finally, Aisha is released with a recommendation to visit her pediatrician's office and a referral to a child psychologist. The child is sent home in a pair of way-too-large surgical scrubs and warm hospital stockings. She loves her outfit and vows never to take it off.

When the weary travelers arrive at the Hayes home, Sarah takes a sleeping Aisha up to her room, tucks her into bed, and kisses her on the forehead. Returning to the living room, Sarah thanks Billy Ellington for Aisha's safe return. Sarah has found her *one good cop,* and Aisha's horrible Detroit to Cedar Ridge experience is now officially over.

Chapter Thirty-Seven

"What the fuck, Micah? How could you let this happen?" Zack Blake is livid.

"She received one or two hours of threatening phone calls, Zack. Complete radio silence from that time forward. The guy never called or bothered them again until the abduction, assuming we're dealing with the same guy who called.

"Whoever the caller was, he left no digital footprint and went completely off the grid. We've been tailing Sarah and her kids for almost two months without a scent of danger.

"She was at work. Her kids were in a licensed daycare center being watched by a director and three aides. There isn't much more I can say. I'd hardly call this *our* fuck-up or something *we* let happen." Love's *very* defensive.

"Yet, it happened. And it happened on your watch."

"If it makes you feel better to blame me, I'll take the heat."

Blake's silent for a few beats, thinking things over. He softens. "Nah. I'm out of line. But, this is so fucking frightening! If we agree that the Detroit cops and Sarah are correct in their thinking and Aisha didn't imagine things, then a Cedar Ridge cop is responsible for this!"

"And that should be our focus, Zack. I'm on this. The Detroit guys are developing leads and suspects as we speak. We may have foreign DNA on the kid's clothes. My people are sharing manpower and equipment with Detroit PD. We'll find this guy and break this whole thing wide open."

"I'm counting on you, Micah."

The phone rings, startling both men. Blake checks the number, cringes, and turns the screen to Love.

"Want to explain things to Sarah Hayes?"

Love looks down at his Apple Watch and heads for the door. "I just remembered. I've got an important meeting to attend to. Good luck with your client, Zack. Say hello for me."

Blake rolls his eyes. "Yeah, yeah, tough guy. Thanks for all your help," Blake grumbles.

"Always here for you, man. We'll get this guy. Better answer your phone," Love points, rushing out the door.

Blake turns back to his cellphone and slides his finger across the screen bar. He takes a deep breath.

"Zack Blake," he whispers into the receiver.

"Zack, this is Sarah Hayes."

"Sarah, so nice to hear from you. I heard about Aisha from Micah. That must've been awful, but I hear she's in pretty good shape. Is that true?"

"She seems okay, Zack. Time will tell, I guess. Thanks for asking. Aisha checked out okay at Children's Hospital, and she's about to get a psychological evaluation for post-traumatic stress. Otherwise, I think we dodged a bullet this time. Aisha's pediatrician claims this psych guy is the best in the business."

"If he's affiliated with Children's, I'm sure that's true, Sarah. If not, I know a terrific guy who treated some young clients of mine a few years back. How are you holding up?"

She called to bitch, but Blake was so quick with expressions of concern and follow up questions, she's rethinking her intent. *He is so disarming. Must be excellent in court. He probably has juries eating out of the palm of his hand.*

"I'm fine, Zack. I called to ask whether you heard anything from Micah. He's supposed to be watching out for us. What happened to our security detail?" Sarah is regaining her mojo.

"But for the initial telephone calls, there's been no contact, nothing, not even the hint of a threat, Sarah. You're at work, and the kids are in a licensed daycare facility with licensed, trained caregivers and aides. Sometimes, excuse my French, shit just happens." Blake finds himself repeating, almost word for word, Love's earlier defense.

"Well, it sure happened here. What about now?"

"Now, we don't take our eyes off you or your loved ones until we get this guy. You have my word on that, Sarah."

"I lost my husband, Zack. The thought of anything happening to my babies . . ."

"We're on it, Sarah. I promise."

"Okay then, moving on now, what's going on with the case?"

"We're about to take Chief Brooks' deposition."

"What's he going to say? He'll just deny everything, won't he?"

"I wouldn't be so sure, Sarah. We've uncovered lots of evidence to suggest otherwise."

"Zack, I just went through three days of complete hell worrying whether my daughter would ever come home again. In my own city, the cops and the media put my child's case on the back burner and prioritized the case of a white kid from the suburbs who's been missing for weeks.

"If Aisha hadn't been fortunate and more resourceful than the average kid her age, we might have had an unthinkable, terrible outcome.

My husband was gunned down before my own eyes by a white cop. I'm not naïve, Zack. We're fighting a form of institutional racism that dates back four hundred years, is embodied in our constitution, and is still alive and well here in the Detroit area."

"Sarah, I can't begin to understand what you're going through. It's hard to argue with your logic. No white person could possibly understand what it is like to be black in America, even someone like me, a descendant of Holocaust victims and survivors.

"I've been a lawyer in Detroit for a lot of years. I've seen the system up close and personal. I've seen the charging differences, the sentencing differences, blacks in white towns harassed and pulled over for the crime of simply being there and being black. But, there are pockets of resistance. There are people out there who are trying to make a difference. I believe Chief Brooks might be one of those people."

"Like Billy Ellington in Detroit and Steve at Nana's in Cedar Ridge. I don't even know his last name."

"Steve at Nana's?" Blake's confused.

"It's the restaurant Aisha walked into after she escaped from the bad guys. Mr. Steve and the people in that restaurant were incredible. We were the only black people in the place—in the middle of one of the biggest nightmares ever, those people were very uplifting."

"See? There's still hope for the world."

Sarah imagines Blake in his office, standing at his desk with that cocky demeanor and those blue eyes . . .

"You are something, Zachary Blake. You must really charm those jurors, especially the ladies."

"You're not the first to notice my considerable charm."

"And your astounding humility?"

"That too. I am very humble."

Sarah laughs and then immediately becomes serious again. "I need you to be Marcus's champion, Zack. I must have justice. I need his death to count for something, to be an agent for change. Otherwise, he lived and died for nothing. I'm counting on you."

"I won't let you down, Sarah. And Marcus didn't live or die for nothing. His life had an impact, especially on you and your children. He'll live on in those beautiful kids. As for the case, it's having an impact on the City of Cedar Ridge and the Cedar Ridge PD. You'll see. I promise."

"Make sure you give Micah some shit before you tell him that I forgive him. Don't let him off too easy."

"I love giving Micah shit. I will lay some tremendous guilt on that guy. You have nothing to worry about on that score."

"But plenty to worry about."

"What do you have to worry about, Sarah? We are on this case. Aisha is home safe. You've got two great kids and a terrific new job. And I'm extremely confident you are about to change the culture of Cedar Ridge. Chin up, kid."

"There you go again, with that charm stuff. I'll bet your eyes sparkle in the sunlight. You were quite the ladies' man in your day, weren't you? Your wife better watch out and protect her turf, Zack."

"She has me completely tamed. I can assure you of that."

"Well, she's a lucky woman."

"No, I'm the lucky one."

"So, when is this chief's deposition?"

"Day after tomorrow."

"Get him, Zack."

"I will, Sarah."

"I'll let you get back to it then."

"Thanks, Sarah. Give those beautiful kids a kiss from their Uncle Zack."

"I will."

Chapter Thirty-Eight

"All evidence points to the fact that a Cedar Ridge cop kidnapped this six-year-old little girl to pressure my client into dropping this lawsuit. Am I missing something? What are you guys doing to find this guy? When will the Cedar Ridge Police start *enforcing* rather than *breaking* the law?"

The attorneys are at Chief Warren Brooks' deposition in Steve Adler's lavish suite of offices at the top of Renaissance Center. Blake stares down Adler before the deposition. Adler's defensive. Chief Brooks remains silent.

"We have the composite drawing, Zack. We have people running photos of every cop on the force. Was this one of ours? Who knows? The guy could be a *security* guard, for all we know. Shit, man, a 'guy in a blue suit' could be a maintenance guy," Adler argues.

"He's a *cop*. You guys know it. I know it, and Sarah Hayes knows it. Don't play innocent with me and do *not*, under any circumstances, take your foot off the gas. It's full speed ahead. *Find* this guy."

"We are looking at leads from all sources," Chief Brooks advises.

"I certainly hope that's true, Chief. My client is very upset."

"Feeling guilty, I suppose," Adler smirks.

"Guilty? For what, may I ask?" Blake's incredulous.

"This lawsuit created the whole mess."

"No, Steve, an asshole cop who broke laws he swore to enforce created this whole mess. Are you serious with this shit?"

"You can't deny that the kidnapping doesn't happen without the lawsuit, Zack."

"Answer this question, Steve. How many lawsuits have you defended in your career?"

"Thousands."

"And how many resulted in the abduction of the plaintiff's child?"

Adler sighs and rolls his eyes. "Only this one, Zack," he concedes.

"And whatever you may think of the city's behavior, you can't honestly say you didn't expect a lawsuit over the Hayes shooting, can you?"

"No, I can't—not in this litigious society that we live in today," Adler huffs.

"Give me a break, Steve. This so-called 'litigious society' is a myth. With lawyers handling cases on a contingency basis, laying out millions of dollars and not getting paid unless they're successful, how does that square with what you're saying?"

"You don't think that the country is lawsuit happy? How about all of these lawyer ads on TV and all the billboards we see all over town?"

"I'm not a fan, but that's not the point."

"What's the point?"

"That people, corporations, and *government agencies* keep fucking up and should be held accountable for their actions. Insurance companies love to take premiums and then smear plaintiffs or trial lawyers in a concerted effort to avoid paying out benefits. Corporate America and the US Chamber of Commerce scream 'junk lawsuits' every chance they get. They want damages caps and will *buy* legislators to get them. What 'junk lawsuit' needs a damages cap? It's a farce.

"Big business isn't after 'junk' cases. They want to minimize the impact of *serious* cases. It's all about the corporate bottom line. Lawsuits and lawyers make wrongdoers pay what they should have paid in the first place.

"Citizens shouldn't need lawyers and lawsuits for fair compensation, but they can't count on *your* clients to do the right thing. How safe would we be if we allowed corporations to do whatever they wanted without accountability?

"Lawsuits hold these bastards accountable and make the world safer. Of course, you disagree; everyone you represent is innocent. Is that what you're suggesting?"

"Of course not."

"Then, let's simply agree to disagree, shall we?" Blake shakes his head in disgust. He turns to Brooks.

"Ready for your deposition, Chief?"

"Ready, Mr. Blake. Fascinating discussion," he chuckles.

Blake turns to the court reporter. She is set up across from Brooks.

"Ready, Judy?" Judy is Blake's other favorite reporter. Comfort and trust are essential in the legal business.

"All set."

"Let's proceed. On the record."

Instantly, the men are in combat mode. Blake begins with Brooks' background, his education, and work experience. He's had a stellar career and has an impressive resume. The man could qualify as an expert in police procedures and conduct on any other case.

After prodding through the preliminaries, discussing career milestones, promotions, and Brooks' extensive resume, Blake moves to the issues central to the case. Is there systemic racism in the Cedar Ridge Police Department? Are Cedar Ridge cops trigger-happy when it comes to black residents and visitors? Is there a police brutality issue?

"Chief Brooks, are you a member of the International Association of Chiefs of Police?"

"Yes."

"When did you become a member?"

"When I was promoted to Chief more than twenty years ago."

"As Chief of Police in Cedar Ridge, are you familiar with the new consensus use-of-force policy that's been adopted through the IACP and eleven other similar organizations?"

"Broadly. When we adopt policies or revise them, that is one of the resources we use. I know they frequently update these policies. In fact, I believe they issued a new policy or a policy upgrade after the incident in Ferguson. Is that what you're referring to?"

"So, you *are* familiar with the IACP model policies?"

"Yes. As part of our IACP membership, we are provided access to those."

"Do you review these policies regularly?"

"I wouldn't say that, but I get all of their e-mails. When something comes up that affects Cedar Ridge, I or one of my lieutenants study them. We also use their position papers and training keys from time to time."

"What are training keys?"

"They are concise, authoritative sources of law enforcement information contained in loose-leaf binders. They contain model practices and procedures on a variety of subjects and help us sharpen our skills or expand our knowledge in a particular area. I am reasonably certain each key is prepared by a leading expert on the particular subject a chief or a lieutenant might be interested in."

"And position papers?"

"Those are official positions that the ICAP takes on particular topics. We certainly take notice of their positions. They are usually consistent with our situational concerns."

"Can you provide an example?"

"Sure. The ICAP has a position paper on firearm violence that I think is of vital importance. Police chiefs all over the country are concerned with firearms violence and particularly interested in ways to prevent it. The assault weapons ban in 1994 was particularly effective in reducing gang violence, for instance, because assault weapons are the weapons of choice for gangs.

"For the ten years the ban was in effect, violent crime committed by assault rifles dropped sixty-six percent. There are position papers on all kinds of things, from body armor to concealed weapons laws. These are common-sense law enforcement recommendations."

"Are there policies on the appropriate use of force?"

"Yes, absolutely. In 2016, the ICAP put out a definitive guide for law enforcement leaders regarding officer-involved shootings. These included incident scene actions and procedures, criminal and administrative investigation procedures, working with the media, and mental health and wellness considerations for both citizens and officers."

"Does Cedar Ridge follow these policies and recommendations?"

"Yes. But there are limits. Not every city or situation is the same. That is the problem with uniform policies. For the most part, these are common-sense recommendations and policies. We implement and follow them as best we can."

"Do you always succeed?"

"Not all the time. Almost all the time, though."

"Is the Hayes case an example of one where set policies were not followed?"

Adler interrupts. "Objection! Calls for a conclusion and for facts not in evidence."

"I'll take the answer. This man is in charge of setting protocol for Cedar Ridge police officers to follow in traffic stops like the one that is the subject of this litigation. These policies and protocols are at the heart of this lawsuit. This is discovery, and this witness is clearly an expert in this field," Blake trains his eyes on Brooks, brushing Adler's objection off like an annoying fly.

Adler gestures to Brooks to answer.

"Obviously, yes. Many of the measures we have implemented to reduce these incidents were in play here, body cams and microphones, dash cam video, and vehicle stop and approach training, to name a few, but, despite all of these preparations, this tragedy still occurred. We must do a better job, especially in the mental health area. Our policies on race and racial profiling are under review following this incident."

Adler squirms. Zack is surprised at Brooks' candor. This helps the case. He presses on. "How do you mean, Chief Brooks?"

"Well, from a mental health and racial sensitivity standpoint, we failed both Mr. Hayes and Officer Jones. Apparently, we failed to see the warning signs regarding Officer Jones's treatment of people of color. His suicide would suggest that other mental health issues could have and should have been addressed. Still, an officer-involved shooting is an infrequent occurrence."

"Do you believe the Hayes shooting was justified?"

"Objection!" Adler screeches. "Calls for a legal conclusion."

"He's the Chief of Police. He's an expert. His previous testimony about his experience and credentials *qualifies* him as an expert. I'll take the answer."

"To be determined," Brooks hedges.

"It's been almost a year. It is still undetermined?"

"Yes."

"What, if anything, would you have done differently?"

"Well, we followed most of the training protocols pre-incident, yet the shooting still happened. So we need to review those protocols. A systemic breakdown failed Mr. Hayes and his family. Post-incident, we have handled the situation reasonably well, except, of course, when it comes to Officer Jones's mental health. We failed him and his family."

"Were there any warning signs, workers' compensation, disability filings, or the like that would have alerted you that Officer Jones had some type of mental health issues?"

"No."

"There was another incident involving Jones and a black motorist, was there not?"

"Yes, but it was a somewhat different set of circumstances. Jones was issued a warning and sent to sensitivity training, which he passed with flying colors. We thought we had it under control. Obviously, we were wrong, but not negligent."

Adler likes that answer much better, and Blake takes it in stride. The deposition is a clear net positive so far. Blake knows the previous incident is similar to the Hayes incident, but he wants and expects Chief Brooks to continue to cooperate. *Don't get in his face about the prior act. It's a distinction without a difference. If the chief continues to testify this way, I can use his testimony to obtain a terrific result in this case without having to go to trial.*

"Did Jones pass all fitness-for-duty examinations?"

"Yes, he did."

"No signs of post-traumatic stress or anxiety disorder at any time?"

"Before or after the Hayes matter?"

"Before."

"No."

"Whose decision was it for Jones to be on patrol?"

"Mine and his captain's."

"Did he have a psych exam before he was released to patrol the streets of Cedar Ridge with a gun?"

"Yes."

Blake turns to Adler. "Steve, do you have those records?"

"Records will be produced pursuant to the discovery order."

Again, Blake brushes him off. "Did you see the report of Officer Jones's psychiatric exam, Chief Brooks?"

"I'm sure I did, but I don't remember."

"But a doctor would have to clear him for active duty, right?"

"Right."

"Chief, did you review the body and dash cam videos of this incident?"

"I did."

"Were Officer Jones's actions consistent with departmental protocols?"

"I would have to say they were not."

"Where do you think he went wrong?"

"Objection! Overbroad. The question calls for a legal conclusion. This man is not a lawyer." Adler is testy.

"I'll take the answer," Blake blusters. "For the record, I am not asking him for his *legal* opinion. I am asking him for his opinion as an *expert in police procedures*. This is a man who literally wrote the book on Cedar Ridge's police policies and procedures. Chief Brooks, will you please answer the question?"

Brooks sighs. *It's going to be a long morning.* "The stop seems to have been unwarranted. The driver did nothing wrong to justify a stop. Officer Jones's belief the driver and passenger resembled the Burger King suspects might be reasonable. But once he approaches the vehicle and sees two adults and two young children, this belief should have been suspended.

"The stop and aftermath seem racially motivated. The officer's inconsistent commands, failure to await backup assistance, which he knew was on the way, in addition to his unreasonable escalation of tensions during the exchange, were all contributing factors as was the officer's failure to follow high-risk stop protocol. Apparently, encountering a black man who admitted to legally possessing a weapon was a circumstance that caused Officer Jones to act irrationally."

"This incident was heavily investigated, was it not?"

"It was."

"By Internal Affairs?"

"Among others."

"Were reports generated?"

"Yes."

"Objection," Adler cries.

"These reports would be work product."

"No, they wouldn't Steve," Blake argues. "That's absurd. If you don't produce them, we'll let the judge decide. Chief, have you seen these reports?"

"I don't know if I've seen them all. I've certainly seen some of them."

"Do they come to conclusions similar to those you've espoused today?"

"Objection, don't answer that," orders Adler. We *will* let the judge decide, Zack."

"And you and your clients will pay the costs and sanctions for forcing me to go to the judge, Steve."

The deposition drones on. Blake establishes that pulling a weapon out is categorized as a use-of-force activity, that Hayes's statement to Jones that he was carrying doesn't necessarily justify use-of-force activity, and that Jones's action of pulling out his weapon placed the officer and all of the vehicle's occupants in harm's way.

Brooks testifies that officers have a responsibility under appropriate policies and procedures, to render aid to victims and that Jones did not do so in the case. In fact, this responsibility didn't even *occur* to Jones. An ambulance wasn't called for until Officer Mickler arrived at the scene several minutes later. Marcus Hayes was already dead at that point.

Blake scrolls through the ICAP manual of policies and procedures and methodically has Chief Brooks admit to multiple violations of its policies and procedures. And Blake has one final trick up his sleeve.

"Chief Brooks, are you familiar with the Aisha Hayes child abduction case in Detroit?"

"Yes, I've heard about it."

"You are aware the principal suspect is a Cedar Ridge police officer?"

"I understand the Detroit Police are pursuing that possibility, yes."

"Have you seen the composite drawing of the suspect?"

"I have."

"Do you recognize the guy/ Does he resemble any Cedar Ridge cop you know?"

"We are scanning our roster. We should have an answer to that very soon."

"And if it turns out to be a Cedar Ridge cop?"

"He will be punished to the full extent of the law."

"Child abduction violates police protocol, doesn't it?"

"Objection!"

"Withdrawn."

When the deposition is finally over, Blake is feeling positive about the prospects of a significant resolution without a trial. Adler needs a stiff drink and a deep-tissue massage.

Chapter Thirty-Nine

"Our investigation reveals a pattern of institutional racism in the Cedar Ridge Police Department. The CRPD engaged in a pattern of stopping, searching, and arresting people of color without reasonable suspicion and without probable cause. Marcus Hayes is the worst example of this pattern. Officer Jones didn't merely pull him over for no reason, he also *killed* him for no reason."

Court-ordered mediation of *Hayes v Cedar Ridge, et al.,* has begun. Judge Berg appoints veteran trial lawyer Barry Frazier as the neutral mediator, charged with leaning on both sides to negotiate a fair settlement, resolve the case, and avoid a contentious and expensive trial. Both sides provide summaries that contain their versions of the facts and interpretations of the laws that apply to the case.

Exhibits include all video and audio recordings made contemporaneously to the shooting, various post-incident reports and findings, as well as deposition transcripts of key witnesses both to liability and damages. Blake also presents Frazier with a video featuring the life and times of Marcus Hayes and his family, produced and directed by Micah Love. Producing and editing trial-worthy day-in-the-life films are two of Love's many talents.

As a veteran attorney who has tried numerous personal injury and wrongful death cases, Frazier is not prone to react to an emotional appeal built around institutional racism. His role does not require him to choose one side or the other. He has no skin in the game. The emotional video and other mounting evidence of wrongdoing aren't presented for Frazier's benefit. Blake isn't arguing this pattern of racist behavior in the Cedar Ridge Police Department for Frazier. He's offering all of this evidence as a prelude to trial. The presentation is made exclusively for Steven Adler and his clients.

Blake senses the city is deeply afraid to try this case. City officials seem convinced a jury will hammer them, not only in the dollar size of their verdict but in the court of public opinion as well.

Blake hopes to capitalize on the city's fear of trial and strategizes that *fear* will motivate a substantial increase in offers made at mediation. Blake wishes to spare Sarah and her daughters the media circus of a high profile trial in *Hayes v. Cedar Ridge, et al.*, but he also wants full jury-trial type damages for their grievous loss.

While Blake's arguments have little effect on Frazier, they are scaring the hell out of Mayor Mendoza. This is, of course, the whole point of the strategy. Mendoza's attendance is compelled by court order, as is the appearance of Sarah Hayes. Parties with settlement authority are required to attend mediation, so meaningful settlement negotiations can take place.

Mendoza has no ultimate settlement authority. He will only *recommend* settlement and settlement amounts to the Cedar Ridge City Council. But he does have a vote and, as city mayor and the man who attends mediation sessions, his vote and recommendation will carry significant weight. On the plaintiff side, obviously, with Blake's advice and counsel, Sarah is the ultimate decision-maker.

Private mediation is a far less formal process than a trial. The questioning is not mandatory; no oath is required. Both sides' attorneys know Frazier well, believe him to be fair and impartial, and recognize his tremendous record of settling cases at mediation. His success rate is greater than ninety percent. Therefore, both parties stipulate to give him broad powers to conduct the mediation proceedings. Frazier has wide latitude in questioning parties and witnesses without placing them under oath.

Frazier is astutely offering the defendants a glimpse of the serious effect of Sarah's testimony under oath and how bad that testimony will be for the City of Cedar Ridge. Blake has mediated several cases with Frazier and is familiar with this strategy. There is nothing to lose and everything to gain.

Mayor Mendoza and Steven Adler can hardly object. How can you settle a wrongful death and survivor case without hearing from the widow or other loved ones? Sarah's deposition has not yet been taken, so this is the defense's first opportunity to hear from her, albeit informally. Frazier asks her to tell the truth, the whole truth and nothing but the truth. She agrees.

Frazier skillfully takes her through her courtship with her beloved Marcus. They met at Wayne State University at the student union. According to Sarah, Marcus was hooked from the moment he saw her. He wasn't shy. He walked right up to her and introduced himself. For him, it was love at first sight. She was no pushover, but he was nice-looking, funny, and very chivalrous, which she liked. He was a force to be reckoned with. In time, he won her over and they fell in love. They dated through college and married shortly after graduation.

Sarah was a history major. She graduated and got a job at the Henry Ford Museum and Greenfield Village in Dearborn. She loved the work, the people, and the acting she got to do as a Greenfield Village tour guide. She was one of only a handful of black tour guides. Marcus was extremely proud of her.

Marcus was a computer science major and got a job at Comp USA marketing computers and computer technology. When Comp USA went out of business in Detroit, Marcus got a job as a manager at Best Buy and worked his way up the ladder to district manager, responsible for four stores in a geographical area. He was earning $75,000 at the time of his death.

Frazier and the two attorneys agree that calculations for present value of future earnings, including expected salary increases, will have to be made, assuming the parties can agree on liability. The parties stipulate to the mortality tables as an appropriate means to determine Marcus's life expectancy had he not been killed. When his wages, future wages, and promotions are combined with the mortality tables and a life expectancy calculation, a present value number for lost wage and earning capacity starts to take shape.

The funeral home, cemetery service, and burial expenses are stipulated to, and the bills are provided to Frazier. These types of damages, the easy-to-calculate ones, are the relatively easy part of settlement negotiations. More difficult calculations are necessary for survivorship loss and loss of society and companionship for Sarah and her daughters. These are the intangibles that increase the value of wrongful death cases, much like a calculation for pain and suffering increases the value of personal injury cases. These so-called "soft" damages are not easy to measure. Love, comfort, guidance, and loss of companionship are difficult to quantify in monetary terms.

Defense attorneys often try to take advantage of marital or childrearing issues in wrongful death cases. In this case, however, there are no marital problems and no domestic issues of any kind. Marcus was a terrific husband and father. Sarah and her kids loved their husband and father. The evidence is clear, and a large number will have to be proffered if the city truly wishes to settle the case.

The next consideration is whether Marcus lived for a sufficient length of time to experience conscious pain and suffering. If so, Sarah and the kids are entitled to compensation. According to Sarah, a brutally honest woman, Marcus died almost instantaneously. In fact, one of the most painful aspects of the case, and a factor that adds value, is that Sarah and her daughters actually witnessed and experienced the terrible shock of the shooting and death of their husband and father.

They had no opportunity to say goodbye to their loved one. In this case, Marcus's relatively young age and the length of time that his family must live without him is a significant driver of monetary damages in the case.

Sarah tells Frazier their household was a true division of labor. They cooked and cleaned together and interchangeably. Marcus cut the lawn and did minor repairs and maintenance around the house. There is no attempt to exaggerate or manufacture household service damages, which both Frazier and Adler appreciate. It is tough to dislike either Sarah or Marcus Hayes. This is a difficult pill to swallow for Steven Adler and Mayor Mendoza.

Finally, the parties return to issues of liability. Adler argues this is an isolated incident, that Cedar Ridge has an excellent record of community service and involvement. There have been very few incidents of citizens suing cops. Furthermore, those incidents were very minor and involved no issues of racial bias.

Blake argues Jones was predisposed to pull over and harass people of color. Chief Brooks and Officer Mickler have testified to at least one notable previous incident involving Jones and a black citizen or visitor.

Cedar Ridge had numerous opportunities to re-train or counsel Jones, but officials looked the other way. Blake makes the persuasive case that Jones's behavior in the Hayes shooting was so egregious, it amounts to gross negligence. A jury could easily award punitive damages as punishment in addition to a compensatory damages award.

"Trust me, Barry," Blake confides during a private session with Frazier. "These guys want no part of a jury and, if they suggest otherwise, please warn them I will kick ass at trial. A jury will *punish* them. You know it's true."

The parties begin to discuss money. Blake formally demands a mid-eight-figure award. He's willing to discuss a structured settlement with a lower present value number but insists the aggregate funds must result in mid-eight-figures.

Adler again argues the case was an anomaly for the Cedar Ridge Police and that Blake's numbers are way too high. The city's offer is $1.5 million. This is a substantial number. However, as Blake points out, the offer doesn't even cover the wage loss and household services portions of the settlement.

Barry Frazier does not discuss numbers with the attorneys in the same room. His policy for these mediation sessions is to place each party in a separate room and conduct back and forth negotiations. This way, when his opinion is sought, he can readily offer it, without giving anyone's negotiating strategy away.

If Frazier has opinions about which numbers are more or less fair, neither party is made aware of it. Frazier points out case strengths or weaknesses for both sides. He tries to explain why plaintiffs should think about reduced expectations, and defendants should think about raising more capital to avoid potential embarrassment at trial.

Frazier does, in fact, have strong opinions about this case, but he refuses to share them. If a number is reached that satisfies both parties, his feelings and opinions are irrelevant. His job here is to facilitate a settlement, not substitute his judgment for the judgment of the parties and their attorneys.

Back and forth they go, with respective numbers inching closer and closer to each other. They're at the end of the second day of two full-day sessions. A structured settlement provider is contacted, and discussions intensify.

Since structures involve tomorrow's dollars, the numbers appear higher to Sarah, even though they are somewhat closer to numbers that Cedar Ridge might consider. A structured settlement also offers security against a plaintiff's carelessness. Paying Sarah large lump sums at strategic times in the future, as her kids reach college age, for instance, is helpful to her and her daughters and saves substantial settlement dollars for the defendants. Structuring a settlement is, indeed, a win-win strategy for the parties.

The second mediation session goes into the evening hours. The City of Cedar Ridge graciously pays for dinner as the parties negotiate into the night. At eight o'clock, Barry asks the parties if they might prefer to continue the mediation the following day. The numbers are closer, he reports, but there is no resolution in sight.

"Jesus Christ, Barry. What is it going to take?" Adler demands.

"More," Frazier advises.

"How much more?"

"According to my reading of the situation, a lot more."

"Would you please ask Zack what his absolute bottom-line number is so we can get him some structured settlement numbers consistent with his wishes?"

"Are you suggesting if he provides this acceptable bottom-line number, your client is willing to pay the number?"

"In so many words, yes. Unless the figure is bat shit crazy. If it's fair, we'll settle. And it must be a structure."

"Does Mayor Mendoza approve?"

"The mayor ordered me to make the overture."

"Has he spoken to City Council?"

"Yes."

"And Council is on board to approve a settlement?"

"That is my understanding."

"To confirm, if on Zack's honor, he provides this bottom-line number, I can provide him and his client assurance this number will settle the case?"

"Yes, Barry, yes," Adler concedes. He knows he can't try this case. A jury will hammer his clients. He's a beaten man, grateful his clients understand the ass-kicking Zack Blake will administer in front of a jury and in the court of public opinion.

Frazier returns to Blake to share this news.

"Let me get this straight, Barry. I have a serious, come to Jesus conversation with Sarah. We determine the least amount of money that would fully and fairly settle the case and the defense pays it? No questions asked? On *my* honor?" *Incredible!*

"So long as the money is paid as a structured settlement annuity and the demand is not bat shit crazy. Those were Adler's exact words, Zack. You should be very flattered that your integrity is held in such high esteem by the defense."

"I am, Barry. I really am, especially coming from Steve Adler. But this puts a lot of pressure on me. I didn't see this coming."

"Accept the challenge and meet it responsibly and ethically."

Blake leans forward, elbows on the conference table, hands on his chin, and deep in thought.

"Okay, Barry," he finally concedes. "I'll talk to Sarah. I'd like to mull this over, meet with her afterward, and return tomorrow. Good?"

"That's fine with me, Zack. I'm sure it will be fine with Adler. We're all exhausted. I'll confirm."

Frazier leaves the room and returns shortly, flashing two thumbs up. All parties reunite in a larger conference room, shake hands and bid each other goodnight.

Blake walks out into the night with Sarah.

"I can't believe what is happening, Zack. In my whole life, I never expected to see money like this. My husband is gone. No money will bring him back, but I can no longer argue city officials are not taking this case seriously."

"Not at these numbers. We cannot say that."

"Should we take their offer?"

"The case is worth more, and I know they're willing to pay more. I have an ethical responsibility to do what is fair."

"How much will you recommend?"

Blake whispers the number to Sarah.

"Seriously?" She gasps.

"Seriously, Sarah. Don't forget this case will be settled with a structured settlement annuity. You and the girls will be paid over many years, not all at once, so the actual number is much smaller than it appears. The present value of the total structure is way smaller than the total amount you will receive over the next twenty-five to thirty years."

"That's a long time, Zack."

"I know, Sarah, but it's a sensible approach. It gets you to important milestones in your lives. We're talking about college for the kids, emergencies, weddings, and even retirement. There will also be a medical trust to assure your family's medical needs are secure. It provides funding for life's important life events. And, I have a surprise for you."

"What's that, Zack?"

Sarah's tired and perplexed.

Blake pulls out an architectural drawing.

"I'm donating a part of my fee and demanding additional settlement proceeds to build this," Blake announces. He hands her the drawing. It's an architectural drawing of the Marcus Hayes Center for Police Officer Training in the Appropriate Use of Deadly Force. "So, Sarah, please tell me. Where would you like to locate this beautiful building?"

"Oh, my dear God, Zack. Are you serious?" Sarah cries. "This is absolutely amazing! I am completely overwhelmed. But I can't accept such a gift. You've earned your fee."

"Sarah, perhaps you didn't hear me. The defendants will pay for most of the land purchase and construction. Besides, thank you very much, but you can't tell me what I can or cannot do with my own money. I will be well paid. I've done quite well as a trial lawyer. I'm *very successful*, don't you know? These kinds of gestures are important to me. They're my way of paying things forward. This isn't my first rodeo. I am grateful to be in this position.

"This is *not* a gift. You have paid for it in blood and tears. How proud will Aisha and Tasia be as they grow up and see their father's name on this beautiful and important structure of teaching and learning?"

"When you put it that way . . ." She nods and wipes tears from both eyes.

"It's settled then," he interrupts her. "All I need to do now is crunch some numbers and come up with a fair resolution."

"I will leave you to it, then, Zack. From the bottom of my heart and on behalf of my kids and my late husband, thank you for all that you have done for us." Sarah leans over and gives him a peck on the cheek. She's beyond touched by his generosity and courage.

"You're welcome, Sarah," Zack blushes. "It has been my absolute honor to represent you and your beautiful children. I'll see you tomorrow."

"Zack Blake. Man, this is something."

"Stop it, Sarah. You'll inflate my ego."

"Is that possible?"

They both laugh and begin to walk separate ways. Sarah turns back to him. "Bye, Zack. Thanks again."

"You're welcome, Sarah. Now go home, kiss those precious babies, and get some sleep."

Chapter Forty

While the litigants inch closer to a resolution in the civil case, Detective Billy Ellington combs through photographs of Cedar Ridge police officers. Chief Warren Brooks has turned the photos over to the Detroit Police Department "in the spirit of cooperation between brothers in blue." Brooks is dubious, but Ellington firmly believes a Cedar Ridge cop is Aisha's abductor.

For Ellington, the idea that the perpetrator is a cop impersonator doesn't ring true. He's convinced the motive behind the abduction is to pressure Sarah into dropping the lawsuit. While any Cedar Ridge official may have had a motive, only cops wear the blue suits Aisha described.

One by one, Ellington selects a photo and compares it to a copy of Aisha's composite drawing. Halfway through the array, he stops and stares at a face uniquely similar to Aisha's composite. He dials Sarah Hayes.

"Hello?"

"Sarah?"

"Speaking."

"Billy Ellington here."

"Hi, Billy. What's up?"

"Sarah, is Aisha awake?"

"No. She's sleeping. Why?" Sarah's curious.

"I may have found a match to Aisha's drawing. When can I swing by?"

So much good news in one day, things are finally going our way. "That's wonderful, Billy. I don't like living with all of this protection. I won't get a good night's sleep until this guy is caught. I don't want to wake her, though. She's had a rough go. Can we do this first thing in the morning? I have to be downtown to finish our mediation. We can do it before or after."

"What time is mediation?"

"Around ten."

"How's it going?"

"Zack thinks we might settle the case as early as tomorrow."

"That's wonderful, Sarah! I'm so happy for you!"

"Thanks, Billy. I appreciate it."

"How about I swing by around 8:30?"

"It's a date."

"When this is over, I'd like to talk to you about that."

"About what?"

"Perhaps the two of us getting a cup of coffee? Getting to know one another better? You and me, a date, maybe?"

Sarah hesitates. "I don't know, Billy. I'm not sure I'm ready for anything like that."

"Anything like *what*; a cup of coffee with a friend? We already had a date, anyway. This would be our second."

"Huh?"

"We had dinner. Remember Nana's?"

"It was a *great* date, actually," she recalls. "And Aisha does like 'Mr. Billy.' She told me so." She smiles at the memory.

"Mr. Billy likes her too. See—it's meant to be. You wouldn't argue with Aisha, now, would you?"

"Well, when you put it like that . . ."

"Look, Sarah. I think you're a nice person. When this is over, I'd like to get to know you and your children. What's wrong with that? Besides, I'm just asking for lunch or coffee. But, I'm getting ahead of myself. Let's get the case wrapped first. Tomorrow at 8:30? Should I bring coffee?"

"Coffee would be great, Billy, cream and sugar, please. And, Billy?"

"Yes, Sarah?"

"Thank you. See you tomorrow."

"Tomorrow. Bye, Sarah."

"Bye, Billy."

***

At 8:30 a.m. sharp, Sarah Hayes opens her front door to greet Detective Billy Ellington. Ellington comes bearing gifts from the local Tim Horton's, an extra-large coffee with cream and sugar for Sarah and a box of Timbits for Aisha and Tasia.

"Say hello and thank you to Detective Ellington, girls."

Tasia and Aisha squeal with delight as they rip open the cardboard fastener at the top, revealing an assortment of glazed, chocolate, and powdered donut holes. They pop donut holes in their mouths as they say thank you to Mr. Billy. 'Thank you" comes out "fufu," and Ellington laughs at the sight and sound. Sarah waits for the kids to swallow the tasty treats. The girls pout when she takes the box away.

"Mr. Billy couldn't hear you. You were talking with your mouths full."

"Thank you . . ." Aisha and Tasia begin.

"Detective Ellington," Sarah interrupts.

"Mr. Billy," Ellington corrects and winks at Aisha.

"Thank you, Mr. Billy," both girls reply.

"Off you go," Sarah commands, smiling. "I need to talk to Mr. Billy."

"Can we take the donut holes?" Aisha pleads.

"I don't know, *can* you?" Sarah prompts.

"May we?" Aisha corrects herself. "Can we-may we" is a regular exercise in the Hayes home.

"No, but you may each take two more. Understood?"

"Yes, Mama." The girls sift through the box, grab donuts, and run to the playroom.

"They are something, Sarah," Ellington praises.

"Thanks, Billy. They are a *handful*," Sarah sighs. She takes a swig of her coffee. "This is *good*. Thanks for stopping by. Do you have the drawing?"

"I've got it right here, Sarah."

Ellington is holding a manila folder. He opens it and removes a photograph along with Aisha's composite drawing. He hands both to Sarah.

"They sure do look alike," Sarah agrees, studying the two images. "What do *you* think, Billy?"

"I think we have our suspect, but there's only one way to find out."

"Aisha's been through so much. I don't want to traumatize her any further."

"We can wait, Sarah. But, the longer we wait, the more distant the events and Aisha's memory will become."

"Who is this guy?"

"A Cedar Ridge cop named Gil Dunham. He was Randy Jones's mentor and training officer."

"The cops are the criminals; the criminals are the cops. What is this world coming to?"

"It isn't fair to paint all cops with the same broad brush, Sarah."

"I know, Billy. But it's difficult. You're an exception." Sarah brightened.

"You make things much easier for the girls and me. The kids really like you."

"Thanks. So, what do you want to do? If you want my opinion, I think Aisha should get this over with, ID the guy, and begin the healing process."

"We'll let her decide."

"Okay by me."

"Aisha! May I see you a minute, baby?" She called, loud enough for Aisha to hear her from the playroom. She and her sister come running. They have powdered sugar all over their faces.

"Yes, Mama?"

"Aisha, do you remember when you sat down with the artist who drew a picture of the bad man who took you from KidCare?"

"Yes, Mama."

"This picture, Aisha." Ellington hands Aisha the picture.

"I remember, Mr. Billy," Aisha whispers.

"Would you mind looking at some other pictures and telling me whether you see the man who took you from KidCare?" Billy cajoles.

"Do I have to, Mama?" Aisha folds her hands together and stares at the ground.

"No, sweetheart, you don't have to," Sarah soothes. "But it will help Mr. Billy catch the bad man so he won't be able to do this to anyone else's child."

Aisha looks into her mother's eyes. "I don't want him to take anyone else's child, Mama. But he's a mean man. Will he be mad at me?"

"He'll never know you looked at the pictures, Aisha," Ellington promises.

Aisha grimaces. "Okay, I'll look at the pictures, Mr. Billy."

She hesitates and looks away as if she would rather be anywhere else doing anything else at that moment.

Ellington pulls three pictures from the manila folder. "Ready?" He coos.

"Ready," she mutters.

Billy hands her the photographs. Aisha gasps in anguish. She views the three pictures and immediately points to one.

"*This* one," she cries, staring at the chosen photo. "*This* is the mean man who took me."

She picks up the photo, turns to Sarah, and hands it to her.

"See him, Mama? This is the bad man who took me from KidCare. He's not nice. He's mean!"

"And we are going to make sure he is punished, sweetheart. Aren't we Mr. Billy?" Sarah assures. She glances hopefully at Billy.

"Yes, we are. And we're also going to make sure he never does anything like this to anyone else, ever again," Ellington promises.

"Good. Can I have another donut?"

"May I?"

"May I?"

"Yes, honey. Take one for your sister, too."

Aisha grabs the donuts and runs off to the playroom.

It is amazing how resilient kids are! Sarah turns to Billy. "What now?"

"Now, we bring this bastard in for questioning,"

Chapter Forty-One

Gil Dunham knows it's only a matter of time. The composite drawing has been on the news. The Detroit Police have photos of the entire Cedar Ridge police force.

I'm surprised it's taken this long or that no one ratted me out. I wouldn't hurt a kid. I just wanted to scare her mother into dropping the case. Randy Jones was a good man. He deserves to rest in peace without having his name dragged through the mud all over TV and the internet. Still, the abduction idea was dumb. My failure to lock the door on little Aisha was even dumber. Dumb and dumber, that's me.

Gil thinks of the movie and wonders which of those two idiots would have made the decisions he made. *Probably both.*

On the other hand, who could have predicted that a six-year-old little girl would have the temerity to try the door, walk out and proceed down a long hallway and out of the building?

I'm in deep shit. I've got to get the hell out of here. Canada is best for now. Quick and easy border crossing before I'm a person of interest. Lay low in Windsor or Sarnia until things blow over. Need to plan my next move . . .

Gil packs a large duffle bag, checks and packs his gun and holster, and heads toward the front door. A knock on the front door startles him. *Too fucking late!*

Gil ducks down and belly crawls to a window at the side of the door. An unmarked police car sits in the driveway, and a Cedar Ridge squad car is parked out front.

Officer Alex Mickler and a man Gil recognizes from the news as a Detroit police detective are perched on his front porch.

Gil belly crawls back to the duffle bag and pulls out his standard-issue Sig Sauer. He lies on the floor, caressing the fully loaded weapon. *Come and get me, coppers!* Gil recalls James Cagney in those old gangster movies. *Top o' the world, Mom!*

The two cops are banging on the door. This time the black cop yells through the mail slot. "Gil Dunham, if you're in there, we don't want any trouble. We just want to talk to you. Open the door."

"Come on, Gil. No one has to get hurt. Open the door, please," cries Alex Mickler.

Sure, Alex, no one has to get hurt. But two people are dead, including my friend Randy, a good kid and a good cop. Gil stays on the floor, hidden from sight behind the living room sofa. He hears a scuffle and some conversation but can't make out the voices or exchange of words. He peers over the sofa and out the side window. Mickler and the black guy are about to look into the window. He ducks behind the couch again and hears a slight bang on his garage door.

Checking to see if the car is there. Suddenly, there's a loud bang on the front door, harder and louder than the first go around.

"Dunham. Your car's in the garage," the black cop yells. "We know you're in there. We can do this the easy way or the hard way. It's up to you. Open the damn door. You're a police officer. How about you start acting like one?"

Gil stays put.

"Come on, Gil. Please. We just want to talk," Mickler urges.

"Have it your way, Dunham," the black cop yells. "We'll be back with an arrest warrant. Cops will be posted here until we come back."

Gil hears Mickler radio headquarters. Mickler requests a couple of cars to stand guard at the home. A short time later, Gil glances over the couch to see two squad cars arrive and park in front. Two cops get out and begin to talk to Mickler and the black dude.

I guess these guys don't like their assignments. Good for you guys. Give 'em hell! Gil's cell phone rings and vibrates, scaring the shit out of him. Recognizing the number, he lets the call go to voicemail. The phone chimes and Gil listens to the message.

"Gil? Chief Brooks. Look, man, I know you're upset about Jones. I get it. I really do. But you're a cop—you abducted a *child.* You have to answer for your actions. The lawsuit's over, settled. No public trial. Randy may rest in peace. You hear me, Gil? *Randy may now rest in peace!*

"The child's fine. No one's been hurt. Please think about your next move. Turn yourself in. Don't make the situation worse by resisting the inevitable. You're an experienced cop. You know there are only a few ways this plays out. Most of them aren't pretty. Call me back. We'll arrange a peaceful and private surrender. Please, Gil. Do the right thing."

Chapter Forty-Two

"Sarah, the offer is in the form of a structured settlement. It has a present value well into the eight-figure range. The rules require that present value not be disclosed, but there are companies out there that can calculate the value of a structure almost to the penny."

Barry Frazier is explaining the latest offer from the city of Cedar Ridge to Sarah Hayes.

"I have a company that evaluates these structures for me, Sarah. Do you want to know the exact figure?" Blake asks. "As far as I am concerned, the more important issue is that you and your children will be taken care of, financially, for a long time. My goal in these negotiations has been lifetime security for you and your children. This offer realizes that goal."

"I'll do whatever you say, Zack. You've never steered me wrong."

"You have the relationship backward, Sarah. You're the boss—I'm the employee. My job is to give you professional advice. Your job is to make the ultimate decision. I do whatever *you* say."

"What happens if I don't take this offer?"

"Well, Barry assures me we've reached the outer limits of what Cedar Ridge will do. In fact, Barry is shocked at these numbers. He never expected the defense to go this high, right Barry? I don't want to speak for you."

"Absolutely true, Zack. Keep going. You're doing fine," Frazier urges, with a smile.

"So Sarah, this comes down to a game of chicken. We can turn this down and proceed to trial. Cedar Ridge has shown no interest in trying this case, and City officials are very fearful of the potential media coverage. Perhaps we can leverage their fear into increased offers later in the game. We can also refuse *any* offers and go to trial, where we can do much better or much worse than what's being offered here today."

"I saw the coverage of your trial against the church, Zack. They paid a lot more money than this, didn't they?"

"Yes, but that was a settlement following a very hard-fought *jury trial*, and the case involved some terrible people who were trying to cover up their appalling misconduct. The people they hurt became my family. I married the mother and adopted the abused boys. The Church was arrogant and nasty. They never made a fair offer. Trial was forced on us and was quite traumatic. It took a considerable toll on the boys. My oldest son collapsed in court and had to be hospitalized.

"We had to *beat them in court* to get them to pay. They never apologized. The jury punished them for the crime and the cover-up. That isn't the case here. Cedar Ridge has done the exact opposite. City officials have admitted bad behavior and have been very apologetic. They've worked hard to craft solutions to combat institutional racism and conducted these negotiations in a very professional manner. They've made an incredible offer to resolve this case short of trial.

"My advice is to confirm present value, accept it if you think it's fair, and begin to move on with your life. Allow the City of Cedar Ridge and your family to heal. That's my honest opinion, but it's *your* case. I'll handle it for you, whatever you decide. If we settle, I'll dot all of the 'i's and cross all of the 't's before we finalize. If we try the case, I will be a passionate advocate in the courtroom. I *love* to try cases, kick butt, and expose bad behavior in court. Ask Barry, he'll tell you."

"I will testify to that, Sarah," Barry offers.

"What do you think, Mr. Frazier?" Sarah is seeking an opinion from someone who has no skin in the game.

"My opinion isn't relevant, Sarah. It's not my role, and you're not my client. As a mediator, my job is to point out the positives and negatives of both sides of the dispute and bring people closer to a resolution. However, I agree with Zack's advice. He's worked tremendously hard for you. This is a substantial offer and one that will honor your husband's memory.

"If you're careful and invest wisely, this settlement should support you and your kids for the rest of your life. But, the ultimate decision is yours and yours alone."

"I wish Marcus were here. He'd know what to do."

"I wish Marcus were here, too, Sarah," Blake agrees.

Sarah hesitates, in deep meditation. After a lengthy pause, she decides, "Let's price the offer as Zack suggests and get this resolved. My children need me. It's time to move on."

"Are you sure, Sarah?" Frazier probes. "No one can force you to do anything."

"I'm sure. I trust Zack and he trusts you."

"We'll adjourn this mediation, then. Zack will call his structure guy, which I'm sure will only be a formality. The numbers will check out, and we'll draw up a settlement agreement. I'll retain an independent structured settlement company to put the annuity together. I'll talk to Adler and let him know where we are. I'm sure he's on board. Nice work, everyone."

Chapter Forty-Three

Billy Ellington returns to Gil Dunham's house with a warrant and a contingent of cops from Cedar Ridge and Detroit. Chief Warren Brooks leads the Cedar Ridge police contingent. The chief does not wish to preside over another cop's suicide and funeral. Brooks and Ellington knock on the door, then back off the porch and onto the lawn.

"Gil, this is Chief Brooks. We have a warrant to enter and search the premises and to take you down to headquarters for questioning. Come on, Gil! This is no way to honor Randy's memory. Please, open the door and let's do this peaceably. I have Detective Billy Ellington from Detroit PD. He's promised to let Cedar Ridge take the lead. But you have to surrender now."

Gil Dunham sits on the floor of his living room with his back resting on the front of the couch and his gun in his mouth. He's tried to pull the trigger more than once, but he keeps remembering Randy Jones's autopsy photos. He also knows how traumatic Randy's death has been to the entire Cedar Ridge Police Force. Every man or woman in blue is still deeply traumatized by Randy's suicide. *How can I do the same thing to them so soon after Jones?*

Slowly, Dunham removes the gun from his mouth, rises from the floor, and walks to the door. In his confused state of mind, he forgets the gun in his right hand, dangling at his side, as he opens the door.

He sees Billy Ellington and Chief Brooks standing off to the side, holding guns. Cops are situated all over the front lawn, weapons trained.

A bewildered Gil Dunham looks down and sees the gun in his right hand. He begins to raise his right hand in surrender.

"Gun!" Someone on the grass yells.

"No!" A frantic Billy Ellington shouts.

The cops on the lawn are firing at will. Dunham is pummeled with bullets and pitches forward, out of the door's threshold, and onto the porch. Brooks and Ellington jump forward and catch

Dunham. His face registers shock and confusion. Ellington turns to the cops on the lawn, cradling Dunham in his arms.

"What the fuck is *wrong* with you guys? He's a *cop,* dammit. Who yelled 'gun'?"

No one moves. No one utters a word.

"Fucking cowards. He wasn't a threat. Did you see his face? He was surrendering. He was devastated and remorseful. He's one of you. Who fired the first shot? I want that person brought up on charges."

Complete silence prevails on the lawn. The irony of a 'standing on the porch while white' shooting by cop is lost on each of them.

Chapter Forty-Four

Zachary Blake calls Sarah Hayes and advises her that her case is officially over, settled via a structured settlement annuity that will provide lifetime benefits. All that remains is to prepare the settlement papers and create the annuity. Five minutes after thanking Zack for his hard work and tremendous result, she receives a call from Billy Ellington. Aisha's abductor had been shot and killed by police.

Ellington provides details of the attempt to arrest and take Dunham into custody. Sarah is surprised to learn that Dunham's fellow cops have gunned him down under circumstances similar to those killed her husband. *Is this a racial thing, a gun thing, or both?*

Sarah sits alone in her car. Her kids are home, playing with their grandmother, under the careful watch of Micah Love's private surveillance team. Since Aisha's abduction, Sarah has been unable to return her kids to KidCare or any other daycare center. Perhaps the death of Officer Gil Dunham will ease her fears. Maybe they can terminate full-time surveillance and security.

For some reason, Sarah is profoundly saddened by the death of Officer Dunham. For Sarah, Dunham's death represents the last of many tragedies that began with a routine traffic stop on the streets of Cedar Ridge.

Driving to work, Sarah thinks about the various exhibits and tours offered by the museum. *Has racial justice improved? Have we moved on from Reconstruction and Jim Crow? Been lifted by Martin and the Civil Rights Act of 1964? It seems that whenever we take two steps forward, we take a step back . . .*

Epilogue

"Thank you for joining us for this first-ever Forum on Race in Southeastern Lower Michigan. We are coming to you live from the campus of Wayne State University in Detroit, Michigan.

"I'm Professor Michael Kendell. I'm pleased to welcome my distinguished guests, prominent trial lawyer Zachary Blake, Cedar Ridge Police Chief Warren Brooks, Detroit Police Detective Billy Ellington, and our special guest, Sarah Hayes, the brave widow of Marcus Hayes. You all know the case. Mrs. Hayes will have a special announcement for us later in the program.

"Each of our guests played a prominent role in assuring that justice was done for Marcus, a black man shot and killed by a Cedar Ridge police officer during a routine traffic stop.

"Welcome, gentlemen. Sarah Hayes will join us shortly. Welcome to our audience. I'm pleased to see a packed house this evening."

The event is pure Michael Kendell, who's riding high from his involvement in the Hayes case. Wayne State has given Kendell carte blanche to develop and run this evening's program, including a free hand in selecting the panel.

Kendell invited Zachary Blake to the event because of Blake's media savvy, his political connections, his wealth and power, and because the movement needs a strong voice in the legal community. Ellington, the black cop, and Kendell, the black activist, do not exactly see eye-to-eye on the issues. Zack Blake will be a solid buffer between these two men.

Kendell invited Chief Brooks for obvious reasons. The man has made impressive strides toward fixing the culture of institutional racism in his department and healing community wounds opened as a result of the Marcus Hayes incident. The chief's blue-ribbon task force was given free rein to craft solutions and included people from all walks of life, all racial and ethnic backgrounds. The task force did not disappoint, coming up with fantastic proposals.

"We've got a serious problem on our hands, gentlemen. Here we are, living and working in multicultural communities. Many communities in Metropolitan Detroit have more African Americans and people of color than Caucasian citizens," Kendell lectures.

"Yet, the problem of institutional racism, especially between white cops and black citizens, seems to be getting worse, not better. If black lives really do matter, our message does not appear to be reaching the white community.

"I look at America's racial and ethnic diversity. I see an asset, a source of pride and community strength. Many of my white brothers and sisters don't see it that way. They see non-whites as a threat to their way of life. And who is the commander-in-chief in charge of pushing this narrow-minded point of view? The *President of the United States* is their champion.

"These people must be educated by any and all means possible. The proliferation of racist viewpoints, whether they are conscious or unconscious, hurt our country at home and abroad."

"I have to agree with Michael," offers Zachary Blake. "The problem is not going away, nor will it solve itself. We can't look the other way and hope that it will. If we ignore that which is directly in front of us, the problems will escalate. We saw some of that in the Hayes-Cedar Ridge incident."

"It's up to us, *all* citizens, regardless of background, to step up to the plate and address these issues," Detective Ellington declares. "We need to share our life experiences and offer honest appraisals of the problems we face. We need to do it at kitchen tables all over the nation. In schools, we need to educate our children to celebrate diversity rather than fight or kill over it. We need to promote our core values at home and abroad. That begins with citizens and police officers respecting each other and treating each other as each of us would want to be treated."

"Amen to that, Detective Ellington," Kendell agrees.

"Billy to my friends," Ellington bows and smiles.

"Thanks, Billy. And I'm Michael. We are only a few years removed from our first African American President of the United States. We are more than fifty years post-Civil Rights Act and the March on Washington, more than one hundred and fifty years after Lincoln freed the slaves.

"Yet, we are still a racially divided country. Many of our people are still victims of institutional racism. When do we stop talking about how and why we aren't a colorblind society and start to become one? Chief Brooks?"

"I don't have an answer to that question, but we do need to continue discussing these issues until we have real-world solutions," Chief Brooks remarks. "And we need to do it *together*. We must *all* address these issues and try to find solutions."

"My parents grew up in the south during segregation, Kendell reminisces. Back in the day, racism was *legal*. Can you imagine that? So, when my parents and I have conversations about those times, they are often difficult conversations. My parents moved to Detroit from Louisiana to escape some of these things only to have them occur here as well.

"There seems to be no escaping these points of view, especially when we are faced with a POTUS who champions the cause of white supremacy everywhere. But that doesn't mean we give up. It doesn't mean we stop talking about the issues or advancing basic human rights and civil and criminal justice for all citizens, regardless of color."

"And, if we are honest, Michael, it appears President John's election was made possible, at least in part, by the election of the first black POTUS, " Blake suggests. "In my opinion, this was some sort of payback from an angry segment of the electorate."

"Don't forget that policemen are being killed by citizens at least as often as citizens are being killed by the police. And the vast majority of police shooting victims, whether black or white, are criminals," Chief Brooks offers.

"No one is arguing police work is not dangerous or policemen being killed in the line of duty is less of a tragedy than citizens being killed by police in the line of duty. Policemen, however, to a far greater degree, accept the risk of harm when they choose the vocation. Innocent citizens, caught in the crossfire, do not get to weigh and accept those risks. It is not a fair comparison," Zack opines.

"Spoken like a true lawyer," Ellington chuckles.

"Amen to that," Brooks smirks.

The audience laughs at the exchange.

"Still true, though," Kendell suggests, in Zack's defense. "Since the election of Ronald John, the frequency of these types of cop-on-black shootings has risen enormously. Many believed after the Civil Rights Act was passed, America had become what they call a post-racial society. If that were true, we wouldn't be sitting here having this conversation. The *Black Lives Matter* movement is a direct response to news reports about young black men being killed by cops all over this country.

"Many people believe blacks commit all the crime in America. Therefore, blacks must have it coming. The problem is this belief is *false.* And, when these incidents became an issue in the presidential campaign, things became very divisive. RonJohn is a catalyst for racist rhetoric and attitudes, even for calls to action."

"Too many police officers are getting killed in this political environment while the president lashes out at the lawlessness of certain communities of color and stirs up even more divisiveness," Ellington opines. "People are very worried about expressing valid points of view on both sides for fear of being called a racist. I believe this is the time to *have* a conversation, not shy away from one. That's why I am here."

"That's also why I'm here. It took an innocent man's death to wake up our community, an event for which the community is extremely remorseful," offers Brooks. "However, there is almost no focus on or attention given to officer deaths or the dangers that cops face every single day. When a cop leaves home in the morning, there is a real possibility that he will not be returning home in the evening."

Brooks turns to and addresses Professor Kendell. "Michael, you mentioned something I'm curious about. People believe America has become a post-racial society. I have not heard that term before. What exactly do you mean by that?"

"Thank you for that question, Chief. We must clarify our words so people will understand them. We had a black president. We have black superstar athletes and performers, black cabinet officials, attorneys, judges, Supreme Court justices, senators, members of Congress, mayors, and other dignitaries. Some of the most famous people in the world are people of color. Hell, just look at Beyoncé and Jay-Z!

"So, the white man's perception is that we've arrived, everything is equal, and we are now a post-racial society. In this society, we're all on equal footing. If you don't succeed, black or white, you have only yourself to blame. These post-racial advocates believe there is only *personal* responsibility and no *societal* responsibility."

"There is a lot of truth to that, no?" Blake suggests.

"Sure there is, Zack," Kendell agrees. "However, whether it is true, partially true or yet-to-be true is a meaningful conversation to have.

"Can a black man succeed today beyond his wildest imagination? Can he experience the so-called American dream? Sure he can! He can overcome the bigotry, societal views, and ideas standing in his way. But that doesn't mean he, unlike his white counterpart, doesn't have to rise above adverse societal views and bigotry. Do you understand?"

"Yes, absolutely. It is a longer and harder climb to success," Blake remarks.

"You've got the idea. But it is worse than that."

"How do you mean?"

"You have a son, right?"

"Two."

"Okay, two sons. How many you have is beside the point."

"Sorry. Please continue."

"Let's assume your son and my son are young, college-educated adults. They are driving home from the same concert. Both are pulled over by separate white police officers. Now, I can't honestly say that there have been no incidents of white-on-white cop-citizen traffic stop shootings, but I have never heard of one reported by the media."

"I see where you're going . . ."

"What are the chances your son is shot by the cop for any reason at all?"

"Slim to none."

"What are the chances my son is shot, regardless of what a good person he is?"

"Still slim, but better. In fact, statistics suggest if that concert is performed in a predominately white community, your son is far more likely to get pulled over than mine. I studied this phenomenon when doing research for the Hayes litigation. I absolutely see your point," Blake concedes.

"And I want to point out this has nothing to do with the clothes he is wearing or his station in life or his education. He's just a black kid in the wrong place at the wrong time, stopped by the wrong cop for the wrong reason. He could be a lawyer, a doctor, a politician, or, simply, my son. Suddenly, *he's* Marcus Hayes, bleeding to death in his car, and I'm Sarah Hayes, mourning the loss of *my* loved one."

"That's not fair, Michael. You act as if there is an epidemic of cop-on- black police shootings, when you *know* they are few and far between. There are thousands of cops, patriotic and law-abiding cops who are laying their lives on the line for *all* citizens, black *and* white, all over this country," Ellington argues.

"I wouldn't use the term 'epidemic,' but I would, absolutely, use the term 'disturbing trend.' I'm not suggesting there aren't good cops. There are two of them up here on this stage. But, what I *am* suggesting is we need methods to weed out and properly train those inclined to make rash and deadly decisions based on race," Kendell argues.

"So, where does *Black Lives Matter* fit into this discussion?"

Blake changes the subject, to diffuse obvious tension between Kendell and Ellington.

"*Black Lives Matter* fits in because, although a member of any race or ethnic group could be a victim of a cop-shooting, in every instance where an officer cited fear of his or her life, the victim was black," Kendell contends.

"But is that a media reporting issue or a factual issue? Maybe these things are happening to white men and women, but those cases don't make headline news," Blake suggests.

"The media is reporting on these cases because they are occurring with increased frequency. In point of fact, that's how and why *Black Lives Matter* was born," Kendell advances. "And we will keep railing against these institutional racist policies and incidents until they become a thing of the past."

"The opposite seems to be true in kidnapping cases. We couldn't get the media interested in Aisha's case. She had to compete with the cold case of a white kid, and the cold case won," Ellington laments.

"I don't want to ruffle anyone's feathers, and this may be racially insensitive, but one of the criticisms of *Black Lives Matter* is that there was almost no reaction when Gil Dunham, a white cop, was killed," Blake suggests.

"Now I realize that Dunham was a criminal, and that fact alone distinguishes his shooting from the Marcus Hayes shooting, but where is the public outrage? And where's the outrage when a black guy is shot and killed by another black guy? Should your movement be called '*Black Lives Matter* when they are killed by white cops, and white lives don't matter at all?'"

"I agree with the first part of your statement, Zack. It is racially insensitive. In fact, your whole premise is false," Kendell scolds.

"This is not indicative of how *I* feel about the movement, Michael, but it does characterize the feelings of many Ronald John supporters and other people who tend to vote with a more conservative slant," Blake clarifies.

"In my opinion, this is another one of those reporting myths, much like the media's failure to cover Aisha's abduction," Kendell argues.

"A black person killing another black person in the hood is no longer news. The black community has grown accustomed to it and the white community expects it. That doesn't mean the black community doesn't care.

"By the way, I'm not giving credence to the suggestion, either. I'm simply saying, rightly or wrongly, this is how some people in the community feel. I agree we should look at broader issues of crime in our communities and search for solutions. The media, however, is focused on our movement and upon black men being killed by police officers, both white *and* black. We must seize the moment and take advantage of this unparalleled coverage of the killings. Usually, these types of crimes are ignored by the media."

"My city, Zack, as you know, is a blue-collar, lower-income city," Ellington remarks. "To Michael's point, education and poverty have a direct impact on crime statistics. Crime in the suburbs is unusual and newsworthy, while crime in the city is an everyday occurrence and less newsworthy. Is that fair? Is that a form of racism? I'm not a big fan of *Black Lives Matter*, but as a black man, I certainly understand the racial and media divide when it comes to these issues.

"We have their attention for once. We need to take advantage of this and try to change things for the better. What Cedar Ridge did following the Hayes shooting is a great example of positive change. Their task force, its findings, and solutions should be applauded and emulated."

"Amen, brother," Kendell nods to and acknowledges Chief Brooks.

The audience applauds. The panel waits before continuing.

Blake actually steps on the applause as he continues the discussion. The audience quiets. "But shouldn't our society prefer to view people and crime less selectively?" He argues. "All lives matter, don't they? Isn't limiting our protests to what the movement calls 'black lives' a form of reverse racism? Why don't we start a movement focused on the reduction of crime, the improvement of education, and the betterment of all people in all communities, regardless of race? Why isn't that a preferred goal?"

Many in the audience nod in agreement. There are also voices of discontent.

"It *is* a preferred goal, Zack. And that's a fair question," Kendell acknowledges.

"However, with all due respect, it's rather naïve. The problems we're discussing tonight do not broadly impact white communities.

"Let's take you and your family as an example. You live in Bloomfield Hills, an upscale, predominately wealthy white suburban community. If your son goes out for the evening and you watch the car roll down the driveway, do you ask yourself if it may be the last time you will ever see him?

"Many parents in the hood—inner-city Detroit, Chicago, Milwaukee, Baton Rouge or other predominately black urban communities ask that question every time their kids leave the house. While focusing on *all* communities sounds good, it should be readily apparent that some communities need no help at all."

"Point taken," Zack concedes. "But how do you respond to a white person who argues, "I don't see things in black or white? I see the person in front of me, and I believe *all* people should be treated fairly." *Black Lives Matter* doesn't do that. In fact, the movement seems to have an anti-white bias. There are a large number of people who feel this way. How do we respond to them?"

"That's a great question, Zack. I don't think the movement is racist, nor do I believe it necessarily accuses white people of being racist," Kendell begins. "The movement seeks to address one issue and one issue only: Black men are being killed by cops. We want to stop this madness.

"My friend Billy Ellington here is a black man *and* a cop. He probably has different goals, broader community goals for Detroit citizens than those I espouse, and that's okay. I would be willing to work with Billy in the city and you in the suburbs to achieve our goals, but for me, my first priority is to stop the cop-on-black killings. To do that, we need *all* communities, white and black, to care about *that* issue."

"But, Michael, the opposite is true, too. Being a cop is very dangerous. When you're a cop, your color isn't black or white. It's blue. When someone shoots at a cop, he doesn't see black or white—he's shooting at the man in blue. Cops bleed too! We're afraid too!" Ellington's emphatic.

"We need compassion and empathy and a little respect for putting our lives in harm's way to protect the very citizens who might one day be shooting at us. This isn't an easy job. In fact, it's *damn* hard! We need to work on this together, people of all colors and creeds, including cops. Cops are people too, man," Ellington pleads.

"I completely agree, Brother Billy," Kendell concedes. "I stand ready, willing, and able to work with all people, on all sides of these critical issues, to put an end to gun violence of any kind on our streets. I know Chief Brooks, Detective Ellington, and Attorney Blake feel the same way. I hope they will join me in this endeavor.

"I promised our special guest, Sarah Hayes, the last word tonight. She has an exciting announcement. Ladies and gentlemen, Sarah Hayes!"

Sarah walks cautiously toward a lectern situated on the right side of the stage. The audience stands and gives her a thunderous ovation. As the applause begins to die down, Sarah signals to someone off to the side of the stage. Two men appear on opposite sides of a large cardboard architectural drawing of an impressive modern building. The men station themselves on stage to Sarah's left as she begins to read from some notecards.

"Thank you for attending this unique and informative forum tonight. What an insightful conversation! Let's give our distinguished panelists a round of applause."

The audience complies with a long and enthusiastic ovation. When the crowd quiets, Sarah continues.

"It's imperative that we, a community of human beings of all colors and national origins, continue to discuss these issues and commit to finding sensible solutions.

"Rodney King posed an important yet simple question, all those years ago in California: 'Can't we all get along?' While it seems like a simple question, we are still searching for answers. We must learn to get along. We must keep talking to one another.

"To assist in that effort, I'd like to announce, as part of the settlement of my husband's case against the City of Cedar Ridge, the Southeastern Lower Michigan Community of Police Officers will build the Marcus Hayes Center for Training Police Officers in the Appropriate Use of Deadly Force right here on the campus of Wayne State University."

The audience responds with a standing ovation. As the applause diminishes, Sarah continues.

"This will be a state-of-the-art facility, for use by all communities seeking to receive use-of-force training and improve use-of-force decision-making skills. We do not suggest use of force is never necessary. However, he recommends it for purposes of self-defense or defense of innocent people. Even then, force should only be what is reasonably necessary.

"While no two incidents are the same, and officer personality and judgment are unique to the particular officer involved, the training is designed to teach officers quick and appropriate responses to unique situations. Officers will receive training in situational awareness, to judge when a particular crisis requires force, and how to establish control with the minimum use of force necessary under the circumstances.

"The center's training goals will be to teach officers that use of force shall be limited to that amount necessary to mitigate an incident, make an arrest and protect the officer and other innocent civilians and officers from harm. Use of force shall be an officer's last option, a necessary course of action to restore safety when all other practices have proven ineffective. Training will use dynamic and interactive principles that include problem-based role-play, lectures, and demonstrations designed to provide students with the skills necessary to implement and train others in the appropriate use of force.

"The center will also be a national data storage center, keeping track of use of force incidents, whether appropriate or inappropriate force was used, providing sensible advice and counsel on how those situations were handled and whether there are safer solutions than those employed.

"The training will include courses in rendering life-saving first aid at the scene of a use-of-force incident and time-is-of-the-essence training in assuring that trained medical assistance teams are dispatched with due expedience.

"The ultimate goal of the center is to achieve that level of force that is permitted by the Fourth Amendment of the United States Constitution. The United States Supreme Court has established a standard of 'objectively reasonable' and has mandated that the 'reasonableness of a particular use of force must be judged from the perspective of a reasonable officer on the scene.'

"As such, officers must receive premium-level training and develop the experience to determine which use-of-force option will deescalate a particular situation and bring it under control, safely and prudently, using an officer's sound judgment and governed by objective, not subjective standards.

"My husband would be proud this center bears his name. It is an important way to honor his sacrifice. As our daughters grow, they may view this center as a reminder their father did not die in vain. We are still a young nation with a lot to learn and important work yet to be done. Thank you, and God bless you."

The audience stands for the third time and gives the project an enthusiastic ovation. Kendell pauses and waits on the crowd.

"This is an amazing development. We look forward to seeing this project become fully operational and a benefit to communities everywhere. Thank you, Sister Sarah. Thanks to my special guest panelists, and thanks to all of you for coming. We have limited time, but we'll be happy to take questions . . ."

***

Three days after the forum, Sarah Hayes is driving home from work. She is listening to WWJ NEWS RADIO 950, the local news station in Detroit. In a late-breaking bulletin, a reporter is reporting the death of a citizen who was stopped by a white police officer on Gratiot near Eastern Market. According to the report, a fifty-year-old African American man was pulled over for a broken taillight.

The apparently unarmed man was told to stay in the car. Instead, he put the vehicle in park, exited, and confronted the officer. A heated discussion ensued, and the man decided to turn and run.

The officer chased him down and caught up with him at the entrance to the market. The two men struggled, and the officer shot the man three times. The officer stated he discharged his weapon during the struggle because he feared for his life. A witness, however, filmed the entire episode on his cell phone.

This is radio, not television, so Sarah listens as the reporter describes, in graphic and brutal detail, what she is seeing.

"This cell phone video displays, rather graphically and clearly, that the victim is running away from the officer at the time of the shooting and shows him being struck by bullets, not once, not twice, but three times.

"The victim does not appear to be holding a weapon of any kind. The officer is walking over to the fallen victim, and he is grabbing the hands from what appears to be his lifeless body. He applies handcuffs. It now looks like the officer is taking the man's pulse and radioing for assistance.

"This is only one reporter's opinion, but I cannot imagine how this man could possibly be alive, nor can I imagine why any of this force was necessary over a broken taillight. The video displays what can only be called a cold-blooded execution.

"Be glad you are not seeing this video footage yourself. It is disturbing. I am certain we have not heard the last of this story. We do not know the status of the officer, whether he has been relieved of duty, is in custody, or is being questioned. We will provide more details when they become available. Reporting live from Eastern Market, I'm Michelle Delaney, WWJ News Radio 950."

Sarah Hayes listens in horror. After Delaney completes her report, Sarah turns off the car radio. She pulls over to the side of the road and weeps.

END

Thank you for reading, and I sincerely hope you enjoyed *Betrayal In Black*. As an independently published author, I rely on you, the reader, to spread the word. So, if you enjoyed this book, please tell your friends and family, and I would appreciate a brief review on Amazon. Thanks again.

Mark

Join Zachary Blake in his next journey into justice in Betrayal High. Please continue for an excerpt.

Betrayal High

Prologue

Kevin Burns is alone in the house.

Mom left early for work. Dad? Who the fuck ever knows where Dad is? Probably spent the night at his girlfriend's house.

Kevin calmly walks into his parent's bedroom.

Where does that asshole keep the keys to the cabinet?

Kevin carefully goes through drawers and cabinets. For some reason, he wants to leave no trace of a search.

What the fuck difference does it make?

The same is true of the gun storage and display cabinet.

Don't want to break into the cabinet, but I will if I can't find the damn keys. Yes! Here they are!

Kevin finds the keys nestled in his father's cigar box. He lifts the box and takes the keys. He also discovers and pilfers a cigar and some matches. *I'll smoke a victory stogie after the deed is done.*

He stuffs the cigar and matches in his pocket and walks from the bedroom into the den and over to the gun cabinet. He uses the key to open the cabinet.

His father showed Kevin the collection multiple times. Kevin is duly impressed. In fact, he's damned excited about the vast array of weapons, even more so at the prospect of using them on some assholes.

Dad has no idea guns inspire me, all part of my plan.

On many occasions, when he and his father debated the Second Amendment, Kevin always took the liberal side of the debate.

Why do Americans need so many guns? Who needs an AK47 Assault rifle? Will the deer shoot back? You're an expert shot. If someone breaks into the house, and you have to shoot him, isn't an assault rifle massive overkill?

Kevin actually believes none of that. He believes the Second Amendment is sacrosanct and grants him the absolute right to *possess* any weapon he wants. He couldn't *own* guns. He didn't have the money and wasn't old enough. Today's plan requires real firepower. His plan is in place, but he continues to go over it in his mind.

Park the Challenger in the south side parking lot. The school officer will be parading around on the north side like he always does, high fiving his favorite students. My hands will be full. Some idiot will hold the door for me. I'll say 'thanks,' if I like him. If I don't, maybe I'll shoot his ass.

I'll get the pressure cooker ready to arm, load Dad's AK47 and Lugar, walk up the south side steps to my locker, and head toward the center of campus. That's where the real assholes hang out, center stage, where they can be seen in all their glory.

Those fuckers are going to die today. Today, it ends for them, the massacre of massacres, a day of reckoning for those who thought I was weak, someone to be ridiculed and picked on. They will feel my wrath, receive my vengeance, and know my power. I will shoot the first person I see who has called me 'tiny' or 'flop ears' or 'tard' or any other of their favorite names.

*You think I'm small? Maybe I am, but my gun is huge. Wait until I shove it down your throat or up your ass! I may walk softly, but I carry a big stick! Ha! Assholes! Once you encounter the size and power of my AK47, you will rethink your notions of size. You've been right all along. Size **does** matter. The bigger the gun, the larger the massacre.*

The dead will know who made them that way. The survivors will remember my name. All will know me. Kevin Burns, school shooter 2019, first of his kind in Michigan, first of his kind in Bloomfield. This will be prime time news on every station.

I'll kill at least 30 with the assault rifle and another few with the handgun. In fact, I'll probably off 35 or so before that dumb-ass school officer, assuming he has any guts, arrives at the school center. You'll all be dying. I'll be laughing. Bang, bang, bang, bang, bang, bang, bang! HA-HA, HA-HA, HA-HA, HA-HA, HA-HA! I can't wait to get there! Death becomes you, all of you, and you become death. Bang—you're dead.

*I hope some teachers or maybe Principal Adams, are somewhere close by. This is **your** fault. You all could have done something to stop this bullshit, but you chose to look the other way while the so-called cool kids made fun of us. Why? Aren't **all** kids important? Or is it just the rich and famous, like Kenny Tracey and his little bro'?*

Hope I run into them. They're good guys; never made fun of me. In fact, I remember when people made fun of them for doing it with the priest. Sorry guys, but I need to make a statement and you're both kind of famous. So, if I run into you . . .

Maybe their hotshot lawyer daddy will take them to school today and I can get him too! Now there is a statement! 'Prominent attorney gunned down by tormented student, details at eleven!'

I hope I run into Drew Moss, the biggest prick of all! What an asshole! Perfect example of someone I am looking to hunt down today. Jake Tracey, if I let him live, will thank me. That asshole Moss once gave Jake a serious beat down.

Mom and Dad will weep. They'll say they had no idea. Bunch of crap, of course, they're responsible. Them and those assholes that have picked on me since fucking grade school are **responsible***.*

'You're a loser. Work harder. Get better grades.' But did they do anything to help me? Did they provide the tools? No! They made sure I was someone who others ridiculed. Others dressed in brand name clothes while I wore hand-me-downs from my loser cousins, shirts for five bucks and pants for ten at Sam's Club. Second-hand stuff from the Salvation Army Thrift Shop.

Mom? Dad? News flash: Life sucks. You made it that way. Your parenting skills suck. I should stay home and kill you guys first, but who knows when either of you will be home? Dad's getting drunk or laid and Mom, the 'responsible one,' is out making a living so Dad can piss it away on booze, guns, and broads. Does she know the truth about her husband? Sure she does, and she'll have to live with an asshole for a husband and a mass murderer for a son. That's punishment enough for any woman, right?

Fucking school. I can put up with a lot. I've got thick skin. Life was never great, but I could cope until I went to that fucking school. Everything in that place is rotten to the core. Teachers, principals, students, even the janitors and cooks are assholes. These people are supposed to be molding young minds—well you shitheads failed big time with this young mind. It's time to pay for your failure.

Who the fuck invited you to mold my mind anyway? It's my damned mind! You can't tell me how to think or what to do. It's my life and my mind. I'm going to kill every damn one of you hypocrites. Feel my wrath!

Jesus saves, but he can't save your sorry asses!

Chapter One

Kenny Tracey studies himself in the mirror. He's now eighteen years old and a senior in high school. The person staring back at him is no longer a boy. The 'adult' version of Kenny looks increasingly like his late father, handsome face, with piercing green eyes.

Kenny tries hard to keep his dad in his thoughts, but he's at a point where he hardly remembers him. Jim Tracey died in a tragic work accident when Kenny and his younger brother Jake were kids. Kenny knows if his dad were still alive, he'd be proud of him.

Kenny is going to Michigan State University in the fall. His senior year in high school is almost behind him. Assuming he gets through his Chemistry final, he'll be off to college in the fall. Kenny remembers his dad's favorite saying and cherishes the memory:

The key to success is a solid education.

Kenny looks forward to a new beginning where everyone doesn't know him as the boy with the lawsuit against the priest and the church. He'll be just one of thousands of college students on the MSU campus. He finishes brushing his teeth and combing his hair. He wipes down the sink and counter, turns off the lights, and bounds down the stairs. Jake calls to him from the upstairs hallway.

"Hey, Kenny."

"Morning, squirt," Kenny yawns.

He's been calling Jake 'squirt' since the day he was born. Jake doesn't mind, that is, until recently.

"Stop calling me that. I'm as big as you. In fact, I'm still growing; be careful what you wish for. I might be calling *you* 'squirt' soon."

Kenny doesn't respond. There's a good chance Jake's prophecy will come true.

"Ready to go?"

"Two minutes. I've got to brush my teeth and comb my hair."

"For all of the freshman and sophomore girls?"

"Yeah. Jealous?"

"I get all the girls I want," Kenny growls. "I'll be in the car."

"Be right down. Got any finals today?"

"One. You?"

"I have two."

"What classes?"

"English and History."

"Easy-peasy. Study?"

"I'm ready. You?"

"Chemistry."

"Shit."

"Shit is right. That stuff is Greek. I'll be in the car."

Kenny walks out to his car. His step-dad, the famous attorney, Zachary Blake, bought Kenny a Jeep Compass after he got his driver's license. In return, Kenny must maintain a 3.0 or better average and drive his 16-year-old brother anywhere he wants to go, especially to school every morning. Kenny and Jake have a great relationship, and Kenny is happy to chauffeur his younger brother around. A 3.0 average isn't too difficult for Kenny.

Kenny is actually quite wealthy from the trial and resolution of his case, but his mother, Zack's wife, Jennifer Tracey Blake, has tied the money up in a complicated trust. She doesn't want the case proceeds to spoil her sons or deter them from getting a quality education. Zack is extremely successful, and the boys have a sweet life. Limited access to their money has caused no family problems.

Jake comes running out of the house, hops into the passenger seat, and throws his loaded backpack into the back seat in one fell swoop.

"You got everything you need?" Kenny asks. "You don't want to have to call Mom or Dad to bring you something later."

"I'm good."

Kenny looks at his younger brother. They've been through a lot together, including that terrible episode with the priest and the trial. They're both tough kids, but they worry about each other. They have each other's backs.

"So, how did you enjoy your sophomore year, squirt? Meet any ladies you want to talk about? Need any pointers?"

"From you, stud? Ha! I don't see you bringing anyone home to meet the folks."

Kenny starts the car and backs down the drive.

"I'm doing fine in that department, thank you very much. I just don't broadcast my conquests."

"Sure, Kenny, sure. Conquests, that's hilarious! So, what are you going to do about Chem?"

"I'll pray for a 'C.' It's a required class. I had no choice. You'll see. You've got to take it, too. In college, I can do a liberal arts curriculum. Science and I are not compatible. I could have gone to Michigan if it wasn't for science. At MSU, I'm going to load up on English, business, social studies, and stuff like that, go to law school and get a job in Dad's office when I graduate."

"I feel your pain. I don't like science or math either, but I do okay. Maybe I'll go to law school, too. Then we can all work together at the law firm. *Blake, Tracey and Tracey, Attorneys at Law*. Nice ring to it, don't you think?"

"We're partners now? Ahead of all those people who already work there?'

"We're family."

"I don't think Dad sees it that way. If you want to advance in his office, you have to *earn* your success. Nothing's handed to you."

"Okay by me. I don't expect anything for free. It'll be a tough seven years. You up for it?"

"State's a party school. I'm going to meet chicks, have a good time, party, and go to class in my spare time."

"That won't work, Kenny, not if you want to work for Dad. There is such a thing as too many parties, you know."

"Too many parties? Not possible. Seriously, though, I've looked through the prospectus. There're so many interesting things to learn about, and I'll have four years to explore and experiment. That's plenty of time. I want to have fun, too. I can decide on a major, later."

"Sounds like a plan. Don't wait too long."

"I really can't wait too long. A liberal arts curriculum prepares you for nothing except for more school. Maybe I'll hedge my bet, get a business degree. But I want to go to law school and work for Dad."

"This is the twenty-first century. How about looking at twenty-first-century careers like tech or environmental stuff?"

"Tech and environmental stuff, as you call them, require science and math. They're certainly important and topical fields. We should all know about and consider environmental issues, regardless of what we decide to do for a living."

"You're right. If you concentrate on the environment, maybe you'd use it in your career. Even if you became a lawyer, you could specialize in environmental issues. You could be an environmental lawyer. Isn't that a thing? Maybe you could work for a green company or something."

"That's certainly possible, but, again, there's that science crap and, besides, Dad's a trial lawyer. I don't think he handles environmental cases."

"He does if there's money in it. Someone has to protect poor old Mother Earth."

"I went on the MSU website the other day. The professor that teaches intro to environmental issues has his own section on the site. He's got this little eco-game on the site. It's very clever. Every action has a reaction. You shoot a wolf, which protects a deer. The deer has babies and eats all the grass which screws up the ecosystem."

"So, you could get a job as a teacher and teach elementary students about the balance of nature."

"No, I told you already. I want to work for Dad."

"Teaching is a good alternative if law school doesn't work out."

"That's true, I guess."

Kenny turns into the school entrance.

"Here we are. Where do you want to park?"

"North side."

"North it is."

"My first class is right there."

"You're lucky I like you. Mine's on the other side. Damn, I'm looking forward to summer. Can't wait to be done with this place and be off to college."

"And leave me all alone with two goofy adults?"

"Mom and Dad aren't so bad."

"I know, but you won't be around to protect me or make me look good." Jake chides.

"Funny. Got your phone?"

"Yeah."

"Text me when you're done."

"Will do."

"Have a great day. Good luck on your finals."

"You too."

Kenny and Jake enter the north side school doors and split at the first hallway. Kenny heads south. At the same time, Kevin Burns walks north, from the south side entrance, on a collision course with Kenny Tracey.

Other Books in the Series
Betrayal of Faith (Book 1)
Betrayal of Justice (Book 2)
Betrayal in Blue (Book 3)
Betrayal High (coming soon)
Supreme Betrayal (coming soon)

About the Author

Mark M. Bello is an attorney and award-winning legal thriller author. After handling high profile legal cases for 42 years, Mark now treats readers to a front-row seat in the courtroom. His ripped from the headlines Zachary Blake Legal Thrillers are inspired by actual cases or Bello's take on current legal or sociopolitical issues. Mark lives in Michigan with his wife, Tobye. They have four children and 8 grandchildren.

Connect with Mark

Website: www.markmbello.com
Email: info@markmbello.com
Facebook: MarkMBelloBooks
Twitter: @JusticeFellow
YouTube: Mark M. Bello
Goodreads: Mark M. Bello

To request a speaking engagement, interview, or appearance, please email info@markmbello.com.

Printed in Great Britain
by Amazon